THE ESPOSITO CAPER

KAREN K. BREES

Black Rose Writing | Texas

This is a work of fiction. Names, characters, businesses, places, events, and incidents are either the products of the author's imagination or used in a fictitious manner. Any resemblance to actual persons, living or dead, or actual events is purely coincidental.

ISBN: 978-1-68513-429-7
PUBLISHED BY BLACK ROSE WRITING
www.blackrosewriting.com

Printed in the United States of America
Suggested Retail Price (SRP) $21.95

The Esposito Caper is printed in Garamond Premier Pro

*As a planet-friendly publisher, Black Rose Writing does its best to eliminate unnecessary waste to reduce paper usage and energy costs, while never compromising the reading experience. As a result, the final word count vs. page count may not meet common expectations.

To John, always

ACKNOWLEDGEMENTS

Thanks to Joyce (FR) who slogged through at least three edits and to Detective Sgt. Larry Stokes of the McCall Police Department (ID) for the procedural information. Thanks also to Pat for his input on wine and wineries. Thanks to Vicki for the use of her name. Hope you like Liz. Any mistakes are mine, not theirs. The SFPD Art Theft Division is a fictional department created for this book. Thanks to my source in the SFPD who wishes to remain anonymous but who graciously answered all my questions.

THE
ESPOSITO
CAPER

CHAPTER ONE

Sardinia: Aeroporto di Cagliari

The online mini-course on assertive behavior, *Using Body Language to Intimidate*, had come with a money back guarantee, and Gino Esposito was wishing he'd kept the receipt. It had been a stupid waste of time and money. One more stupid thing to add to all the rest of the stupid things he'd done in the past month. He'd overlooked the obvious—Italians had invented body language. So now, forced to abandon subtle postural moves, he cleared his throat and drew himself up to his full height, a less than intimidating five-foot-six, and took the more direct, vocal approach.

"What do you mean there's no car?" he screamed at the desk clerk, a large man with an adenoidal voice whose name badge identified him as *Peppino da Palermo*. "I've got a confirmation number. Just get the car and get it now." Gino cleared his throat, stood back, and waited for the car to be produced.

"*Si, signore*, but that is last week's confirmation number. We have upgraded the system." The clerk shrugged. "An unfortunate mix-up, *signore*, but there's nothing to be done. Not even if *Il Papa* himself should arrive would there be a car for him."

"But I've got a confirmation number." Gino grabbed the edge of the counter with both hands. His left eyelid twitched and a vein above his right temple throbbed. "Look, Peppy from Palermo, I don't want the Popemobile. *Capisce?* I want a midsize sedan—the one I reserved." He stabbed an index finger at the paperwork he'd spread on the counter. "I want my car."

"*Si, signore*," Peppino said, pushing the paperwork aside to make room for his coffee mug. "This is indeed most regrettable, but..." he threw up his hands as if to cast blame upon the terminal's stagnant air.

Gino lifted his hands from the counter, clenched his teeth, and pulled the money clip from his pants pocket. He slapped a hundred Euros on the counter. Peppino responded by producing a nail clippers from his own pocket and attending to a rough edge on his thumbnail. Gino peeled off another hundred. Peppino clipped a hangnail. When the stack had grown to five hundred Euros, Peppino snapped closed the clippers and returned them to his pocket.

"*Signore*, perhaps my brother-in-law's car would be available." He flicked an invisible piece of lint from his jacket sleeve and tugged at the cuff.

It took another hundred Euros before Peppino produced the keys. Counting the money twice, he jerked his head in the direction of the door marked *Employees Only*. Gino let out a heavy breath. He hoisted his bags and followed Peppino out the door to the parking lot to inspect the 1976 Fiat with most of the body damage hammered out and much of the primer peeling away.

"You want insurance?" Peppino stood beside the relic, hands clasped behind his back.

"Insurance?" Gino circled the car. A wire coat hanger stabilized the muffler, a horizontal crack at eye level ran the entire length of the windshield, one headlight was missing, and two of the tires were balder than his uncle Vito. "You're kidding, right?"

Peppino smiled, revealing a mouthful of nicotine-stained teeth. "One hundred Euros. For insurance, and you have it back with the gas tank full by five o'clock Wednesday afternoon. Don't be late. My brother-in-law needs this car Wednesday night."

Gino reached for the money clip again. "Does he have a date? Never mind. Does the gas tank leak? Forget it. I'm sure it does." He jammed the money into Peppino's outstretched hand. "Don't worry. I'm not going to be here a minute longer than necessary."

"I no worry. You be late, you worry." Peppino's eyes swept over Gino with a careful look. "Have a nice day." He stuffed the insurance premium in his pocket, consulted his watch, lit a cigarette, and strolled back into the terminal, leaving Gino with the road-weary Fiat and a bad case of buyer's remorse.

Gino tossed his luggage into the back seat, in the process snagging his suit pants on a jagged piece of metal protruding from the inside door panel. While trying to bend the metal back into place, he merely succeeded in slicing open his thumb. He gave the door a savage kick, and it responded by springing a hinge. He slammed the door shut and kicked it again for good measure but opened the driver's door with more caution. The door frame was intact, but the seat upholstery was torn. The rough edges of the vinyl dug into his back, and the seat was loose. The passenger side was littered with crumpled food wrappers, and Gino shuffled through the debris until he found a greasy napkin which he wrapped around his thumb to keep the blood from dripping onto his ripped trousers. He folded his suit jacket and placed it on the seat cushion, both to protect his own seat and also to give him a quarter inch of visibility above the windshield crack. He eyed the clutch with suspicion. It took several tries before he found a gear the car approved of. It wasn't first, so he and the Fiat lurched out of the parking lot in second.

Once outside the city and off the main arterials, Sardinia remained as it had for centuries. The battered sedan rattled through one sleepy village after another, raising dust and scattering chickens. With each kilometer, time seemed to slow until Gino could almost feel the moment the clock began to move backward. Traffic ceased to be a concern. The only other vehicle for miles had been an abandoned delivery van at the edge of town. When he took his eyes off the road to see if there was anyone at the wheel, a child toddled into the road in front of the Fiat. He slammed on the brakes and jerked the steering wheel to the left, causing the car to spew dirt and gravel as it fishtailed and nearly collided with the child's mother gossiping with an old woman by the side of the road. The plastic rosary hanging from the Fiat's rear view mirror clicked and swayed, keeping an annoying celestial beat, until finally, his hands still trembling, Gino jerked it free and flung it out the window.

While straightening the mirror he'd tweaked while ridding himself of the rosary, he glimpsed the old woman stoop in the road behind him to retrieve the beads and kiss the crucifix. He tightened his grip on the steering wheel and pressed hard on the gas. The car responded with a rattle and a sputter. He'd asked too much and broken their uneasy truce. Gino backed off the gas but the motor coughed once and died. He checked the mirror again. The mother held her son's arm in a vise grip, and the old woman was standing in the middle of the street, hands on her ample hips, the rosary safely tucked into her belt. She narrowed her eyes and nodded.

"Christ," he muttered. *Malocchio.* She'd given him the evil eye. Nothing new there. He'd been pissing off women since he'd turned twelve. He raised his arm in a salute and tried the ignition. "Come on baby. Come on," he coaxed. The motor wheezed and took a breath of life. He eased the Fiat into second, and they coughed on down the road. He caught himself before he gave one last glance in the mirror. "Don't look back," he mumbled. "Never look back."

CHAPTER TWO

New Haven, Connecticut

"Get your ass onstage, Carla! This ain't the fuckin' *Folies Bergère*. We got a schedule to keep." Tony's voice burst into the dressing room a microsecond before his beefy frame wedged itself through the doorway and past the sagging pink vinyl shower curtain tacked to the doorjamb.

"A gentleman knocks first, asshole, but pardon me, I forget—you ain't a gentleman, and we don't got no door. When you gonna get a new door, Tony? It got busted down two weeks ago, and it's drafty, not to mention it ain't respectable."

"Do I look like a fuckin' repairman?" With his thick neck, thick body, and thick head, Tony Vitale was built more along the lines of a large, cumbersome appliance than a repairman, and the woman he was snarling at had thought more than once that his looks could only be improved if somebody would take a wrench or a hammer to his head.

Bent over a pair of fishnet stockings, Carla Catalano was working on a ripped seam. She bit off the thread. "This ain't working. You got any glue, Tony? The Stop and Shop was all out."

"Do I look like your fuckin' mother?"

Carla arched an eyebrow. "You got that backwards. If we had a house mother, which we don't, you'd be out on your ass. You got such class, Tony." She eased on the stockings, smoothing them with care as she went, but the fishnet sprang a new hole on her left thigh for spite. She grunted and propped her leg back on the wooden stool. She reached across the counter for a black eyebrow pencil and drew a couple of lines on her skin under the hole in the fishnet. She set her leg down and turned to check her work in the mirror. "Think it'll pass until I can get a new pair?" "Do I look like a fuckin' beauty consultant? Quit screwing around and get onstage."

"Do us both a favor and go screw yourself." She positioned the pointy fox ears on her headband so they tilted forward and kicked the stool so it glanced off Tony's shin on its way to the floor.

"Bitch!" Tony grabbed the stool just as Frankie Genovese pushed the shower curtain aside and looked in.

"Problem, Carla?"

"No, Frankie. No problem." Carla glanced down at her leg and drew another line.

"Tony?"

"Just getting Carla onstage, Mr. Genovese." Tony set down the stool and shoved it back towards the counter. Carla did a quick step to the side to escape its path.

Frankie's gaze shifted from Tony to Carla and then back to Tony again. He pointed at the shower curtain. "Get this fixed, Tony. Tomorrow, before the Club opens. You've got to assume responsibilities if you're going to get respect. Respect is important. Remember that, Tony."

"Yes, Mr. Genovese." Tony turned to the entryway and examined the doorjamb, running his fingers along the rough edge as if he were noticing it for the first time. "I'll take care of it right away, Mr. Genovese."

"That's good, Tony. That's taking responsibility. We've got to take care of the upkeep. It's good for morale. And Carla, you come see me after your last set." Frankie gave them both a disgusted look before returning to his office.

Carla held her tongue as she watched Frankie's exit. She tied the black laces on her bodice into an artful bow and then buttoned the red fur collar around her throat. Morale? It would take a bulldozer to improve working conditions, but a new door was all they were going to get, and she had a pretty good idea what it would look like. Knowing Tony, the door would come out of the salvage yard or the dump. But what did she expect? Even with a fresh coat of pink paint and a new neon sign, the PussyCat Club was still a minor blemish on New Haven's backside.

As far as the dressing room, it didn't take a genius to figure out what the Club thought about its dancers. She'd seen bigger clothes closets, but that had given her an idea. She needed to limber up before her sets and for that she needed some basic equipment. At the least, she needed a *barre*, but there was no way in hell Tony would get her one. So she'd jacked the clothes rod from her apartment closet and installed it on the short wall. Tony hadn't noticed. No big surprise there. He didn't notice shit. Above the rod, she'd tacked her photograph of Marie Taglioni performing *la Slyphide*. And that was it. Not much as a dance studio went, but it was hers and she could focus on Taglioni instead of the Club while she stretched and exercised before she danced.

As far as the rest of the dressing room went, pegs nailed into the far wall passed as clothes racks for the house dancers. The opposite wall was a row of mirrors with a string of bare light bulbs above and a chipped Formica shelf below. Someone had taped a poster of kittens playing with a ball of yarn on the empty wall to the left of the pegs. Amber had drawn a pink lipstick border around her section of mirror. A drinking glass with a wilted red rose draped over the rim sat on the shelf by Carla's section. She frowned. Should have pressed that one before it croaked. Yep, Carla thought. No expense spared for morale for sure.

Pushing past Tony, who was still fondling the doorjamb, she made her way down the dark corridor to the stage which was actually in the next building, the former site of Johnny G's Bar and Grille. When the Mob had moved into the neighborhood, they'd bought up the entire block and renovated. You could now get from one building to another without having to use any outside entrances. It was all very convenient. The whole block was one big suite of rooms with the connecting doors carefully concealed behind sliding panels. The PussyCat Club was just one enterprise. The pawn shop two doors down was the front for the bookmaking, the dry cleaners on the corner housed the drug operation, and the motel next door bedded the girls. It was a full-service commercial enterprise, and Frankie Genovese managed it all.

After her third set, Carla stepped into her street shoes and slipped into her robe. Frankie's office was down the end of the corridor, away from the noise of the bar and close to the rear exit. She gave a quick rap on Frankie's door and let herself in.

"I'm here."

Frankie was seated behind a massive mahogany desk working on the books. The room was dark, and the light of the computer screen cast an eerie glow across his face. About forty-five, balding, and slight of build, Frankie favored three-piece suits with bow ties, Italian loafers with silk tassels, and single malt Scotch. At Carla's knock, he took off his glasses and set them down by an open bottle and a half-filled glass. He rubbed his eyes with the back of one hand while reaching for the glass with the other.

"All work and no play, Frankie. You're gonna die young." Carla reached across the desk and switched on the floor lamp. "You're also gonna die blind if you don't get no light."

Frankie took up the glass and leaned back in the swivel chair. "I have no plans to die young or blind either, for that matter. I'm going to retire a rich man with everything I could conceivably want." He looked her up and down. He was a leg man and Carla had legs that went halfway to her neck. With skin like ivory, red hair the color of a summer sunset, and eyes as green as a martini olive, the rest of her wasn't hard to look at either, but her temper was a problem. So was her mouth. She danced under the name of Vixen, and it suited her.

"What about you, Carla? You got plans?" He tossed back the rest of his drink and handed Carla the glass.

"I'm gonna get my break real soon, Frankie." She poured him another two fingers of Scotch. "My friend knows a big shot who's got an in with this director guy at the Shubert, and he says they're gonna need a girl for the chorus line. This is probably my last week here, Frankie."

"Yeah. Sure, sweetheart. I hear that a dozen times a day. I thought your big break was last month, or was it last year? Better make it while you can, Carla. How old are you? Nineteen now? Maybe twenty? You've got three, maybe four years if you're lucky. Time isn't on your side."

Carla handed him back the refilled glass and shrugged. "Maybe."

"No. Not maybe. Anyhow, you've got a big break tonight if you play your cards right. Sal requested you personally, and you get to keep your tip. Don't piss him off, Carla. If he likes you, he can make your life easy." Frankie reached into the top desk drawer, pushed aside a Sig Sauer, and pulled out a bank envelope with a padlock hanging off the zippered top.

"Give this to Sal when you get there. And hustle. He's sending a car for you. It'll be here in twenty minutes."

Carla reached across the desk. "How much in here, if you don't mind my asking?"

Frankie clamped onto her hand. "I don't mind you asking. I mind telling. Just be sure it gets there safe and sound and there'll be no problems. Understood?"

"Sure, Frankie. Sure." She waited until he released his grip and then picked up the bag. "Don't work too late. You got circles under your eyes." She let herself out and returned to the dressing room to collect her street clothes. She found them wadded up in Tony's sweaty hands with the rest of him framed in the doorway with the shower curtain draped around his shoulders looking like Superman's fat brother.

"I'm your escort, Sunshine. Here to make sure nothing happens to you before your ride shows." He held the curtain aside. "After you."

"Gimme those," Carla said. "You're wrinkling my best skirt." She grabbed her clothes and pushed past him to retrieve her pocketbook from the counter. "I'm changing in the powder room, and I don't need no company. Move." She marched down the hallway to the bathroom reserved for the girls.

Unlike the men's room, the ladies' room had a lock on the inside. She slammed the door and slid the latch closed. She flipped on the light switch, hung her coat and hat on the hook on the back of the door, shook out her skirt, and draped it and her blouse over the counter. She turned on the water faucet, and it was then, waiting for the water to warm up, that she saw her reflection in the mirror.

She reached out and touched the glass, tracing the outline of her face. How old did she look? Frankie said she had three or four more years of this.

Of this? Her eyes stung as tears threatened to spill over and add their saltiness to the tepid water filling the cracked porcelain sink.

Waiting. Always waiting for the big break that didn't seem to want to come. She clutched the sink, forcing the tears back. A night with Sal. And then what? Another night? Until he tossed her aside like used goods and latched onto some new, young fuck with wide eyes and no brains. No future there. The bathroom seemed to get smaller the longer she stood there. She straightened and dabbed at her eyes with a paper towel. No future here either. She sold herself by the piece. A percentage to the house for the stage fee. A percentage to the house for every private dance. Every lap dance. Every everything. A tip out to everyone who worked at the Club, even Tony. She blew her nose. She had to pay Tony. She laughed but the sound was hollow. She stared at the girl in the mirror. She didn't know her. She didn't even recognize her own face any more. She took a bar of soap and smeared it across the glass. *No more. No more.*

She fished through her cosmetic bag until she found her nail file and went to work on the lock securing the money pouch. A few quick jabs and the hasp sprung. A peek inside the bag told her all she needed to know. There was a hundred thousand there, easy, but time was short.

"Get your cheap ass out here. I don't got all night." Tony banged on the door again.

She took a sharp breath. "I'm coming. I'm coming," she called to Tony. "Hold your water."

She dumped her cosmetics out of the plastic bag and stuffed the money pouch inside. She flushed the toilet and ran some more water in the sink. Then, lifting the top of the toilet tank, she dropped the plastic bag into the water, reset the top, and scrambled into her clothes. She stole a final glance at the toilet. Whatever. It was done. She'd started something, and there was no going back now. She'd figure out the rest of the idea later. It was a start. Hopefully, it wouldn't be the end of her. She slid back the latch and opened the door only to connect with Tony's fist coming down one last time. His pinky ring snagged her cheek below the eye and she went down hard.

"Jesus, Mary, and Joseph, Carla! Christ!" Tony's strange litany brought Ginger and Nanette running from the dressing room. Carla lay sprawled on the floor with Tony bent over her, his fist still clenched. The girls screamed. Tony sprang back, jumped up, and made a move towards the girls but that just cranked up their volume.

Carla shook her head and opened her eyes to see Tony looming. He looked hard at her, then shot a glance down the hall at Frankie's door before he turned and fled through the door into the bar. "Let me at him," she rasped. "Where'd he go?" She squinted to get a better view.

"He's gone, honey," Nanette said. "He's long gone."

CHAPTER THREE

Sardinia: Castel del Mare

As the grade steepened, the Fiat labored around hairpin curves and across switchbacks. Gino hunkered over the steering wheel, contending with the ruts and potholes of the rural secondary roads and their lesser cousins. Adding to those hazards, the weakened roots of the parched grasses clinging to the cliffs could no longer hold back the rocks and arid soil that tumbled down the mountainside, littering the road with debris. Avoiding obstacles and correcting for the Fiat's tendency to pull to the left commanded Gino's full attention.

Late September should have been pleasant, but a heat wave held the Mediterranean in a vise grip and the sun was a hot hole in the sky. The scirocco blowing in hard from the Saharan south stirred the road dust into brown clouds, further obscuring his vision. The Fiat's air conditioner wasn't working, but at least the heater was. Gino had it going full blast to keep the radiator from boiling over.

The windows might have been closed, for all the good they were doing. His blue silk shirt was soaked with sweat, and he sat forward to keep from sticking to the vinyl seat back. He reached for his water bottle at the exact moment a small herd of goats emerged from the dust and capered across the road in front of him. Gino wrenched the wheel to the right, overcorrected, and ran over what might have been the sharpest rock in Sardinia. The goats, safely across the road, disappeared down the hillside. With the tire sliced as neatly as a piece of provolone, there was nothing to do but collect his bags, abandon the car, and do the final three kilometers on foot. He picked up the rock and heaved it at the ruined tire. His mood didn't improve.

Gino coaxed the last drop of water from the plastic bottle he'd brought from the plane and tossed it into the car. He put a hand to his forehead to shade his eyes and wished he'd thought to pack a hat and his sunglasses. Heat shimmers danced across the road like wraiths escaping the fires of hell. He looked up at the sky half expecting to see vultures circling, but there was nothing but unrelenting heat and brutal hot wind.

He waited by the car, hoping someone would come along but gave it up as a futile effort after twenty minutes that seemed like two years. There would be no other vehicle coming down the road. There was no service on his cell. And so, resigned to his fate, he trudged up the long hill to the final switchback, where the terrain mercifully leveled off and the glaring sun was hidden behind the arching branches of the olive trees bordering the vineyards of *Castel del Mare*. Another two hundred meters and he reached the gates where he collapsed against the cool stone of the archway and pushed the buzzer on the intercom.

There was a blast of static followed by a tinny voice demanding, "*Che cosa voi desiderano?*"

"I want to see my grandfather," Gino said. After a brief pause, the gates swung open in reply. Inside the grounds, he walked along the drive in the shade of the olive grove baking in the late afternoon heat and past cactus-filled crevices in the rocks. The driveway curved one last time and the villa, low and white with its red- tiled roof, came into view.

Under the portico of *Castel del Mare's* whitewashed walls, the housekeeper, Celestina Borghese, was picking spent blossoms from the bougainvillea and stuffing them into the bulging pockets of her black dress. She'd cleaned an area about a meter up and was scowling at the higher branches but brightened when she heard Gino's voice calling her name.

"Celestina, what are you doing? You should be inside in this heat."

"Gino! I was about to get a ladder." She wiped her hands on her work apron and turned away from the troublesome vine.

"You are too old to be climbing ladders. You leave that kind of work to the men." He stooped to kiss her wrinkled cheek and smiled when she drew back. "Yes, I look like hell. I want a cold drink, a bath, a change of clothes, and a clean bandage. I'm probably incubating some disgusting infection already." He offered his thumb as testimony. "I'm going to my room."

"Where is your car?" She looked to either side and then behind him, as if he'd somehow managed to hide it in his shadow.

"I had a flat." He waved his arm in the direction from which he'd come. "I walked."

Celestina took a handkerchief from her pocket and a few petals fluttered to the ground. She spit on a corner and began rubbing at the dirt on Gino's face. "He's been asking for you, Gino."

"Don't, Celestina." He pushed the kerchief away. "I'm not six years old any longer, and it's going to take more than that to get my face to come clean. I can't see him like this. Let him ask another half an hour. This cursed dust gets into everything."

Celestina looked at the sky. "Tomorrow it will rain, and the dust will become mud."

"Not much improvement."

"The priest is with him."

"Priest," Gino snorted. "What good is a priest? Taking up space and eating your food. Tell Aldo the car is three kilometers down the road. He'll find it easily enough. It's the only one of its kind. My bags are in the car."

Celestina frowned. "It is not good to speak lightly of these matters. You were seen in the town, Gino. The awful thing you did. The Rosary." She shook her head. "It will not go well with you." "It already hasn't gone well with me. Just have my things brought up. I'll see *Papa* as soon as I'm presentable." He moved through the portico and stepped into the tiled entryway, Celestina at his heels twittering like a small bird.

Castel del Mare was a masterpiece, perhaps Emiliano Esposito's finest. Like his paintings, it had begun as a thought—a vision. He bought land as the owners abandoned their own dreams and left in search of easier lives. He added a piece here and a piece there until his holdings exceeded nine hundred acres and spread across the hills in a wide swath of barren soil and rock. The land had produced nothing except weeds and dust for years, but he labored over it with the same intensity he brought to his paintings. He terraced the hills, amended the soils, introduced an irrigation system, and planted his grapes. And as a result of his efforts, the vineyards flourished, and the *Castel del Mare* label became an important one.

The mansion itself was sequestered deep inside the grounds, and from his studio windows on the second floor, Esposito could look out on the distant sea from which he drew inspiration for his art. Throughout the home, the thick stone walls that kept out the summer heat and the winter cold were pockmarked with recessed alcoves that served as nesting grounds for the villa's ceramic saints. In Gino's quarters, the Virgin and St. Joseph regarded each other with beatific indifference across the room, while above the bed their Son hung on the cross. The crucifix was counterbalanced and softened on either side by two watercolors of fishermen repairing their nets. The symmetrical as well as allegorical effects weren't lost on Gino, who now draped his coat jacket over the Virgin and stripped down.

When he emerged from his bath, he found his bags had been delivered and unpacked. One set of clothes had been laid out on the bed, and his shoes had been polished. There was also a box of sticking plasters for his cut. The jacket had been removed from the Virgin and hung in the wardrobe, and a votive candle burned its penance at the Virgin's feet. Gino muttered but left the candle burning, a small victory for Celestina waiting for him outside the door.

"That is my Gino." She nodded in approval while glancing inside the room to be sure the candle still glowed. Satisfied, she patted his cheek, took him by the hand, and pulled him down the hallway to his grandfather's room. Rare and fragile tapestries on the walls muted the sounds of their footsteps on the tiled floor.

"You must hurry, Gino," she said. "He hasn't much time left."

****

The curtains of the master bedroom had been drawn against the light, and a small lamp shone on the nightstand next to the canopied bed. The priest sat on a straight-backed, wooden chair reading his breviary in the lamplight, while the old man, shrunken with age and illness, plucked at the bedcovers. Gino walked to the bedside and took one of the old man's hands in his own.

"Grandfather, *Papa*, it's me, Gino."

"I know who you are. I'm dying, I'm not senile," his grandfather snapped. "Help me sit up. Get me some pillows. Get this priest out of the room. Hurry up." He closed his eyes. "I'm waiting." The voice was weak, but it still commanded obedience.

"*Si, Papa, si.*" Gino helped his grandfather to sit up and positioned two pillows behind his back for support. The priest closed the prayer book, blessed them, and left. "Is he on paid staff now?" Gino asked, taking the vacated chair. He moved a claw-footed table aside, careful not to disturb the chess game in progress.

"He's a Jesuit, which makes him something more or less than a priest, depending upon your point of view." The old man coughed. "His presence is for Celestina more than anything else, and he's company of a sort. He's also a terrible player." He glanced at the chess set. "His king is always in checkmate. Probably a message, but he's too dense to see it." He gave a toothless grin. "At least he keeps the mourners at bay. If Celestina had her way, there would be wailing heard throughout the countryside. She is convinced my immortal soul is still a marketable commodity." He shook his head. "Foolishness. Open the door. I want to make sure nobody is listening behind it."

"It's open, *Papa*. No one's there."

"*Bene, bene.* Come close, Gino, let me see you." The old man reached out and touched Gino's cheek with a cold hand, then gave him a pat. "*Bene.* You are a man now, Gino. You come when I ask for you. That is good. *Bene.*" He looked into Gino's eyes, and his gaze was steady. "Gino, I am going to tell you a story. When I am done, I am going to ask you to commit a sin. A mortal sin." Now he studied Gino's face with concern. "From what I am hearing, that will not be as big a burden as I had feared."

"*Papa*," Gino began, but his grandfather held up his hand.

"This will take some time. Something you have a great deal of, and I, not so much. But there is time enough for this. Indulge an old man and listen to his ramblings. You will understand in due course."

Gino looked about the room for a chair that might hold up better if the old man's story proved to be a lengthy discourse, but he came up empty. It was either the wooden chair or standing. He settled himself as best he could and prepared to endure.

"It begins after the War," his grandfather said.

Gino did some fast math. Sixty years, more or less. Not a story, but an epic saga was in the works. His eyes made one more fruitless search of the room for a better seat.

"The War," his grandfather continued. "We were poor before it and even poorer afterwards. Mussolini was a fool." He leaned over the edge of the bed and spat on the hardwood floor. "I survived the war, but I wasn't doing so well surviving the peace. I was twenty-four. There was no work and little food. What was I to do?" He looked at Gino and shrugged his frail shoulders. "I had nothing to lose and so I gathered my paints and my brushes and went in search of my future." He looked into his grandson's face. "It is easy to be poor, when everyone else is. And so I went to Florence. Desperation gave me courage—a kind I never found in the trenches. All I cared about then was living through another day and another night. But now? Now I wanted something more." His voice gained strength as he spoke.

"Can you understand, Gino? It was a hunger greater than any hunger for food. I went to the home of Angelo DeMontana and asked for a job. Crazy. I had the confidence of youth and the naïveté of an idiot. But you know what happened?" He raised a bony finger toward the heavens. "He hired me! Not quite that fast, of course. But he let me in, and he looked through my portfolio, and he said he could teach me. I, Emiliano Esposito, would be taught by the Master." Emiliano chuckled. "I moved in that same day. And within the week I was joined by two others—Dominic and Giovanni.

"It wasn't charity on Angelo's part, you see. He had a plan, and we fit that plan perfectly." Emiliano took a sip of water. "Open the drapes, Gino. The sun will be setting, and I like this time of lengthening shadows. *Chiaroscuro.*"

The French doors along the western wall of the bedroom extended from the ceiling to the floor and opened onto a balcony that overlooked the gardens. Gino pulled the heavy brocade drapes aside and secured them with the braided gold cords that hung from hooks fashioned from brass and shaped like fish.

"Yes, that's better. We will stop for a while. Celestina will be invading with my dinner tray in a moment and she'll hover over me until I've taken all my pills. Then she'll reward me with a glass of wine. Maybe two, if I flatter her." He winked at Gino and patted his hand.

On cue, Celestina arrived with the medications, a bottle of wine, and two glasses. "He gets one glass, Gino. You see to that." Celestina wagged a finger first at Emiliano and then at Gino. "He will drink too much otherwise, and then he will not sleep well. One glass," she repeated, taking a vase of yellow flowers from the dresser with her as she left.

"She's moved into the main house," Emiliano said, watching her form move down the hall back toward the kitchen. "It's for the best. She worries too much. She's afraid she'll miss my exit. She hovers like one of the bees in her garden."

Gino smiled and handed his grandfather the bottle. "She is always worrying. Mostly about me."

"And for good reason." Emiliano turned his attention to the wine. "This is our label," he said, cradling the bottle in his hand. "A Cannonau. It's a good vintage." He handed the bottle back to Gino. "Pour. There is time enough to sleep later." He watched with approval as Gino filled the glasses.

"Where was I? Oh, yes. To continue," Emiliano said. "We were ambitious and arrogant—Dominic, Giovanni, and myself. Talented, of course—and so sure of ourselves. Young cocks. After all, we had been chosen to apprentice under DeMontana." He waved the glass in the air and the wine sloshed nearly to the rim with the sudden motion. "By the time we understood what we had agreed to do, it was far too late to turn back." Emiliano saw Gino's puzzled expression. "What was it we were asked to do, you wonder? Oh my Gino, we became accomplices in an ingenious scheme. Unwitting ones at first, to be sure, but later, as we watched our wallets swell, we were as guilty as DeMontana." Emiliano studied the remaining wine in his glass and frowned. "If the truth had gotten out, we would have been ruined. Perhaps even jailed. But I get ahead of myself." He took a sip of his wine and smacked his lips in appreciation. "Yes, a very nice Cannonau. "DeMontana was clever. He began slowly, but he began the first day. When we arrived at the atelier, he had our canvasses set out on their easels, and he'd sketched rough outlines on each one. We were to fill in the outlines and complete each painting, while he studied our strokes, choice of color, and technique. He encouraged, berated, and humiliated us. But we persevered. We learned. Two years this continued. Two years! We became experts at following his directions. Then one day, the canvasses were bare. We were told to create a seascape. We had been set free. It was a moment both welcome and unsettling. We knew it was a test, and each of us approached the task differently. Would we be good enough? I didn't know about the others, but I was confident in my talent. I knew I was good enough. And so I painted. I painted fishermen, those who labored in the sea and pulled its harvest onto land. They became a passion. Fortunately for me, it was a passion of which DeMontana approved."

"The fishermen above my bed," Gino said.

"Yes, among many, many others. And Dominic and Giovanni found their own passions. Dominic painted storms at sea with roiling waves and complex skies. Color was his strength, and he played light against dark with great skill, if not originality. Giovanni, however, abandoned the sea and turned to coastal work. Imposing cliffs, rocky beaches, and all that sort of tripe. Very romantic. Very cluttered and heavy. It didn't set well with DeMontana. Dominic and I passed the test, but Giovanni didn't. He was let go. I heard he died shortly afterwards. He intervened in a barroom brawl and got a knife in the side for his troubles. It was a fitting romantic end for a fool." He held out his glass and Gino obliged him.

"Ah," Emiliano sighed. "I shall miss good wine. Perhaps there will be some in the next world. I must ask the Jesuit his opinions on this." He cradled the glass in both hands. "The man drinks like a Sicilian. Anyhow, to finish my story, and yes, Gino, it is drawing to its conclusion. Do not worry. DeMontana was preparing for a showing of his work. Canvasses were crated up for delivery to the gallery. It was chaos. We helped, of course, running here and there and attending to all kinds of details. He kept us very busy." He laughed, the sound barely a whisper. "We were supposed to be busy."

Gino nodded and the old man continued. "The show was a huge success, and DeMontana made out quite well. Imagine our surprise the following week when we each received an envelope from him. Inside the envelopes was more money than either of us had ever seen before. So many *lira,* we were giddy with our good fortune. He asked us to sign a receipt, which we did without hesitation. And then he nodded with satisfaction and motioned for us to have a seat in his office. Oh yes, he had an office, a very large one." Emiliano gazed out the window at the sky's changing canvas. He squinted to gain a clearer perspective and held up one hand, framing the remaining thin light of dusk between thumb and index finger. He dropped his hand and turned again to Gino.

"DeMontana began by applauding our efforts and telling us how satisfied he was with our work. He told us he had sold some of our paintings at the showing and had received a good price for them. He knew we'd be pleased, and we were. The money he had given us was more than fair compensation for our labors. We had arrived. Or so it seemed until he explained further. He had signed his name to our work. He explained that no one would have bought our paintings had we signed them. It was his name that people were looking for. We were nobodies. Perhaps in time we would have our own following, but for now, this was the way things would be. This was the arrangement, and he reminded us that by accepting the money and signing the receipt, we had agreed to the terms.

"To put it bluntly, we'd been had and had good." Emiliano fixed his grandson with a hard look. "I told you it was an ingenious scheme. There was nothing to do but keep painting. The money was fine. We had no complaints about it and after a while, the whole thing became just a business arrangement. Our moral outrage was short-lived. It is difficult to remain outraged when one's wallet is bulging.

"DeMontana kept meticulous records. He used a combination journal and account ledger in which he recorded each transaction. Each one, mind you. He identified every piece of art by number and next to it wrote how much it had brought him and how much he had given us. A separate page broke down the coding system so the paintings could be easily identified.

"I suspect that over the course of the next ten years we produced a couple of hundred paintings for him. Some he used and some he didn't. But we were paid, regardless. He had his own code of ethics." Emiliano reached for his grandson's hand. "I had lost mine. But there is something in a man that won't let him totally accept someone else's plan for him. Maybe I had realized this from the start because I found a way to paint my initials into each piece I worked on. I started during my apprenticeship during those two years of training. Soon, it became an interesting diversion and ultimately quite a challenge to keep finding new ways to sign my work without making it visible, even to a trained eye. I suspect I might have been a good forger, if I had turned my hand to that occupation instead of art. As it was, DeMontana was the forger, but I derived a measure of satisfaction all the same.

"Riding on DeMontana's name, I became a wealthy man, and you have enjoyed, sometimes perhaps too much," Emiliano closed his eyes, "the benefits of that fortune. DeMontana owes me nothing. He was quite right. I would never have become rich in my own right. He is dead now, and so is Dominic. And now you and I are the only ones who know the truth." He opened his eyes, released his grandson's hand, and drained the last of his wine. Gino raised the bottle to refill the glass, but his grandfather shook his head. "It is enough," he said.

"That is the background of my story. Perhaps you think me a fraud, and perhaps I am." He paused. "The past cannot be changed. It is the future that concerns me now. Not my own. I have precious little future left, but I live on in my work. I am not proud of what I did, but I take some satisfaction that the world appreciates my art, regardless of whose name it bears. I have had that comfort— until now."

"Papa," Gino said, "what has this to do with me?"

The old man clenched his jaw. "Yes, of course. You grow impatient. All right then." He looked at Gino. "It began about six years ago. The thefts. At first, I thought it was random crime, but that is not the case. My work is being systematically stolen from galleries and private collections. Dominic's, as well. Other valuable paintings are passed by while mine and Dominic's are taken. Why, I do not know. My ego, even at this late stage of my existence, cannot let this continue. It must be stopped."

"Interesting," Gino said, "but difficult, if not impossible, to prove."

"Without the diary, yes. But each theft increases the value of DeMontana's works and reduces the chance that someone will discover the truth—that there are initials in each painting that reveal who the real artist is, that prove I am the genius." The old man's voice wavered. "Bring me the scrapbook on the desk. It explains better than I can."

Gino, glad to stand at last and stretch out the kinks in his back, walked to the writing desk, where the scrapbook was nearly buried in the papers cluttering the desktop. It was a large black book with embossed gold lettering on the cardboard cover. The corners were bent with time and use. The pages inside were crammed with yellowed newspaper clippings. Some clippings were glued to the pages, but others had simply been inserted between the leaves, as the old man's strength had left him.

"Read the book. Then you will understand." Emiliano closed his eyes again and sank back against the pillows.

Gino stood, watching his grandfather's labored breathing. The old man soon slept. Gino took the scrapbook back to the hard chair and began to read. The first entry told of DeMontana's death at the age of eighty-six in 1987. The June eleventh edition of *Il Testamento* proclaimed "Art World Mourns the Passing of the Master." It gave a brief biography along with mentioning several of the artist's more popular works. Cause of death was attributed to a heart attack.

Subsequent clippings added over the next twenty years chronicled the escalating value of DeMontana's works which seemed to increase with each new revelation of his sexual liaisons. Adulterous affairs weren't anything newsworthy in Italy where mistresses were an add-on clause in most marriage contracts of the rich and powerful. What was noteworthy, however, was the emergence in 1988 of one particular woman as a potential power player in the disposition of the artist's fortune. Donna Napolitano claimed to have a signed and notarized copy of DeMontana's most recent will, bequeathing her a large share of the estate along with villas in Tuscany and Milano. The looming litigation was heaven-sent for the press, but before a court date could be determined, Napolitano died in a skiing accident in Grenoble after plummeting headlong into a tree. After a few days, the story died with her, and later that year, DeMontana's widow, Bianca, departed Florence to take up permanent residence in the United States.

The *San Francisco Bay Reporter's* Society page led with the story "Bianca DiCicco DeMontana Welcomed by San Francisco Society." It was a full page spread showing the merry widow attending a gala celebration at the DeYoung. Gino studied the photograph of a tall, willowy, ash blonde in a Dior gown accented with a queen's ransom in jewels. She held a cigarette in a jewel-encrusted holder and a wreath of smoke swirled around her head like a dirty halo. His interest ratcheted up a notch. He continued turning the pages. Then six years ago, just as his grandfather had said, the thefts had begun. To date, eight paintings by DeMontana had been stolen from showings and private collections. The first had been taken from a collection on loan to the Brancicci Gallery in New York City. The gallery owner hadn't been insured, and the insurance company of the painting's owner was refusing to pay. It was a legal quagmire.

In two other thefts from private homes in Los Angeles and San Francisco, a crowbar had been found outside a jimmied window. The art had been taken while the owners were attending a society function. In the remaining cases, the burglars had gained entry without setting off the alarm system. The police speculated the thieves had keys to the homes and, once inside, were able to disarm the systems. Police were pursuing several leads and were questioning "people of interest," but no arrests had been made. In one clip, a harried-looking Inspector Liz Paone of the SFPD's Art Theft Division was shown fielding questions in a roomful of reporters. She didn't have any answers to give them. "Police Come up Empty in Art Thefts" the headline chided.

Gino flipped through the remaining pages. A shaky hand had scribbled "Mine! Mine!" or "Dominic!" in the margins of all the theft accounts.

"Do you understand now?" Emiliano had awakened from his nap and was watching his grandson read. "Bianca has the diary and wants to make sure no one ever discovers what DeMontana did. She won't stop until she's taken all of my work to protect her fortune. You must stop her, Gino. You must get the diary and keep her from completing what she has begun. If she succeeds, there will be nothing left of my art for the future generations to appreciate. It will be as if I never was. That my life has meant nothing. That is a pill much too bitter to swallow.

"It is time the world knows that DeMontana is not The Master—I am. This is my legacy, and it is yours as well. Perhaps I have the woman to thank for this decision—maybe yes, maybe no—but regardless, my mind is made up. I am The Master and you must protect my art while there's still time. If there's still time," he added, pressing his thin fingers to his forehead. "If it's not too late. You must break the Seventh Commandment. You must steal. Gino, will you do this?" The effort and the weight of what he asked caused his voice to tremble.

Gino considered the potential consequences of what the old man asked, weighing risk and balancing it against the possibility of success. There had to be an angle he could work. The diary? Blackmail, perhaps? There was always an angle, but finding it could take some time and that seemed to be in short supply.

"Then, Gino," his grandfather continued, "use the diary against her. Make her pay." His eyes burned into Gino's.

So there it was, hidden like the old man's form under the bedcovers. *Vendetta.* It was about more than the art. Revenge fired the old man's spirit. Pride, too. And who could say he was wrong? Gino was in no position to cast stones.

"I have something that may make it easier for you," Emiliano said. "Turn to the last page of the scrapbook."

Gino flipped to the back where a folded piece of paper had been inserted in the cover's sleeve. He removed the paper and unfolded it, smoothing out the creases, and then looked up at his grandfather, questions in his eyes.

"It is the list, as complete as I can make it, of all the works I did and where I hid my initials in each one. By itself it means nothing, but with the diary, it proves what I say is true. Guard it with your life, Gino."

Gino refolded the paper without comment and returned it to the jacket sleeve, buying time. *Vendetta.* He had enough trouble without taking this on. He'd already dug a hole so deep the casino could use it for his grave. Launching a *vendetta* for his grandfather could finish him off. This was Italy, for Christ's sake. Did his grandfather not know that the DeMontanas were connected? On the other hand, it didn't seem that anything, including this, could make matters worse.

He looked at the old man who'd raised him. How could he refuse? Maybe there'd be a way out of his own problems through this. He really had nothing to lose. He slapped his hands on the table and turned to face his grandfather. "*Si, Papa, si.* I will do this thing for you," Gino said. He kissed the old man on the cheek, took the scrapbook and let himself out, closing the door quietly behind him.

He walked back down the silent hallway to his room where darkness had been banished through the ministrations of Celestina, who had not only resupplied the Virgin with a fresh votive light but had also placed one by St. Joseph for good measure. Additionally, two smaller candles flickered before the rosary-draped portraits of his mother and father, their young faces frozen in time. He took the beads from his mother's picture and spun them around his hand before stuffing them into a corner of his suitcase. In Italy, it was wise to hedge your bets, all the dead being potential sources of divine intercession or sources of torment. One never knew. It didn't matter if God wasn't listening. The angels might be. The devil certainly was.

Celestina had closed the windows against the night air, but Gino threw them open. He flipped on the light switch and the gauzy curtains danced and trembled in the air currents drawn in and tossed about by the ceiling fan.

Timing. Timing wasn't his strong point. That was one thing he knew for sure. He pulled the money clip from his pocket, counted the remaining bills, and frowned. Not enough there to do anything. Not enough to finance a *vendetta.* Not enough to pay the casino. Not enough to do jack shit. He was a slow learner. That much he'd figured out. The roulette wheel had been rigged, but he hadn't caught on soon enough, and they'd taken him to the cleaners. They had his IOU. And now the cash cow, or rather the cash bull, was dying. Bad timing. He took his suitcase from the closet and opened it on the bed. Hitting the old man up for an advance on his trust fund wasn't going to work out. He collapsed onto the overstuffed chair across from the bed, laced his fingers behind his neck, and contemplated his sorry excuse for a life. The pictures of the fisherman on the wall above his bed beckoned to him, begging to be lured away from their dead companion. The whole house was a freaking mausoleum. "I wonder," he said softly, as he walked to the bed, set the suitcase on the floor, and lifted first one picture and then the other from the wall and laid them side by side on the bed.

Ten minutes later, he hadn't found anything in either one that could have been the old man's initials. He'd followed every line and stroke and he was damned if he could see what was supposed to be there. The corners were bare of initials. The borders, likewise. Gino took the paper from the back of the scrapbook and used it like the roadmap his grandfather had said it was. And then there they were, plain as day. *EE* was inscribed in the line of clouds as they intersected with the spars on the fishing boat. The masts were the long strokes and at their base and where sails met sky the completed strokes of the double letters were clearly visible. He'd been looking for something small, but the initials took up nearly the whole damn painting.

"Son of a bitch," Gino said to the fisherman on the left who kept a silent counsel. The old man was telling the truth after all.

A soft knock on his door and a voice calling from the hallway interrupted his thoughts. "Gino, Gino, are you asleep?"

"No, Celestina. Just a moment, please." He replaced the pictures on the wall and returned the code key to the folder. "Is it *papa*?"

"No. He is resting. But when I checked him just now, he told me to go to bed and give this to you before I did." She handed Gino an envelope. "He also told me to tell you not to wait for him to take his last breath but to go now." Her face was a nest of worry, and she was on the verge of tears. "What is going on, Gino? He calls you here and then sends you away the same day. I don't understand."

"It's all right, Celestina, really it is." Gino wrapped his arm around her shoulders. "Don't worry. We did not argue. Quite the contrary. We had an excellent visit. There is just something I need to do for him. That's all." He smiled at her. "God's honest truth, I swear."

She tilted her head, assessing his words, and finally her face registered acceptance.

"I will say my goodbyes before I leave in the morning. Now go to bed." He turned her towards the hall and gave her a gentle push. "Good night, Celestina." He shut the door and slit open the envelope. Inside the envelope a scrap of paper was clipped to a neat stack of bills. He counted them quickly. There were five thousand Euros in the stack. *Travel Expenses*, the note said. Gino tossed the envelope into his suitcase. Not enough to pay off his debt but maybe a down payment on one last chance. "You old bastard," Gino said, looking toward the door. "You're not ready to go yet. I'll do this for you. I owe you that much, but it's going to pay off for me as well...somehow."

CHAPTER FOUR

New Haven

Screams from the hallway brought Frankie out of his office for the second time that night. "What the hell's going on here?" he bellowed, stopping in mid-stride when he saw Carla on the floor and Ginger and Nanette hovering. "What the hell happened to you?" He looked down at Carla slumped against the wall, wiping her bloodied face with the back of her hand.

"Tony slugged her, Frankie," Ginger said. "I seen him. He was standing right where you are Frankie, and he had his fist just like this!" She raised her hand to demonstrate. "Then he seen us, and he started for us like he was gonna punch us out too, but then he kinda like panicked or something."

"He ran that way!" Nanette pointed to the door leading back to the bar. "He just about knocked me down. I yelled after him! *Cicciobomba! Fannullone!* Creep! But he didn't stop." Her dark eyes flashed. "What's going on, Frankie?" She turned to Carla. "Why'd he hit you, Carla?"

Carla, struggling to her feet, was hit again, but this time by an inspiration. She grabbed her pocketbook and dumped the contents on the floor. "The bag!" she shrieked. "He got the money bag!"

"What are you talking about?" Ginger moved close to Carla and stared into her eyes. "I think you hit your head when you went down, honey. There's no money bag." She held her hand in front of Carla's face. "How many fingers am I holding up?"

Carla pushed her hand aside. "I don't got no concussion. I been robbed!"

"What money?" Ginger asked.

"Where's my money?" Frankie's face was a mask of red rage. He slapped Carla, and she pitched back against the wall, whimpering.

"What money?" Ginger asked again.

"Shut the hell up!" Frankie yelled. "Everybody just shut the hell up!" He put his fists to his temples to ease the pounding in his head.

"Gee, Frankie," Nanette began, but Ginger gave her an elbow in the ribs. "Oh!" she said, nodding. "Right!" She stood looking as prim as a girl could, dressed like a French maid. She patted down her ruffles that had gone askew and waited.

"You three wait here. Don't move an inch." Frankie spun on his heel and moved toward the door. "Tony," he muttered. He glanced back at the girls huddled together against the wall. "Stay right there."

Raucous laughter and loud music drifted into the hallway as the door from the bar opened. "Mr. Genovese, we got a problem out here." The bartender was standing in the doorway, a polishing cloth in one hand and a highball glass in the other.

"Now what, Rico? I don't have enough trouble already?"

"Tony knocked some geezer down, and we think the old guy's having a heart attack."

Frankie looked back at the girls who hadn't budged and then at Rico. "Where's Tony now?"

"I dunno, Mr. Genovese. He ran out the door. Nobody sure wasn't gonna stop him or nothing. What's wrong?"

Frankie gave a mirthless laugh. "Wrong?" he said, "Everything's wrong. Think, Rico. Did he have anything in his hand?"

"Hand? Geez, Mr. Genovese, it all happened kinda quick. Maybe. I dunno. What do you want me to do about the old guy?"

Frankie threw up his hands. "Put him in a cab. Get him out of here."

"Sure thing, Mr. Genovese. A cab." Rico jammed the cloth into the glass and reached for the cell clipped to his waistband. He hit the speed dial. "Tony coulda had something, come to think of it, I guess. But he was kind of a blur, if you know what I mean." Rico mumbled something into the phone and then shoved it back in the holster.

"Get back to work, Rico. The guy goes in the cab, regardless."

"Right, Mr. Genovese. Understood. I'll take care of everything." Rico pushed back through the swinging door, barking orders at the wait staff as he went.

****

"I quit! No more! No way! I'm outta here!" Carla squinted at Frankie. Her left eye was swollen shut and her cheek was purple. "I don't know where the bag is. I sure as hell don't have it here." She reached for her pocketbook, staggered, and Nanette caught her.

Ginger had collected everything Carla had dumped and stuffed it back into the pocketbook. "I'm taking her back to the dressing room for an ice bag. All right, Frankie?" She handed Carla the purse and wrapped an arm around her waist for support.

"Yeah. Yeah. Take her back and keep her there." Frankie ran his hands through his hair. "The car's coming. *Merda!* I've got to make a phone call. Nobody leaves. Understood?"

"Yeah, Frankie, what's going on?" Ginger asked.

"Just do as you're told." He strode back down the hall to his office, slamming the door so hard the wall shook.

"Carla, what's going on?" Ginger's voice came in short bursts as she half-carried, half pushed Carla along with Nanette offering vocal support.

Carla shook her head and said nothing. Back in the dressing room she slumped on the stool in front of her makeup mirror and surveyed the damage to her face. "Think I'm gonna need stitches?" She winced as Ginger pressed an ice bag against her face.

"Here. Hold this against your cheek. Tight. First thing is to get the bleeding stopped. Then we see what we got." Ginger wrung out a wet cloth and peeled back the ice bag to begin cleaning Carla's cheek. "It's not too deep. Tony must've just hit a bleeder. Why's everybody hitting you tonight? What the hell did you do to piss everybody off like that? That ain't smart, Carla. Frankie don't never get mad. I never seen him lose it like that."

"My head hurts. I don't want to talk. I want to get outta here." Carla pushed the cloth and the ice bag away and leaned against the mirror.

Amber shook her head. "Not right now, you don't. You leave now and Frankie'll kill you for sure. You got something he wants Carla, or he thinks you do." She shook her head again. "I sure hope for your sake you ain't got whatever it is."

CHAPTER FIVE

New Haven

At three in the morning the city streets were as quiet as they get. The winos had stumbled and crawled into the doorways and alleys. The homeless had returned to their shopping carts and spread out their bedrolls, and the crackheads had disappeared into the bowels of the wrecked real estate of the boarded up storefronts on Dixwell Avenue. The cops on the beat were drinking coffee at Betty's donut shop, their squad cars cooling down at the curb. The street sweepers wouldn't be out for another hour. It was a lonely time of night.

Salvatore "Sally the Pipe" Puglisi shouldn't have been among the lonely. He should have been enjoying Carla's considerable charms but instead was en route to handle a business problem. Pushing sixty, Sal had the physique of a man ten years his junior and worked hard at keeping it. His hair had silvered, giving him a distinguished look that he favored, but his broad face, fleshy cheeks, and heavy-lidded brown eyes told a different story. His hands were soft, his nails were manicured, and his cologne was overpowering. But tonight, his only companion, aside from his dark thoughts, was Maximus, a toy poodle with a diamond studded collar and a flatulence problem. An ebony steel cane was propped against the passenger seat of the black Lincoln MKS that now cruised along the Wilbur Cross Parkway. Sal stifled a yawn and made the turn onto Dixwell.

Inside the Club, Frankie paced the confines of his office. The bottle of scotch beckoned. He hesitated, then poured a healthy measure but set the glass down. There wasn't enough booze in the world to help. He slicked back his hair, put on his suit jacket, added a bow tie, and settled in at the desk. He opened the top drawer enough to permit easy access to the Sig inside, then called up a program on the computer, printed two pages and stuffed them into a folder which he locked in the attaché case. He drummed his fingers on the desktop and rehearsed his story while he waited. It wasn't a long wait.

Within twenty minutes, Sal pulled up to the curb outside the Club. With Maximus tucked under his arm, he used the tip of his cane to push open the swinging door at the front. Frankie's office was down the hall to the right, but Sal turned left into the girls' dressing room.

****

"What a cute little puppy," Nanette cooed at Maximus who returned the compliment with a snarl. "Ooh, you've got sharp little teeth, don't you, sweetheart?" She smiled. "Just like my Rufus," she said, turning to Ginger. "He'd bite the balls off a bull." She nodded at Maximus. "You tell 'em what's what, little guy."

"This room's off limits, mister," Ginger said, glancing up from tending to Carla. "Just go right back through that curtain and take that monster with you."

"Uh, Ginger, zip it quick," Carla grabbed her arm. "It's okay."

"Whatever," Ginger shrugged. "Nothin' tonight is anything like normal. What do you want, mister?"

Sal didn't reply. He walked over to Carla where she was perched on the stool, elbows on the counter. A perfect study in misery. He took the ice bag from her cheek. "I find Tony and he doesn't have my money..." Sal lifted his cane and brought it down hard on the Formica counter. Carla tensed. "Such a pretty face," he said. "A shame to see what can happen." He left the girls and made for Frankie's office.

"Who was that, Carla?" Nanette asked. "He sure seemed to know you."

"Let it go, Nanette," Ginger said. "The less we know about all of this, the better off we'll be." Nanette shrugged and looked at the new chip the cane had made in the counter. She returned to removing her makeup. "When I see a man, especially one like that, you don't got to tell me twice."

****

Sal settled himself in the leather chair across from Frankie's desk and rested his cane across his knees. He deposited Maximus on the floor, and the dog promptly lifted his leg against Frankie's desk. Frankie clenched his teeth as Sal patted the dog on the head. "The money's not here? You sure?"

"I'm sure." Frankie rubbed his temples. "Sal, I searched the place. I searched Carla. The bag isn't here. It's gone and so is Tony."

"Nobody stopped him?"

"You ever seen Tony? The guy's built like a truck." Frankie shook his head. "It doesn't make sense. Tony's not that bright, but he's been loyal. He's worked for me five years. And then he just all of a sudden decides to steal from me? He's had plenty of opportunities and never done anything against me before."

Sal stroked the cane. "Perhaps he's not as stupid as you thought. Perhaps he was waiting for the right moment. Regardless," Sal gave a dismissive flick of his hand, "you have employee problems. A good manager deals with employee problems. Are you a good manager, Frankie?"

Beads of perspiration glistened on Frankie's forehead. There wasn't any good answer to that question.

"There something you're not telling me, Frankie?" Sal stroked the cane.

"No. No, Sal. Nothing." Frankie's eyes were fixed on the cane but he forced a smile. "You'll have your money in the morning. I've already made out the withdrawal slips from my own accounts." He pointed to a small pile of papers on the desk. "See. You're not out anything." His eyes narrowed. "But I am, and I'm going to get it back." His hands were shaking, and he felt Sal's eyes on him. He hoped Sal would think the tremors came from rage.

Sal nodded. "I trust you, Frankie. You're like a son to me." He continued to stroke the cane. "You made one bad decision. Don't make any more." He lifted the cane, scooped up the yapping Maximus, and looked at the wet carpet. "You should get that cleaned up," he said.

Frankie waited a good five minutes, and when he was sure Sal had gone, he buzzed Rico.

"Yeah, Mr. Genovese?"

"Lock up and tell the girls to go home."

****

"About time we get outta here," Carla mumbled. "I'm going to the can. I'll meet you out front." She grabbed her coat and pocketbook and was nearly to the door when she stopped and returned to her exercise barre. She pried away the tape that held Marie Taglioni's picture to the wall, tucked the picture into her pocketbook, and went down the hall to the bathroom. Once inside, she shut and latched the door, and then pressed her ear against the wood. Satisfied, she lifted the lid from the toilet tank and retrieved the plastic bag containing the money pouch. She shook off the water and jammed the bag in the bottom of her pocketbook, covering the pouch with cosmetics and cotton balls. She slipped the strap over her shoulder, flushed the toilet for effect, grabbed her coat, and went to join Ginger, waiting for her at the front door.

The club smelled like stale booze and cheap cologne. The floor was sticky, and she picked her way around a pile of broken glass Rico had swept up but not disposed of. She gave a last look around. The sign above the bar warned patrons about the house rule: "No Touching." She felt her cheek and winced.

"I'll drive you home," Ginger said. "You could pick up your car tomorrow." "No way. I meant what I said. I'm not coming back to this place for nothing. I can drive. I don't got that far to go."

Ginger, hands on hips, protested. "You ain't in no condition to drive. You can't even see."

"I can see well enough to get home and once I'm there, I ain't going nowhere." Carla rummaged through her pocketbook for her keys.

"Here. Let me help. I can hold that." Ginger reached for the bag, but Carla held on tight.

"I can manage," she said.

"What are you going to do if you're not coming back here? You're not gonna get that chorus line job looking the way you do right now. How you gonna eat?"

"Don't worry about me. I got plans. I'll be fine."

"Frankie ain't through with you, you know. Don't think he is," Ginger said, searching for her car keys. "I'm pretty sure you're making the biggest mistake of your life."

"Yeah, well I'm through with Frankie. And the Club. And this shit-assed excuse of a life. In that order."

"Don't be so sure," Ginger said. She crossed the street to the lot where she'd left her car.

Carla tightened her grip on her bag and walked the hundred yards down the street to her own car, parked in the cheap lot. A warm gust of wind stirred up a pile of trash huddled in the gutter. The tiny vortex spilled across the sidewalk and piled its contents up against the locked security gates of a pawn shop. A siren's wail pierced the night and she quickened her step.

CHAPTER SIX

New Haven

In her car and just two blocks from the Club, Carla hit the brakes, and her fairly reliable Ford Escort screeched to a halt, grinding two ribbons of black rubber onto the asphalt in her wake. She gave herself a head slap and winced at the jolt.

What the hell was she thinking? Why go home? Hell, she didn't have a home. Home was where families lived and laughed and talked and fought. What she had was a two-room walkup flat with no air, dirty laundry, an empty fridge, and a roach problem—not one of which was worth her life, and that's what going home might cost her. She drummed her fingers on the steering wheel and then swung a left onto Whalley and aimed her car for Westville. By now, chances were pretty good Sal's goons had found Tony and he'd either gone back to the Club to spill his guts and take his medicine or else he'd been given a lethal dose and was now food for the mutant bottom fish in Long Island Sound. Either way, she was next in line and she hated the water. She racked her brain. *Home? Not going there. But where? Where to go?* It had to be close to four in the morning and by five, traffic would pick up. An hour after that, the morning commute would be in full swing. She could jump onto 95 and disappear in the crowd on their way to NYC. She pressed her lips together and checked her mirrors. "Get off the road, Carla, you dumb shit," she muttered, as a white Jeep Cherokee cruised past, the driver giving her the eye.

****

The Daisy Dineraunt on the main drag in Westville was a salvaged railroad caboose that had been gutted, remodeled, and painted an intense yellow that time and weather had faded to pale. A ten foot tall daisy, petals and stem outlined in yellow neon, beckoned from the roof, where two guy wires worked hard at keeping the stem straight. Bypassing a parking space out in front, Carla pulled into the rear lot, bumping over ruptured asphalt slabs and the deep divots they'd created. Tufts of weeds and shaggy grasses had established a base of operations in the exposed dirt, and Mother Nature was winning the battle to reclaim her turf. Remnants of white lines that had once marked parking spaces were reduced to jagged slashes across the blacktop. A GMC diesel pickup with a cabover camper pulling a trailer with a red and white '54 Buick Roadmaster aboard straddled most of the slashes and took up a good two-thirds of the lot. She wedged the Escort between the GMC and a dirt berm at the back of the lot.

Carla pulled the rear view mirror toward her and considered repairs to her face. She slathered on concealer and, while it did a fair job of covering the bruise, it didn't do much for the swelling. She ran a brush through her hair and tried fluffing it up around her face then letting it hang loose about her shoulders. She tilted her head a bit and her hair fell forward, covering most of her jaw line. She let out a long breath. That was as good as it was going to get. She got out of the car, straightened her shoulders, and smoothed the wrinkled jersey of her red mini-skirt that clung like a second skin to her slim hips. She grabbed her pocketbook, slung the strap over her shoulder, and entered by the back door, sliding into a booth near the rear exit.

"Coffee, hon?" The buxom waitress held the carafe at hip level, the murky contents sloshing against the sides of the glass like waves crashing on a muddy beach. She tossed a menu on the table and filled the heavy ceramic mug in front of Carla without waiting for an answer. "You need a minute?"

"No. Just apple pie. A big piece." Carla squinted at the name stitched into the uniform's yellow fabric. *Angie* was positioned strategically across her left breast, the letters pulled against each other, victims of the fabric's ongoing attempts to confine the woman's ample bosom. Carla raised her head to smile and her hair fell back from her face, revealing her bruised face.

"You okay, honey?" Angie was on the downward slope of fifty but built to last. Her peroxide blond hair was pulled back into a lopsided bun. Her voice had the gravelly texture of a woman who liked her booze. She smelled of cigarettes and cheap perfume.

Carla flipped her hair back into place. "Yeah. I'm fine. I was just wondering what you call the other one."

Angie patted her right breast with her free hand and let out a hoot. "Gloria." She leaned in and studied Carla's face with deliberate eyes. "Your old man do this?"

"It was an accident."

"Yeah, sure, honey. Whatever you say. Looks like an accident to me. Looks like a hit and run."

Carla reached for the cream and sugar. "Just the pie. Thanks."

"You got it, honey." Angie tucked the menu under her arm and worked the aisle on her way to the order station, refilling coffee mugs and dropping a bit of chatter here and there along her way.

Carla wrapped her hands around the thick porcelain mug emblazoned with the cheerful face of a daisy in full bloom and lowered her face to the rim to catch the steam, letting the moisture seep into her pores—a poor girl's moisturizer. But she wasn't poor any longer. Nope. The thought warmed her as much as the coffee. She settled back to wait for her food and looked around.

The Daisy wasn't much on the inside, but it was yellow everywhere you looked. The high-noon effect of all the décor had dimmed, but the regulars didn't seem to care and the transient trade was too tired or hungry to notice. Ground-in grime filled the cracks in the linoleum on the scuffed floor. Scratched chrome accented the chipped and scarred plastic surface on the tables and counters. Rips on the plastic upholstery of the booths were hash-marked with random applications of silver gray duct tape. Grease tracks marched up the walls and across the ceiling. The only break from the shabby and faded yellow was above the cash register, where a daisy clock's dusty face was framed by a generous overlay of greasy white petals.

At the counter, an old woman had wedged a metal shopping cart in the space between the neighboring stool and the counter. Her snarled gray hair billowed out from under a frayed Tyrolean ski cap. Her cheeks were heavily rouged, and her pink lipstick had bled into the lines around her mouth. She turned to stare at Carla, who smiled at her and lifted her mug in greeting. The woman raised a hand, and then turned back to her coffee, blotting her lips with a pink napkin after each sip.

A few seats down, a stocky middle-aged man shoveling in the steak and eggs blue plate special made notations on the daily racing form he'd propped against the sugar bowl. Close to the front door, a young couple shared a bowl of ice cream, a battered suitcase waiting outside the booth. Angie stopped and patted the young man on the shoulder and said something Carla couldn't hear. The girl blushed.

Her closest neighbors, two men arguing in the adjacent booth, caught and kept her interest. She leaned back and cocked her head to better catch the drift of their conversation.

"Admit it, Morrie. You are the world's—no, I stand corrected—the universe's worst navigator. If Columbus had had you on board, they would have landed in Tucson."

"Tucson doesn't have a shoreline, Jeffrey. And I knew exactly where we were going. The shortcut should have brought us out on the main highway. The construction road blocks weren't posted. It wasn't my fault, and if you mention the Donner Party one more time, I'm going to cram that pork chop where it'll do some good." "We should be through New York City by now."

"If you'd stopped and gotten new maps, we wouldn't be trying to read through ripped creases that obviously had important information on them."

"If your friend's wife hadn't taken the sledge to the GPS, we wouldn't need maps."

Carla strained to listen but the two men had settled into stony silence and were concentrating on their food. No better time to get acquainted. She edged out of her booth, bumping the one called Morrie with her pocketbook.

"Excuse me. Just on my way to the can." She looked down at the torn map. "That's kind of like a treasure map, ain't it? Looks old enough to be one."

"No, it's no treasure map, and it's not doing all that great a job, as you can see by our presence here." Morrie cast a disapproving glance around the diner.

Carla sat down on the edge of the seat and motioned for Morrie to scoot in.

"Where you guys going?" she asked.

"I really don't see as that's any of your business, Miss," the one called Jeffrey said.

"Carla. Name's Carla. Pleased to meetcha." She nodded at both men and extended a hand. With no takers, she shrugged and withdrew the offering. "Well, the way I see it is if you need to go somewheres, you got to tell me where that is before I can tell you how to get there. You guys brothers or something?"

"Unfortunately," Jeffrey said.

"You can always tell family. You've got the same cleft in your chins," Carla said. "Guys with cleft chins have a strong jaw line."

Jeffrey raised an index finger to his chin and ran it along his jaw.

Carla nodded. "Yep. Definitely brothers. Brown eyes, brown hair— what I can see of it with those shaved heads. You got the same build, too. Big. Kind of chunky. You got to be careful about that. You could get fat easy." Morrie turned to Carla. "Do you know the way out of this place?"

"Sure. I can get you back on the interstate, no problem," she said, pulling the map towards her. "Here's where you got turned around." She raised her eyes to Jeffrey. "I couldn't help overhearing. You guys weren't exactly quiet." She traced a route with her index finger. "You should have turned here," she said, pointing to a spot along the crease.

"Finally," Morrie said. "Deliverance."

"Yep," Carla said, bobbing her head decisively. "You won't get lost again. I'm going with you."

"What?" Jeffrey sputtered a mouthful of coffee.

"I'm going with you. How far you guys going?" Carla asked. "It don't matter though. You need me." She watched Jeffrey dabbing at his coat. "You better get that coffee off of your jacket before the milk sets. It'll get all hard and everything if you don't."

"Morrie, I'm going to the men's room. Would you care to accompany me?" Jeffrey asked.

"I don't see why..." Morrie began.

"Now," Jeffrey repeated, tossing his napkin on the table after a futile attempt to sop up the coffee.

****

"Excuse us, Carla," Morrie said. "We'll be right back." He shot an encouraging smile as Jeffrey grabbed his arm and propelled him to the restroom tucked down the hall to the left of the kitchen. Slamming the door behind them, he pinned his brother to the wall with a well-placed elbow. "Have you lost what's left of your freaking mind? We don't know anything about this woman. Were you not looking at her face?"

"Yeah. So? Did you get a look at that body?" "Morrie, you miss my point. We don't know shit about her. She could be a murderer or a nutcase or a professional assassin who will off us in our sleep."

"She looks more like the victim. Besides, we're lost. "

"Define lost."

"Here."

Jeffrey released his grip on his brother. "You have a point. We could ask her if she has a weapon." He brightened. "You ask her."

"Me? Why do I have to ask her? You're the one who wants to know. I trust her. I just have a feeling. I think she needs us."

"You trust anything in a skirt."

"We'll flip for it."

"Fine," Jeffrey said, checking his pockets. "I don't have a penny."

Morrie patted his own pockets. "Me neither. Maybe we could borrow one." "Right. Who's gonna give us a coin? The axe murderer? 'Excuse me,

Carla, but we're flipping a penny to decide if you're going to kill us or not and we're a bit short of funds.'"

"You're overreacting, as usual. Just give her a chance," Morrie said. "All right. But if we wake up dead, don't say I didn't warn you."

The two men stomped out of the men's room and back to their seats to find Carla adding a dollop of ketchup to Jeffrey's scrambled eggs which she had scraped onto her pie plate.

"They were getting cold," Carla said, wiping her mouth with the back of her hand.

"I'm going to be ill," Jeffrey said.

"You gonna finish those hash browns?" Carla asked, waving her fork over Morrie's food.

"No. By all means, help yourself," he said, shoving the plate toward her. "I like hash browns and scrambled eggs. Never had them with apple pie before, though," she said. "You gotta keep yourself open to new ideas. That's my motto. That's where all the good recipes come from, you know. New ideas. Yep." She nodded her head with conviction and tucked into her food.

"I'm sure," Jeffrey said and signaled for the waitress to bring more coffee. "You ever watch the food channel?" she asked. "That's one of my favorites, although in my line of work I don't have a lot of time for cooking."

"What exactly is your line of work? If you don't mind my asking," Morrie said. Carla straightened her back and lifted her chin. "Dancer."

"Really."

"Yep. I've been working some but now I'm headed for the big time. Finally got my big break."

Morrie and Jeffrey exchanged looks. "Really. Where is this big break happening?" Morrie asked.

"San Francisco. I figure it's got a lot of culture. You need culture if you're a dancer. Culture is high class, and that's what I'm workin' on. I got a plan for my life. Yessir. San Francisco is where I'm going. I'm gonna be high class."

"Quite so," Morrie agreed. "You shouldn't have a problem there."

Carla glanced at the daisy clock and shoved the rest of her food into her already stuffed mouth. "So, you comin' or not? Make up your mind. I'm headed out." She took a fiver out of her wallet, set it on the table, and anchored it with a fork.

"Yes," said Morrie, ignoring Jeffrey's mutterings. "We're coming."

She held out her hand and wiggled her fingers. "Keys. It's easier to drive than tell you every turn to take."

Jeffrey's mouth moved but he couldn't seem to form any words, so he dropped the keys into her waiting palm. "You're the Jimmy out back," she said, examining the key fob. "I can't wait to hear the story about the Buick. Bet it's a scream. Let's go then. Get a move on," she said, shouldering the purse and leading the way out the back door like a school chaperone with her charges.

"What about your car?' Jeffrey asked.

"Not a problem," she said. "Forget about it. It's all taken care of." Taken care of was right. In this neighborhood the car would be up on blocks and stripped before sundown. Even the Mob couldn't move as fast as Eddie's Chop Shop.

"It's almost sunrise," Jeffrey said, pointing to the mountain looming behind them where dawn was a smudge across the crest.

"Yeah," Carla said. "That's Mount Carmel but nobody calls it that. The Indians called it Sleeping Giant. If you look close you can see him. Takes some imagination, though. I never could get it" She negotiated her way across the littered parking lot and past the dumpsters to the Jimmy. The air was damp in the early morning chill and smelled like rain. She clicked her tongue against her teeth. Rain meant fender benders and other minor accidents that would cause traffic to snarl up like a rat's tail hairbrush. It would slow them down. She walked around the truck, checking the tires with a practiced eye, supplemented with a few good kicks. "Quite a rig you got here," she said.

"It's not ours," Morrie said.

"It's hot?" Carla stopped in her tracks.

"It's not stolen," Jeffrey said. "It belongs to a friend. We're doing a favor." Carla studied Jeffrey's face. "You got an honest face. I can read character good. I wouldn't take a hot truck anywheres." "Good to know," Morrie said.

"Yeah, I seen some bad shit out there. I used to ride with my old man." Her eyes softened. "He was a long-haul trucker. You'd be surprised what you see on the road. You don't wanna get mixed up in no auto ring, that's for sure. They don't play nice. What's with the car?"

"It's going too," Morrie said. "It's a classic—a '54 Buick Roadmaster, and it's worth more than the truck pulling it."

Carla gave the car a glance and shrugged. "Let's go. We're burning daylight." She climbed into the driver's seat, Morrie claimed the passenger side, and

Jeffrey crammed himself into the back bench. "You guys never told me where you're going once we get on the interstate."

"San Jose," Morrie said.

"No kidding?" Carla said. "We're headed the same direction, sort of. Who would've thought?"

"Who indeed," Jeffrey agreed, leaning his forehead against the window. "What happened to the GPS?"

"It got busted." Jeffrey said.

"I can see that. It's all crumpled. How'd it happen?"

"It's a long story," Morrie said.

"We got time. The way I figure it, we drive in shifts round the clock. Four hours apiece, and the guy off duty crashes on the bunk in the camper. Fifty hours to San Jose, give or take, depending on food and fuel stops. It's I-80 all the way. So you got plenty of time to fill me in. Hang on a minute," Carla said, rummaging through her pocketbook until she found her cell. She punched in some numbers and frowned as the voice mail menu options came up. "Shit," she muttered. "Call me," she said and disconnected. "Where were we? Oh yeah," she turned to Morrie. "You were gonna tell me how this happened." She pointed at the ruined piece of technology dangling from the console.

"Wanda," Morrie said, his lips curling into a snarl that added a few extra n's to the name. "Wannnda." He gave a shudder. "She got a thing against technology?" Carla asked.

"She's got a thing against Freddie."

"Who's Freddie?"

"Her husband," Jeffrey said. "At least he was. Is. Was. She's been busting up everything he owns before the divorce is final. And she's using his tools to do it. But when she started in on his truck—that was too much. I mean, his truck, for Chrissakes." Jeffrey's eyes showed the depths of his pain at this outrage.

"Freddie asked me to get the truck out of her reach before she trashed it," Morrie said. "Get it to his brother's house. That's why we're headed to San Jose, and that's why the GPS looks like it went ten rounds with a kook. It did and she is."

"She coming after him?" Carla asked.

"Even Wanda wouldn't go that far," Morrie said. "The truck, maybe. I dunno."

"You never know about these things," Carla said. "Sometimes people get one idea in their heads and there ain't no room for another. I'd tell your friend to watch his ass. Especially if the divorce was his fault."

"She's got a point, Jeffrey. If Freddie hadn't been screwing around, he'd still be married."

"Yeah, Morrie, but he'd still be married to Wannnnda."

Seven and a half hours into their drive, they'd left the traffic problems of New York behind and were cruising through Pennsylvania, keeping an eye out for radar sweeps. They'd already passed two strings of cars pulled over to the side of the road awaiting their turn with the highway patrol officers working the crowd. In Pennsylvania, there's no such thing as safety in numbers.

"I think we're good to go now," Morrie said, reaching for the accelerator lever on the steering wheel to bump up the cruise control.

"Not a good plan," Carla said. "It's kinda like deer. Where there's one, there's more. There'll be another one about ten miles down the road. Wait and see." "There've already been two."

"It's psychology. That's a high class word. I learned about it on television. They had one of those lady shrinks on and she explained how your mind works. She said it was psychology—the mind thing. Anyhow, people do what they see other people doing and figure it's okay. Like now.

The second group got caught because they were thumbing their noses at the first group. There'll be one more, trust me."

Morrie huffed but put his hand back on the wheel. Three cars sped by them in the passing lane. "I feel like we're standing still," he complained.

"In a couple of minutes, it'll be the other way around."

"Five bucks says you're wrong."

"I never take a sucker bet," she said. "Look to your left." She pointed at a small copse of trees in the median that hid a patrol car with a radar gun aimed at the cars passing by. "The chasers will be up ahead. And so will the guys who passed us." She tapped her index finger to the side of her head. "Psychology."

Morrie whistled through his teeth. Sure enough, the cars were being herded to the side of the road like stray cattle. "You were right on the money," he said.

Carla looked out the window. "You got no idea." She crumpled the last candy wrapper and tossed it on the floor where it joined a growing accumulation of empty chip bags and other snack wraps. "It's time for a break," she said. "DuBois is coming up, and there's a big box store about five minutes off the highway. You and Jeffrey can grab some fruit and drinks or whatever. I need to get some things to wear. This outfit ain't gonna be enough."

"Sounds like a plan," Morrie said, flexing his shoulders and rotating his neck to an accompaniment of snaps and cracks. "Jeffrey can fuel up and we'll meet back at the truck. How long?"

"Fifteen minutes should do it," she said. "I'm a quick shopper. I work fast." Morrie raised an eyebrow. The parking lot was full but not jammed, and he finessed the truck into a space just south of the main entrance and well away from the cart caddy. The truck didn't have any scratches on its silver paint job, and he wanted to keep it that way.

They split up at the entrance and Carla, true to her word, was back waiting at the truck fifteen minutes later. Morrie climbed into the back of the camper with an apple. Carla took the wheel, and Jeffrey settled into the passenger seat. In ten minutes they were back on the interstate. Jeffrey stared at the road ahead, and Carla decided he was less of a conversational asset than his brother.

"You don't like me much, do you?" Carla asked.

"I don't know you," Jeffrey replied.

"You're sure kind of a stuffed shirt, if you don't mind my saying so. You should open up more to people." She checked her rear and side mirrors.

"You've got a mouth that doesn't know when to quit. Not everybody likes to talk all the time. That's my opinion, in case you're interested and even if you're not. Now if you don't mind, I'm going to listen to the radio."

"Not for long, you ain't."

"What's that supposed to mean?"

"Psychology," she said, as if the word defined life itself. "Just reading you. You're the type who probably likes jazz. Maybe alternative. You ain't going to find what you like here."

Jeffrey ignored her and worked his way through every station and then tried one more time. He shut off the radio and glared at Carla who smiled sweetly.

"It's the Jesus stations. That's all you're gonna get until we get close to the big cities. That and the farm reports. You don't strike me as the kinda guy who's into either one. Although some of them preachers can really get worked up into a clammy sweat about hell and damnation." She leaned slightly toward him and confided, "I don't hold with any of it. Hell is on earth. So's heaven." She checked the mirrors again. "You should relax more. You're very tense." She took her right hand off the wheel and fished around in her pocketbook until she found a CD, which she handed over to him. "Pop that in the player, will you? I need to burn off some negative energy."

Jeffrey opened the CD and stared at the label, then turned to look at Carla. Carla shot a glance in his direction. "What? You don't like Prokofiev? I got a
Stravinsky if you'd rather hear that."

"It's just," he began. "I didn't...you...I never..." he stammered.

"Tense," Carla muttered. "Way too tense."

CHAPTER SEVEN

New Haven

Seven months until retirement. It might as well have been seven years. Frankie Genovese leaned against the bar in the club's main room and thumbed through the calendar hanging behind the cash register. He considered his options, but there weren't many and none of them looked good. He massaged his throbbing temples. Thinking clearly was essential but he was tired. His brain wouldn't focus. Staying and riding this out wasn't going to happen. He slammed a fist on the bar and swore. How could it all have gone so bad so fast?

He'd been meticulous in the planning. He'd worked out a plan and done everything according to that plan. The money followed if you did it right and were careful. And he was a careful man. Consistency was the key. He'd been nothing if not consistent since Day One. He also wasn't greedy, and that was why his daily withdrawals from the receipts had gone unnoticed.

It all came down to routine. Nothing out of the ordinary. Nothing unusual to raise suspicions. Just careful and methodical bookkeeping. Straight and steady. Each night he'd skimmed five bills off the receipts and deposited the cash in an offshore account. Two hundred from the booze, two from the drugs, and one from the girls. When the receipts were high, he took his five. If they were low, he took his five. Consistency. Greed never entered into the plan. He was never tempted to take more than his five. It wasn't complicated and it had added up. Over fifteen years, it had turned unto a very nice IRA. Nothing had gotten in the way, and nothing had gone wrong—until tonight when Tony had pulled this stunt. And just like that, the planning didn't matter any more. Now Sal would be looking really close at everything Frankie did. Too close. It was over. It was time to close the books and take early retirement.

Frankie squared his shoulders and strode back through the empty club and down the hall, his shoes making sucking noises on the sticky linoleum. He shut his office door and snapped the deadbolt. Time was short. Sal would expect him with the money before ten and that was only six hours away. Time enough. It had to be.

Draping his suit coat around the chair back, he unclipped his bow tie and dropped it on the filing cabinet. He pulled the chair up to the desk and brought up his personal files on the computer. A few clicks of the mouse and the final transfer of funds to his offshore account was complete. Not that it mattered, but he'd taken the usual five hundred tonight anyway. No reason to deviate now. That part of the plan had worked. He'd started that way and he'd finish that way. He sat back in his chair and snipped the end off a *Romeo y Julietta* No. 5, poured himself a last two fingers of scotch, and began to sort through the desk drawers. He flipped through the pages in his planner to the last entry. The date was circled in red ink. April fifteenth. His personal Red Letter Day. The taxes would be filed, and he'd planned to be long gone, enjoying the sand, surf, and babes in bikinis on a tropical beach in the Caribbean. He closed the planner and shoved it into his briefcase. Plans change.

He turned his attention back to the computer and brought up his bookkeeping program and both sets of books. He had no delusions about his chances of living out the day without insurance. He uploaded the files to flash drives and placed each one in a separate mailer. He addressed the first to himself in care of his bank. He took a business card from his wallet, jotted off a quick note, and clipped the note to the card. He slipped these inside the second mailer, addressing it to his wife in care of her sister in Jersey. The third flash drive he slipped into his pocket. Then he picked up the phone.

****

Anna Marie Genovese slapped in the general vicinity of the lamp on the bedstand and finally connected with her land line. She fell back against the covers and mumbled, "Hello?"

"Wake up. Are you awake?"

"Ummm."

"Anna Marie. Wake up."

"Frankie?"

"Don't ask questions. Pack a bag and go to Eleanor's. Do as I say and do it now. Don't talk to anyone until you've heard from me. Do you understand?"

"Uh huh."

"Goddammit! Wake up and listen. Do you understand?"

"All right. All right. Yeah, Frankie, I understand. Go to Eleanor's." "All right." He disconnected.

****

At the other end, Anna Marie, phone still cradled to her ear, pushed up her eye mask and glanced at the glowing green LED numbers on the face of her bedside clock. It was 4:45. The middle of the goddamn night. She grunted and swung her legs out of bed, fishing in the dark for her slippers.

****

Almost everything was done. Frankie watched the ash build on the cigar, breathing in the aroma. He removed his Sig from the desk drawer. First things first. Paying Sal was business. Paying Tony was personal. He searched through the employee file until he found Tony's address, a cheap apartment north of the Club. "What are the odds he'll be home?" he wondered. "What the hell? He's just stupid enough to go there."

In his panic, Tony had left his car at the Club and Frankie took the precaution of lifting the distributor cap and removing the rotor, just in case Tony doubled back to get it. Unless he boosted a car parked along the street, he'd still be legging it. His apartment on Bassett Street was a fair distance and on foot would take him maybe half an hour, if he kept up the pace. The initial adrenaline rush wouldn't take him all the way home. He'd have to slow down or collapse along the way. Frankie half expected to find Tony's body sprawled somewhere in an alley, dead of a heart attack. Nobody could run that far that fast for that long and Tony was no athlete.

Frankie straightened the papers on his desk. He picked up the framed photo of Anna Marie, taken on their honeymoon when she was beautiful and slim and young. He put it back down. The office needed to look like he'd be returning to it that night. He shouldered the Sig and let himself out through the office door that opened onto the alley where he parked his Cadillac Sedan. He fobbed open the door, slid into the driver's seat, started the engine, and turned left onto Dixwell, slowing for each driveway and cross street—any place Tony might have stepped aside to rest. Maybe Tony'd already made it home and this was wasted effort. Still, it didn't hurt to be thorough. He could get lucky.

A black and white sped past, siren blaring, and Frankie startled. He tightened his grip on the steering wheel. Three blocks down and to the right he turned onto Bassett. Another three intersections down he was met by a roadblock, crime scene tape, three cruisers, and the film crew from WNHC. Nothing out of whack there, they probably had the neighborhood on their regular schedule. Frankie strained to see past the cop directing traffic, what little there was of it, to the figure sprawled on the sidewalk. It wasn't Tony. Too small. Just a punk kid. Dead, though. Real dead. The cop started toward him. Frankie waved and made a quick turn onto Shelton, looking for another way in.

Garbage cans and trash bags heaped at the curb meant tomorrow was pickup day. If somebody had forgotten to latch a side gate after lugging the cans through, Frankie'd be able to cut across a back yard and come on to Tony's place from the rear. He cruised the street slowly, checking every yard, and at the third house he got lucky. A rusted gate was propped open with a brick. You take your luck where you find it. He parked the Caddy, setting the alarm before he sprinted through the gate and across the back yard. Apparently he wasn't the first guy to have taken this route. Wire cutters had chewed through the metal and the rough ends had been bent back, providing a smooth and handy portal to Tony's back yard. Frankie made his way around the piles of trash that hadn't made the final trip to the curb. A pit bull on a short chain was dozing by a wooden box next to a locked storage shed. The dog paid him no mind and Frankie returned the favor.

New Haven might not have invented urban blight, but it sure as hell had perfected it. Urban renewal had been going on for over half a century and if the number of parking lots created was the goal, the effort had been a resounding success. In the slums that had survived the wrecking ball and the dozer, there was little to distinguish one building from another. All were the same three stacked stories of despair with their cracked and chipped asbestos shingle siding. There were bars on the ground-floor windows and expansive porches that nobody ever used, unless they wanted to watch a drive by. Tony's digs had the distinction of housing the Cazbah Mini-Mart and Liquor Store on the ground floor. The dead kid in the street had most likely tried to stick up the store and hadn't counted on the proprietor's gun under the counter or the guy's aim with it.

The kid's luck had run out but Frankie's held. Wooden stairs up the backside of the house opened onto narrow landings at both the second and third floors. Recessed entryways off the landings led to stairwells that reeked of rancid cooking oil and urine. At the second landing, a rat was chewing on a piece of something putrid amid a pile of crumpled beer cans and used hypodermic syringes.

The door at the second landing was unlocked and Frankie pushed it open, waiting for his eyes to adjust to the dim light cast by a single bulb hanging from the ceiling by frayed wires. With this open invitation and his Sig in hand, Frankie moved along, hugging the wall. Tony's front door was wide open but the apartment was dark. He inched around the doorjamb, feeling against the wall for the switch. His fingers connected and he flipped on the lights. Silence. He eased back around the jamb and scoped out the room.

The place had been tossed. More than tossed. Trashed. Frankie stood briefly in the doorway, taking in the damage, then closed the door behind him and began his own search. There weren't all that many places to look. The main room was part living room, part kitchen. The bedroom and bath were off of that. The kitchen was bare bones—some dirty dishes piled in the sink, empty pizza cartons and fast food containers piled in the corner next to the fridge, a hot plate on the counter. A round wooden table lay on its side up against the wall, a smashed kitchen chair beside it. A few pots and pans were stacked on some shelving attached to the wall by metal runners.

The other side of the room made up the living area. The only furniture was a beat-up second hand sofa, its cushions slashed and thrown on the floor. The only decent thing in the room was a 52 inch HDTV on the far wall. It wouldn't be there for long once word got out Tony had split.

The bedroom and bath told the same story. Someone had gone through the place with a vengeance. Dresser drawers had been pulled out and emptied. The mattress was half off the bed, the sheets in a heap alongside. The closet door was open revealing a few clean shirts, slacks, and a pair of dress shoes. If the money had been there, it was gone now, and so was Tony. Where the hell was he?

Frankie returned to the living room and peered out the window at the activity on the street below. The cops were bullshitting and the meat wagon was loading up the kid's body. Whatever had happened in the apartment hadn't been heard down on the street. He stepped away from the window and surveyed the room one last time. If he was going to get his money back, it sure as hell wasn't going to happen here. A car alarm sounded and Frankie bounded out of the room and down the stairs.

CHAPTER EIGHT

Sardinia: Aeroporto di Cagliari

It was twelve-thirty the next afternoon when the flatbed truck was buzzed through the gates into the airport's employee parking lot. Two minutes later, Aldo Borghese activated the hydraulics, and the Fiat slid off the truck and onto the asphalt. It hit the ground, rear bumper first and flipped over, coming to rest on its roof. Peppino from Palermo stared bug-eyed as the car shuddered before collapsing into a pile of metal scrap.

"Idiot!" Peppino screamed. "No ramps! You forgot to put the ramps on. Idiot!"

Aldo thrust a clipboard into Peppino's hands. "Sign here," he said, pointing at a signature line on a grease-spotted Waiver of Liability form. He offered a pen.

Peppino opened his mouth to yell again but changed his mind when Aldo shifted his stance just enough to reveal the shoulder holster beneath his grimy, oil-stained jacket.

"Sign here," Aldo repeated.

Peppino scribbled his name, and Aldo grabbed the clipboard, tossed it onto the front seat, and drove away whistling—a cloud of black diesel smoke obliterating the fuming Peppino standing amid the crumpled remains of the Fiat.

CHAPTER NINE

The Skies above San Francisco

It had to be love. Gino had fallen hard shortly after takeoff and nothing during the flight had changed the way he felt. It was possibly lust—definitely lust—but this woman had the potential for being The One. She had been his seatmate and the object of his adoration since they'd left JFK. Her name, which he had yet to learn, was undoubtedly something exotic, musical. She was slender with raven hair and almond eyes, and from the little he'd seen of her legs, they were shapely. She was no more than twenty-five, certainly no more than twenty-eight. An added bonus was that she wasn't going anywhere anytime soon. It would take at least half an hour for this current spin over the water to run its course.

He'd tried a few conversation openers but the weather hadn't gone anywhere and she apparently didn't follow football, so he hadn't had much luck until he remembered some sage advice from his mini-online course on assertive dating, "Seven Pickup Lines That Never Fail." The fifth Line advised making an unexpected yet enticing comment. As the plane began a wide arc over the Pacific for the third time, he crossed his legs—a difficult action, given the miniscule space provided in coach—and ventured forth. "Did you know that eighty-one-point-two percent of landing delays at SFO are for reasons other than weather?"

"Excuse me?" She looked up from the book she'd been reading and stared at him.

Gino repeated the statistic and waited, a serious expression on his face and his eyes focused intently on hers.

"You're making that up." She closed her book over her right hand and looked at him. "Yes, I am," he agreed. "But it's as good a statistic as any, and it got you to look at me."

She blinked twice and then laughed. It was a beautiful sound. Soft and gentle and musical. He upped the ante. "I see you like to read." He pulled the Boeing 737 Safety Features and Emergency Evacuation Procedures folder from the seatback pouch and offered it to her. "Do you ever read these? A strange mix of topics, aren't they? You know, one page telling you how invincible the airplane is and another telling you what to do when it starts plummeting to the ground. Wouldn't you think they'd put them on separate pieces of paper?"

She shuddered. "Read them? Nobody reads them. Besides, would it really make any difference if I did?"

"Probably not, but they are nicely laminated."

"You're very strange." She removed her hand from the book and it closed all the way. "I don't usually talk to strange men."

Gino smiled. "Strange? Perhaps I am. But I'm not dangerous, and I finally got you to put down your book and talk to me." He flashed a grin. "How about dinner, if we ever see ground again?"

"When. Not if. Asians are superstitious."

"So are Italians. Although we add guilt for seasoning."

"That's a religious burden, not a cultural one." She shook her head. "No dinner. If we don't work together, dinner is a long time to suffer. Believe me. I've learned that lesson and it's a place I'm not going again. Drinks. Maybe."

"Maybe is a yes," he said.

"Maybe," she agreed.

"What's the worst that could happen? You decide you don't like me and we part company. My heart will be broken, but I will be strong."

This time she really laughed, causing a woman in the seat ahead to crane her neck to see what was happening behind her.

Gino moved in as close as the armrest would allow. "Since we may be meeting for drinks, will you tell me your name?"

She hesitated only briefly. "Francesca. Yours?"

"Gino."

"It suits you."

"Yeah, I know. It's short."

"No, I didn't mean that. Short, I mean. You don't look short. Oh, shit, this isn't coming out the way I meant. I'm sorry. Truly. I didn't mean anything wrong. Open mouth, insert foot, Francesca."

He winced. "That's okay. It's as good a name as any. They have to call you something, short or tall." His mind raced. What to say next? Pressure tactics never work. He settled on something safe. "What do you do?"

"Did, not do. As of yesterday, I'm officially downsized." She shoved the book into her bag. "Going home to family to sort things out. You?"

He looked out the window where dusk had given way to night. What hadn't been visible in the waning daylight was now clear and sharp. What appeared at first glance to be stars were actually dozens of planes circling, above and below them, waiting for clearance to land, their flashing lights winking encouragement. He forgot all about the course suggestions. "Do," Gino repeated. "I grow grapes," he said. "And I make wine."

"Really." Her eyes were warm and radiated genuine interest. "I love wine." "Yes," Gino said, warming to the topic. "My vineyard..."

The pilot chose that moment to announce they were finally cleared for landing. Opportunity lost. There was no way this was going anywhere. He needed more time. They'd had hours and nothing had happened. Now he'd finally done...said something right, and it was doomed. She was probably too tall for him anyway. Her legs were a dead giveaway. Too tall. She'd laugh when he stood up and had to ask her to get his carry on from the overhead compartment. Too damn tall. Tall women didn't like short men. Period. End of discussion.

Francesca used both feet to jam her computer bag as far forward as it would go. And then she took a business card from her pocketbook and dangled it between her thumb and index finger.

"I want to know more. Use the cell," she said. "The other number's no longer mine."

"Count on it," Gino said. At least his mouth did. The rest of him was in cardiac arrest.

Twenty minutes later they'd touched down and gotten the official okay to use their cell phones. In the ensuing techno-frenzy, Francesca scanned her incoming messages and wrinkled her forehead at an unfamiliar number.

"You should answer that," Gino said, a knowing look in his eyes.

Francesca shook her head.

"No, really. See, that would be me," Gino said leaning closer. "I'll save you the trouble of answering. You can save a lot of time by going directly to the source. I said I'd call. I'm a man of my word. So, how about it?"

"Look, I'm really sorry, but I've got plans tonight." She studied his face. "How about tomorrow?"

"Tomorrow? Tomorrow's good too. Top of the Mark at seven."

"Maybe." And she smiled.

CHAPTER TEN

New Haven and environs

Freshly showered and shaved but minus two hubcaps and with a busted out driver side window, Frankie turned his wounded Cadillac left off Grove onto Temple and cursed his luck. He had luck all right, but lately it had all been bad. First Tony grabbed the receipts, then Sal paid him a visit, then that crackhead punk tried to chop his car, and now he couldn't even get a parking space outside the bank where he was going to have to withdraw a hundred thousand of his own money and go groveling with it back to Sal.

Even then he wouldn't be out of the woods. He'd hand over the cash and get out of Sal's in one piece, he was fairly sure, but how long he'd last before the whack came was anybody's guess. Not long. Sal didn't give second chances. That's why Frankie planned to be out of town as soon as he'd made the delivery, and he wasn't coming back. By tonight he'd be long gone and beyond Sal's slimy tentacles. Change his name maybe. Leave the country. Whatever it took. He'd be gone. But right now, Sal was waiting for his money at his home in Orange and Frankie was stuck in a holding pattern in downtown New Haven.

The third time around the block, he struck gold. A dark green SUV with heavily tinted windows pulled out from a space directly outside the main office of the Greater New Haven Savings and Loan and Frankie swooped in. He shifted into park, set the e-brake, and was about to kill the ignition when he caught a glimpse of the SUV in his rear view mirror. The car seemed to be double-parked just across the intersection. Frankie waited, but the car didn't move. He let out a low whistle and slapped the steering wheel. One thing about luck. Once it started going downhill it picked up speed until you crashed and burned. But then again, maybe not. Time for a new plan. Frankie shut down the engine, grabbed his briefcase, and exited the car without giving the SUV so much as a sideways glance. It would still be there waiting for him when he emerged from the bank with the cash. He hummed softly as he climbed the seven marble steps that led to the revolving door that opened onto the bank's main floor.

GNHS&L had undergone a few name changes in its existence, but the interior had remained the same. The bank had been built to inspire confidence in its customers. It was rock solid. Black and white marble Corinthian columns with ornate capitals lined both sides of the massive interior and supported the ceiling some thirty-five feet above the marble floors. Marble was everywhere—marble counters, marble floors, marble pen holders at the tables housing deposit and withdrawal slips. A row of cashiers operating behind wrought iron screens occupied one side. Along the other was a tasteful arrangement of oak desks polished to a high gleam where bank officers entrusted with the personal touch in banking sat and waited for prey. The vault occupied the mid-section of the rear wall.

Frankie made his way to the desk with the Customer Service placard and stood by the chairs aligned before a low rectangular table where copies of *The Wall Street Journal* and *The New Haven Register* were neatly arranged in separate piles.

"May I help you?" The officer, a heavyset woman in her late forties with too much makeup and a frizzy perm, spoke to him while cradling the phone to her shoulder. Her name plate identified her as Florence.

"I need access to my safety deposit box, Florence," Frankie said, declining her motion for him to have a seat.

"Just a moment. I'll be right with you." Just a moment became several and Frankie spent them staring at her until she'd finally gotten the message. She ended her conversation, returned the phone to its cradle, and greeted him with an official smile that had all the sincerity of a politician's handshake.

"Yes?"

The word seemed more of a challenge than a greeting, but Frankie pressed on.

"I need access to my safety deposit box," he repeated.

"Certainly, sir." She offered a clipboard with a sign-in sheet attached. He entered his name, the time, and the date in the appropriate spaces and handed the clipboard back to her.

"I'll need some ID, sir," she said.

Frankie pulled out his wallet and handed her his driver's license.

She made some further notations on the sheet and then made a good show of scrutinizing his face and matching it with the photo on the license.

"Would it help if I smiled or frowned or whatever you need so we can move this along?" Frankie said. "I really am in a bit of a hurry."

She returned his license, made still another notation on the sheet, and then reached into her center drawer for the bank key. "Follow me," she said, leading the way through the open iron vault doors to the rows of safety deposit boxes. She paused before box twelve oh five and waited while Frankie inserted his key. She inserted hers and then withdrew the box from its niche. She handed it to Frankie and then opened a door to a room just large enough for a small table and two desk chairs. "Press the buzzer once when you've finished," she said. "Once," she repeated. She turned and left him alone, closing the door behind her.

Frankie set his briefcase on the table, opened it, and removed a flash drive, which he placed in the safety deposit box. He rifled through the papers in the box, but there was nothing he needed. The deed to the house, the kids' Baptismal papers, his marriage license. He checked his cell but there was no service in the vault. He closed the box and buzzed one time, as instructed, and waited for Florence to return. Within a few minutes she opened the door and they went through the procedures in reverse. He took a seat at Florence's desk this time and checked his cell service. Plenty of bars. He requested a phone book, which Florence extracted from a bottom desk drawer and shoved at him. Nobody used a phone directory anymore, her action told him, but he ignored her and thumbed through the listings in the front of the book until he found what he needed. He punched in the numbers and bypassed the menu of options by pressing 0 for operator. A few seconds later a real person came on the line.

"Federal Bureau of Investigation. How may I direct your call?"

"I'd like to speak to an agent. The call concerns income tax evasion, racketeering, murder, and a few other things. I'll hold."

Florence's eyes grew wide. She said nothing but continued to straighten the same stack of papers over and over again.

"If you don't mind," Frankie said to her, "I'll just wait here."

"Take all the time you need, sir," she said, pulling a file folder from her inbox and straightening those papers as well.

"McManus." The voice on the other end of the phone listened without interrupting while Frankie outlined the situation and the price for his testimony.

"I'll wait," Frankie said. While he waited, Frankie electronically transferred the entire balance of his GNHS&L account to his offshore account. He smiled. There was no reason now to make a withdrawal for Sal. Screw the plan. With no 100K withdrawal to complicate matters, he wasn't out a dime.

Ten minutes later two FBI agents strode into the bank and proceeded to Florence's desk, where they presented their IDs. Frankie stood, locked his hands behind his head and said, "You don't know how happy I am to see you. I assume I'm under arrest. There's a Sig in my shoulder holster. Before we leave, you'll want to check out a green SUV double parked in the next block. They may wish to interfere with our business."

Agent McManus spoke into his Bluetooth and nodded to Frankie.

"We're clear. Let's go."

At the front door, Frankie searched for the SUV. It was effectively blocked front and back by two unmarked Government Issue cars. It wasn't going anywhere. But he was, and while it wasn't the Caribbean yet, it was a far better place than Sal had slotted him for. He smiled for the first time that day.

CHAPTER ELEVEN

On the Road

"Why do you people do that?" Morrie looked up from the map to fix Carla with a hostile stare.

"Do what? What people? What the hell you talkin' about?" She didn't take her eyes off the road. "You wanna speak English or something?"

"That cross thing."

"What cross thing?"

"This cross thing!" He made a rapid sign of the cross and kissed his fingertips.

"Oh."

"Well?"

"What?"

"Why? It's a simple enough question," he said.

"Okay. What about the 'you people' thing?"

"You people. You people. What's not to understand? I don't do that. You people do."

"You people? Okay. Fine. My people. My people do this when we hear a siren or see a hearse or on a whole bunch of different occasions. It's what we do. My people, my ass."

"Don't get huffy. It's an honest question." "Then ask it with some respect, asshole."

Morrie took a careful, measured breath. "This isn't going well. Let's start over," he said. "Why do you do the cross thing?"

Carla nodded. "Okay. Starting over. It's consideration for somebody who might need a prayer. Nothing complicated." She glanced at him. "Sounds like you resent it on some level. What do you people do?"

"My people? My people don't do anything. I'm Jewish." "Okay. I'm Catholic. What's your point?"

"We're different."

"No shit."

"Would you two cut the noise up there? I'm trying to take a nap." Jeffrey's voice wafted up from the depths of the back bench. "Where are we? I don't think I can take another hour of your bickering."

"We ain't bickering," Carla said. "We're discussing. Morrie has issues and we're working them out."

"I do not have issues," he said.

"That's an issue," she said. "You can't live and not have issues. I have issues. Everybody has issues."

"Where are we?" Jeffrey repeated.

"Coming up on exit 284, Walcott, Iowa. You're gonna love this place. It's the world's largest truck stop. It's got everything we need. Fuel, food, showers. Some of us could really use one. Shouldn't take more than half an hour and we'll be back on the road. I made a list of stuff we need. We can split up and meet back here."

"Jeffrey can take care of the diesel," Morrie said. "I'll go in with you."

"Suit yourself," Carla said, "but you ain't following me into the showers."

CHAPTER TWELVE

Top of the Mark, San Francisco

"I wasn't sure you'd be here," Gino said.

"I said *maybe*, didn't I?" Francesca reached across the cocktail table to touch Gino's hand. "After all, we never had a chance to finish our conversation." She shook out the linen napkin and arranged it on her lap. It was a slow night at the bar and the waiter appeared promptly, brandishing the drink menu.

"Give us a moment, please," Francesca said. "We're not in any rush."

"I like the sound of that," Gino said. The waiter melted back into the scenery, and Gino picked up the menu and scanned the wine list.

"I would have taken you for a Scotch man," Francesca said.

"*Italiano, signorina,*" Gino bowed his head slightly. "'Where there is no wine, there is no love.'"

"Is that original?"

"Euripedes. Even the Greeks loved wine. I'm not sure about the Scotch." "Ah, the benefits of a classical education."

"Such as it was. I didn't pay very close attention." "Too busy chasing women you meet on airplanes?"

"Something like that." He set the menu down. "Actually, a great deal like that. I appreciate women. And I find them vastly more intelligent than most men."

"So it was my mind that attracted you to me."

"Mostly your legs."

"You're hopeless."

"Yes, I am, but I do know wine."

"Then, my fate is in your hands. They make a hundred different kinds of martinis here, but I've never developed a taste for any of them."

Gino set down the wine list at the edge of the table, a gesture that re-activated the waiter. "We'll have a bottle of Dark Mountain Pinot 2011."

Francesca raised an attractive eyebrow and shrugged out of her evening wrap, revealing a form-fitting black dress with a nice degree of décolletage.

"Excellent choice, sir," the waiter said, retrieving the menu. Gino was unsure whether he was referring to the dress or to the wine.

"Dark Mountain," Francesca said. "It's got a mysterious and sexy appeal." Gino felt the last bits of anxiety melt away and he settled back in his seat, warming to the topic. "And that's just the label. Wait till you taste the wine." He unfolded his napkin. "I really am glad you decided to join me."

"I am too. After the day I've had, this is a welcome interlude. It's hell out there applying for jobs. Nobody's hiring, and even if they are, there aren't any benefits." She spread her hands, palms up. "I think I've got a possible, though, but it's only part time and temporary at that." She leaned towards Gino. "Know anybody who needs a good event planner?"

"Not off hand, but I've got your card. Ah. This should help smooth out the rough spots of your day," he said, as the waiter approached with their wine bottle in one hand and two glasses dangling by their stems in the other.

Gino waved the waiter away after he'd uncorked the wine. "We'll let it rest a bit. Even a pinot can benefit from a little breathing room."

Francesca nodded. "You're right on both counts. Breathing room. That's for darn sure. I let today get to me. Maybe tomorrow will bring better luck," she said. "The right job is out there. I just have to find it."

"Most of the time—well, some of the time—I've found that things work out if I don't try too hard." He frowned. "At least that's what I'm counting on." Gino lifted the bottle, took a sniff of the contents, and poured a little wine into his glass. "Sometimes breathing is overrated. Have you thought of starting up your own business? There are benefits to being your own boss." He set the glass down at an angle against the white tablecloth and studied the wine's color with a schooled eye. "Of course when you work for yourself, it seems like you never get a day off." He swirled the contents and inhaled deeply. Satisfied, he finally tasted the wine and approved. "This will do nicely," he said, pouring a glass for Francesca and himself. "Tell me what you think of it."

Francesca inhaled and closed her eyes, and then took a sip, letting the warm liquid move across her tongue. "Very nice." She brought the glass up to her nose and sniffed again. She shook her head and then sniffed once more. This time she made a connection. "Cherries, a hint of raspberry, and possibly chocolate."

"You do know wine," he said.

"I love good wine. I can't afford it, but I love it."

Gino nodded approval.

She took a sip. "I love this."

"Dark Mountain Vineyards. It's my label," Gino said, his eyes shining. "Are you serious?" She extended her glass. "This is really yours?"

"I'm not serious about many things in my life, but I am serious about wine. Yes, this is mine, and I'm happy you like it."

Francesca picked up the bottle and studied the label. "Dark Mountain," she read, tracing the letters with her index finger. On the label, a silhouette of a jagged mountain crest was set against a backdrop of a sunset-streaked sky where a lone bird soared toward the distant horizon. "It's beautiful," she said. "Haunting and mysterious."

"And sexy?"

"And sexy too," she replied, swirling the wine in her glass until it released more of its aroma. "I'm detecting a certain trend here. Where's your vineyard?"

"Not too far from here. In the Santa Cruz Mountains, just south of Los Gatos and past the summit. It can be difficult to find. The locals have a habit of getting rid of road signs. Kind of a remnant of the counter-culture thing, I guess." He hesitated. "If you'd like to see it sometime, I'd be happy to take you there. It's where I live," he added as an afterthought. "At least for now. Things might work out."

"I'd like that very much," she said. "Although the last thing you said..."

"Forget it. We could toast your part-time job success," he said.

"It's not much, but it could be an in, I suppose. I thought I'd gotten past this part. I'd been building my portfolio. Slowly." She grimaced. "Too slowly to do me much good right now. Anyhow, I did two weddings, a Bar Mitzvah, and a waterfowl hunters' convention. I figured that last one would make my name."

"And it didn't, I take it."

"Nooo. Bad timing or bad karma," she said. "Take your pick. I booked them next door to a group of animal rights activists. It got ugly, and I got fired." She picked up the wine bottle again and then set it back down. "Bryan was a first-class creep. My ex-boss," she added. "You know, I would love to get back at him. He set me up. I would never have done that kind of a booking. Only an idiot or somebody who wanted a big scene would. He'd arranged for the mismatch and let me take the heat. Then... Oh, what's the point? There isn't any." She made a fist and pounded her forehead. "No. I'll finish. You know what he did?" Her eyes blazed. "He accused me of embezzlement. And I can't prove him wrong. The money is in my bank account."

Gino set down his glass and gave her an intense look. "You want to run that one by me again?"

She threw her hands in the air. "All I can think of is that he took a deposit slip from my checkbook when I was out of the room. It wouldn't have been hard to do. I kept my purse in my bottom desk drawer. I never made any secret about it. He steals the money from the company, deposits it into my bank account, and then gives me a big wink and a nod. We're co-conspirators now. He figures I'll feed him leads and he'll rake in the loot. He's bought my silence." She ran her finger around the rim of the glass.

"But I refused to help him, and that's when he set me up. I can't do a damn thing about it or I'll take the heat. The money's still there. Not enough to make him worry about it but just enough that I can't explain where it came from. I haven't touched a penny of it. I won't touch a penny of it. Even if I withdraw it and send it to the company, there will still be a record I had it." Her shoulders sagged, and she let out a long breath. "But who knows? Maybe someday I'll find a way to get out of this. I keep hoping. But back up. You said something about things working out?"

"Yeah. Everybody's got problems. You, that guy at the bar working on his fourth martini, everybody. Why should I be an exception?"

"Well?" she prompted.

Gino finished the last of his wine and set the glass down. He took the napkin and folded it carefully, pressing down the creases with the side of his hand. He opened it again and dropped it back into his lap. "This wasn't the way this evening was supposed to go. I'm not sure where the hell it's going. All right. You really want to know?" He propped his elbows on the table, resting his chin in his hands. "To begin, I'm Sicilian. That alone carries a shitload of freight. I owe a debt I can't begin to figure out how to pay, which is not a good thing. And, oh yes, my grandfather wants me to begin *vendetta*, which will involve at least three felonies and God knows how many misdemeanors. Outside of that, my life is just wonderful. Terrific. Couldn't be better." He sat back in his chair and waited. "You asked."

Francesca paused, her wine glass nearly to her lips. "Really."

He waited. What would she do? Toss the wine at him and make a scene before fleeing from the bar and out of his life? Laugh at him? Maybe she'd think he was making the whole thing up to best her story. Once again, he'd managed to turn something good into nothing at all. But he waited.

"Hmm," Francesca said. "I knew you'd be fun. I like Italian men."

"You're not leaving?"

"Why should I leave?" she said. "This is just beginning to get interesting. *Vendetta.* It's a great word, if not a great idea. Shakespeare used it, so you know it's got to have some value. *Vendetta* sounds so much more sinister than *feud*. More sophisticated. Even your lips and your mouth work more when you say it." She mouthed the word and Gino got the idea. She continued. "*Feud* sounds like you've eaten something that didn't agree with you. *Vendetta* rolls off the tongue— waves on the ocean. But then, Italian is a much more picturesque—no, a much more expressive language than English. Life is more exciting when there's an element of danger, don't you think?"

"I'm not sure exciting is the word I'd choose, but if it works for you..." Gino hesitated only briefly, then went for broke. "So, just checking here. You're not leaving."

"Nope. Not going anywhere. I want to see what happens next."

"Next is dinner. Are you ready for some food?"

"Definitely."

"There's a Moroccan hole in the wall about three blocks from here. It's got four tables, but the food is out of this world. Sound okay?"

"Sounds terrific. I think I've got the big picture, but you can fill me in on the rest of the details of your sordid life while we munch." She finished the last of her wine, retrieved her wrap, and draped it across her shoulders, while Gino settled the bill.

****

The trip from the Hopkins to Omar's had been seven blocks more or less downhill. At the second intersection, Francesca took off her heels and donned a pair of flats she'd stowed in her purse. "Girl Scout training," she said, dropping her pumps into a net bag with a pull tie she slipped around her wrist. "Be prepared. It's also the event planner's motto." At the entrance to the restaurant she debated changing back into her heels but didn't. With her flats on, she was just a couple of inches taller than Gino and her feet were comfortable as well. It was a no brainer. She caught him watching her and the expression in his eyes warmed her. "I'm starved," she said.

"So am I. After you" He bowed and she curtsied.

"This is nice," Francesca said. "Intimate. Elegant." She fingered the silken fabric suspended from the ceiling that formed the walls of their dining tent. "Romantic. I don't know how all these small restaurants stay in business, but I'm glad this one is doing so well." The four tables were full and they'd had to wait while a party of two finished their meal. Gino's pointed stares in their direction may have had something to do with hastening their departure because the couple left without lingering over coffee. But now they were seated, and their orders had been taken.

Francesca shook out her napkin, placed it in her lap, and then leaned forward, resting her chin in her hands. "So. I'm all ears. Shoot."

Gino winced. "An unfortunate choice of words there."

"Oops. Sorry. Let's start again." She took a bite of salad and set her fork down. "You know you've piqued my curiosity, but why are you telling me this? You don't know me. I could be anybody. A cop. A crook. Anybody."

"I've got to tell somebody. It's eating me up inside." He touched her cheek. "I trust you. It's as simple as that."

Francesca nodded. "You can."

"I know," he said. "God knows I don't know why, but I do. You aren't, are you?"

"Aren't...?"

"A cop or a crook?"

"Nope. Just me. What you see is what you get."

"And I very much like what I see. Oh, boy. Where to begin?"

"I've found it usually works best if you begin at the beginning," she said. "Just start. It'll get easier once you've broken the ice."

"Right. Here goes nothing." He took a deep breath and let it out slowly. He picked up his fork and studied the tines, running his index finger over the points. He set the fork down and nudged it until it aligned perfectly with the tip of the knife. Then he looked up and met her eyes. "Okay. I'll give you the condensed version. My grandfather in Italy is dying. He raised me after my parents were killed in a car crash. He's a very wealthy man, and I've spent my share of his money. I gamble. Used to, at any rate. Once I got started, I couldn't stop. I was at a casino in Monte Carlo and lost at the Roulette wheel. They took my mark."

"How much?"

"Five hundred thousand and change. Pretty dumb, huh? I thought I was smart but I got sucked in by the royal treatment. You spend big and they comp you suites, meals, and all kinds of stuff, and you think you're pretty hot shit. But you're just another sucker, and they know they'll get you in the end. They got me and got me good."

"That's a lot of money." There wasn't any judgment in her words. Just a simple statement followed by a simple question. "Can you pay it?"

"The honest answer? No. I don't know. I'd have to sell the land, the vineyard, the label, everything I own. If I ever got in so deep that that was the only way out, I knew I'd reached bottom. Well, I'm there now, and I've got to tell you, bottom is not a good place to be." He clenched his jaw. "Fast forward back to my grandfather. He made his fortune as an art forger, and now that he's ready to leave this world and head for the next, he wants to be sure his good name stays intact."

Francesca choked on her salad and reached for her water glass and then her napkin. Her eyes were watering, and she blotted at her lips. She cleared her throat. "Is that it?"

"Oh, no. That's just the beginning. Somebody is stealing my grandfather's work. There's a diary that can prove he's the genius behind another artist's output. That would be the world famous Antonio DeMontana. My grandfather wants me to steal DeMontana's diary that his widow probably has, recover the lost art, and make sure that the family responsible for the thefts—that would be the DeMontana family—pays. *Vendetta*. And, did I mention, that I'm Sicilian? When you add forgery, theft, and all the background stuff together, you don't come up with the Boy Scouts. So basically, I'm screwed any way I go. That's the story. Sorry you asked?"

Francesca pushed her salad plate aside and took Gino's hands in hers. "There's always a way out," she said.

"I don't have the guts to kill myself, if that's what you mean."

She slapped his hand. "Don't. Don't even go there. There's a way. There has to be a way."

"Sure. Whatever you say. I'll just hop on the next trolley to Alpha Centauri and start over as an illegal alien."

Francesca chuckled. "One thing I know for certain. You're telling the truth. It's not possible to make up a story like that."

Gino threw up his hands. "That's my sad tale. I don't know how it ends. I'm not expecting a happy ending, but stranger things have happened. I figured if I got a little distance from it, something would occur to me. So far, nothing has. What I do know for sure is that my marker is due. The casino will take me to court, and I'll be ruined. Right now, I'm on borrowed time. Literally."

"Don't lose hope. I'm not exactly my family's shining star of achievement." She paused. "I know. I'm just feeling sorry for myself.

Something will come up. I just have to be positive. It's not easy, though. It was tough enough landing the first job. They say it's much easier to get a job when you've got one. And I don't."

Gino nodded. "Finding a job isn't ever all that easy, especially now. But you're going to be fine. What's the part time gig?"

She sighed and then laughed at herself. "I sound like some kind of tragic heroine. It's actually kind of neat. I'm taking over the planning for a classic car rally. I've got about five days to pull everything together, and walking in cold isn't a picnic. But it'll work." She looked at Gino. "It has to. If I pull this off, I'll come away with a good recommendation that may open some doors."

"You'll do it," he said.

"Maybe. I used to be a lot more certain than I am now. I'm using my grandmother's name. Well, her last name, anyway. Kim. I figured it'd be safer in case the job somehow runs across El Slimo's radar. "

"Probably a good move. Unless your name is Kim, too."

Francesca crossed her eyes at him. "It's Kelley," she said. "My father's Irish." The music from the stage where the belly dancer was undulating increased in volume as her routine kicked into overdrive. Gino's eyes traveled from the dancer to Francesca. "You know what I think? I think your boss was a fool. I think you'll find a way to kick his ass. And I think you are the most beautiful woman I've ever known."

Francesca took his hand. "You've known me less than forty-eight hours. This is all moving very fast."

"*Life* moves very fast." He signaled for the check. "I'll take you home. You ready?"

She reached for her purse. "You bet your ass I'm ready."

CHAPTER THIRTEEN

On the Road in California

"What are you guys gonna do after you deliver the truck? You going back East?" Carla and the men were just outside Sacramento and traffic was light. Morrie was taking his turn at the wheel while Jeffrey napped in the camper. Carla, bare feet on the dash, was filing her nails.

"That's a good question," Morrie said. "We're both out of work. Actually, that's not entirely right. Jeffrey's out of work. He's a house painter and nobody's spending money on dressing up their real estate right now. Uncle Sam and I parted company last month, and I'm not ready to jump into anything with rules and regs just yet. Jeffrey, though, he's willing to do just about anything. It's bad out there." He checked his blind spot and changed lanes to pass a minivan spewing oil and fumes out the back.

"Does he get the cross?" Morrie asked.

"No. He ought to get the finger and get pulled over besides. Asshole."

"One more rest stop up ahead and we'll be there," Morrie said, pulling off the interstate. "I'll get Jeffrey up and we'll be ready for the final push." He turned to Carla. "We can take you to San Francisco. We're ahead of schedule now and there's time."

Carla touched him on the shoulder. "You're a nice guy, Morrie. But I changed my mind. I think I better wait a while before I do San Francisco. I got something I need to do first and it ain't that far from where you guys are headed. I'll get out there. Even you two can't get lost on your way to San Jose. There's only one main highway, if you catch my drift." She grinned.

CHAPTER FOURTEEN

Dark Mountain Vineyards

"Lunch," Francesca said, lifting a wicker basket by the handle. "And a few things I thought I might need for tomorrow when we get down to business and solve all our problems." She tilted her head toward the small overnight bag hanging by a strap from her wrist. With the addition of her purse, Francesca looked more like a photographer going on location than a woman heading off for a tour of a winery. She grabbed a copy of the newspaper from the hall table and jammed it into the picnic basket. "Tablecloth," she said, handing him the picnic basket.

Gino's eyes cut straight to the small overnight bag. He cleared a space for her bag and the picnic basket in the back seat, shifting his own belongings to the side. His cell picked that moment to ring and he ignored it.

"I feel like Italian royalty," Francesca said, as they hung a left onto Skyline Boulevard, Gino's Maserati Quattroporte's 4.21 V8 engine accelerating into curves and owning the road. "Maybe I'm royalty touring the coast of California. Or maybe I'm riding with an international espionage agent in a high-tech car. As long as I'm fantasizing, might as well dream big. Regardless, it feels great." She looked around and then under the seat. "Any secret devices installed in this beauty?"

"None that I'm aware of," he said, "but it sure would be handy to have something to ward off the bad guys."

"Tomorrow, remember?" she said.

"Yes ma'am. Tomorrow. Picnic lunch first, and then for tonight, I'm thinking steaks and pasta on the back deck at Dark Mountain with a private view of the lights of Monterey," he said. "There are about five days a year when it's not fogged in, and it looks like tonight will be one of them. How does that sound?" "Terrific. See, our luck's changing already." She stretched both arms out in front of her and wiggled her fingers. "I can feel it!"

"Francesca," Gino began, but she held up a hand, and he knew that gesture.

Every woman he'd ever known used that gesture. There was no getting around it.

He shut up.

It was one of those warm, clear autumn days that could make you forget your troubles, if only for a few hours. It was wonderful to be alive and driving along the California coast, the surf pounding on the rocks below the cliffs, and the scent of the salt air intoxicating the senses.

Fields of pumpkins dotted the east side of Highway 1 below Half Moon Bay, and the roadside stands were gearing up for fall business with displays of apples, cider, and pears. Gino and Francesca stopped at one of the stands and added a few crisp apples to the picnic basket. Francesca sorted through the pile of pumpkins until she found a behemoth she couldn't live without.

"Where are we going to put that thing?" Gino asked, scratching his head and taking a mental measurement of the pumpkin's girth.

"It'll fit. Trust me. I know about these things," she said, "and we can carve it tonight and put a candle in it. It'll look great." Her eyes were twinkling and Gino caved.

"I haven't had a jack-o'-lantern since I was a kid," he said.

"Then it's way past time you did. You have to get into the spirit of the seasons. There's magic there." It took both her arms, her right hip, and a last-minute boost from Gino to angle the pumpkin up to the counter to be weighed. It came in at twenty-three pounds and took up a fair section of the back seat. Francesca fastened a seat belt around its middle to keep it in place.

About ten miles outside of Santa Cruz, Gino pulled off the road. "You stay there," Francesca told the pumpkin. "You have important work to do tonight, and we want you all in one piece." She patted the pumpkin's seat belt. They carried their picnic lunch down a rocky path to the beach where they watched dogs chase balls and couples stroll hand in hand along the shore. It was easy being together, and by the time they'd finished their lunch, there was an unspoken understanding that they'd found something worth keeping.

It was late afternoon when they returned to the car and got back on Highway 1, taking the Soquel exit to head north on Old San Jose Road. A few miles out of town, the road began its slow ascent into the mountains, sometimes following Soquel Creek and sometimes carving a path through dense forest. Homes were few and far between, and those that could be seen were nestled deep in the woods, affording only a glimpse as the car passed by. Finally, Gino turned off onto a private road, punched a code into a keypad, and a wrought iron gate swung open to admit them. Redwoods flanked the mile long drive to the estate, and for a short distance they drove alongside a creek that burbled over rocks in the stream bed. They crossed a one lane bridge and came to a fork in the road. Gino took the gravel road to the right, and they climbed for another half mile, around hairpin curves with a sheer drop off, until the first sight of Dark Mountain Vineyard came into view.

"It's beautiful," Francesca said. "It feels like we're on top of the world." Her eyes couldn't seem to take everything in fast enough. She turned her head from left to right and then back again. "Gino, this is absolutely wonderful." She squeezed his arm. "Wonderful," she repeated.

"It's home," Gino said, pulling into the driveway and parking.

"It's like it goes on forever."

Gino rested his hands on the steering wheel. "Not forever. Just about twenty-five acres, but that's a considerable piece around here. I could show you more of it, if you'll ever decide to get out of the car." "Right. Good idea," she said and scrambled out of the car, grabbing her bags from the back seat. She set them down on the asphalt and then unfastened the pumpkin's seatbelt. "What about the pumpkin? Getting him out is going to be a lot trickier than it was getting him in."

"I'll get a dolly out of the garage and we can wheel him to the front door. Then, let's take some wine out onto the back deck. From there you can get a good view of the vineyard on the slope below the house."

"Sounds great. Everything about today has been absolutely perfect," she said. "That's a great omen. If it's possible, it can only get better."

CHAPTER FIFTEEN

Dark Mountain

"Hi Gino, who's your friend?" Carla was sprawled on the leather sofa in the Great Room, an iced drink in one hand and the remote in the other. "Hope you don't mind. I made myself at home."

Gino froze in midstep, his eyes nearly bugging out of his head. "Carla? What the hell are you doing here?"

"Me? Well, right now I'm watching a foodie show and getting hungry. When's dinner?"

"Maybe I should..." Francesca's voice trailed off. She looked uncertainly around the room.

"Hold it! Everybody hold it!" Gino's normally smooth baritone had morphed into a squeak. He wrapped one arm firmly around Francesca's shoulder as if to keep her from bolting and spun her around to face him. "Francesca, this," he pointed at the figure on the sofa, "is Carla." He turned to Carla. "My cousin." He looked at Francesca to be sure the last word had registered. "Cousin."

"Cousin," Francesca repeated, relief flooding through her. "Cousin. Got it." Gino released his grip on Francesca's shoulders. "She does this from time to time, although usually, she calls first." He glared at Carla who switched off the television and got up off the sofa. She set her drink and the remote on the coffee table and wiped her hands on her pants.

"Pleased to meetcha. And I tried to call." She directed her eyes toward Gino. "More than once. You never answered." She offered her hand to

Francesca and made no pretense about checking Francesca out from head to toe. "You Gino's girlfriend? His taste is improving," she said. "We've just met," Gino said. "And we were about to take a tour of the vineyard. Alone," he added.

"Right," Carla said. "And that bag," she pointed to Francesca's overnight case, "is probably a snakebite kit."

Francesca's eyes widened and the corners of her mouth twitched. She took Carla's hand. "I'm Francesca. And yes, I'm Gino's girlfriend." She glanced at Gino.

"About time he found somebody with some class. That last one," she began, but Gino interrupted.

"Carla, I'm sure you'll want to freshen up before dinner. Why don't you go do that now? You know where the guest house is. You've been there often enough."

"Nah. I already got cleaned up. This is a new outfit. I went shopping with Morrie. He got good taste, but I think it could fit a little snugger, you know?" She turned her head to check out her rear. "By the way, the hot water faucet in the shower drips. I'll fix it tomorrow. Morrie's comin' by to take me to lunch. I'll get what I need then. You'll like him. He ain't nothin' like you." She frowned. "I didn't mean that the way it came out. What I meant is that he's tall and big." She looked at Francesca, confidingly. "I like big men. They make me feel feminine, you know?"

"Carla," Gino said. "Shut up."

"Not that you're not masculine or nothing, Gino," Carla said. "But you gotta admit, you're short and kinda on the skinny side. 'Course ol' Blue Eyes was like that, and he didn't have no trouble with women. You can't sing but you still got good hair, though. Morrie's not too good in that department. But at least he don't do no comb over." She turned to Francesca again. "Guys that do that got all their priorities messed up. Morrie shaves his head. He looks good, too, for a white guy. Usually it's the black guys that look good that way." "Let's take our wine out on the deck and have a little chat, shall we?" Gino said, pushing Carla ahead of him with one arm and taking Francesca's hand with the other. "I'm sure Carla won't be staying long, will you, Carla?"

"Matter of fact, I got some free time and so yeah, I figure about a week or so oughta do it. I mean, ought to be a nice visit," Carla said, as Gino propelled her out the door and deposited her into a wicker chair by the patio table.

"Sit! Stay!" he growled. "We'll be right back. I mean it, Carla. Stay put. Francesca, come with me, please."

Francesca sent a reassuring look back to Carla who winked at her as Gino led the way back inside. "I like her," she said.

"I bet you pick up stray puppies and abandoned kittens."

"On occasion."

"If there's a bad time to show up, it's like she's got radar. I had plans to give you the whole inside tour this evening. Starting here," he swept his arm around the Great Room with its open floor plan and vast expanse of logs and glass windows and warm wood accents, "and ending upstairs in the master suite."

Francesca cradled his face in her hands. "Poor baby," she said. "I can see everything I need to see from here." She kissed him. "And there's more where that came from. I can be as patient as I need to be. Anticipation stokes the fires."

"This fire doesn't need any more stoking." He looked back at the deck where Carla was comfortably ensconced in her chair with her feet on the table. "All right. All right. Come on, at least I can show you the wine cellar." He paused before a set of ornately carved double doors and entered a code into the alarm system. There was a faint chirp and then the sound of a lock being released.

Francesca ran her fingers across the wood. "It's beautiful," she said.

"Manuel did the carving many years ago, when my parents owned the estate," Gino said. "It was the last thing he did for us. He's gone now. And so are they. But I have this." He took her hand and traced the delicate filigrees of the vines and grapes that spread across the wood. "The doors are birdseye maple. Their light color gives a good background. The grapes are African purpleheart, the vines are walnut, and the leaves are canary wood. But the best," he said, "awaits inside. Shall we?"

Gino opened the doors with a bit of a flourish, a rather unnecessary gesture, Francesca thought, as she entered an empty room. Empty of wine, that was, and furniture as well. The room, backlit by the Great Room, was beautifully appointed with recessed mahogany wooden panels on the walls and ceiling and a marble floor of a deep, verdant green.

Francesca stood with her hands on her hips, looked around the room, and then threw her hands into the air. "Okay," she said. "I give up. Where's the wine cellar?"

"Close," Gino said. "In fact, you're right on top of it."

Francesca looked down at her feet. "Marble," she said. "Not wine."

"True. But after all, it is a wine *cellar* and the way to it is right over there."

He turned on the lights and pointed to the opposite wall where a wooden spiral staircase rose gracefully to the floor above and descended to the basement below. "Come on." He led the way down the stairs and waited for Francesca at the bottom.

"I'm right behind you," she said. Sliding her hand along the banister, she kept her eyes on the risers and placed her feet squarely in the middle of each one. "You know, I've never been on a spiral staircase before. It takes a little getting used to." She reached the bottom stair and looked up for the first time. "I...oh...wow," she said. "Wow. Gino, this is...wow." She leaned against the newel post and took a deep breath. "I must be Alice. I think I've fallen down the rabbit hole."

Gino waited, Cheshire cat grin on his face, in front of a glass door that provided a clear view of the wine cellar inside. "Welcome," he said, pushing a button on a keypad that opened the door and released a chill burst of air.

"Gino, this is the most beautiful place I've ever seen. But it's cold." She hugged her shoulders.

"The temperature is kept at a constant fifty-six degrees Fahrenheit and the humidity at seventy percent." He opened one of the wood panels, revealing a temperature monitor and controls. "I told you I am passionate about wine," he said. "Good wine deserves good treatment."

Francesca entered the cellar, noting the stone arches that graced the walls where recesses showcased oil paintings. Between the arches, mahogany bins extending from the floor to the ceiling eight feet above her head cradled hundreds, maybe over a thousand bottles of wine. She tried to take one bottle from its bin but was stopped by a ring attached to the bottle's neck and anchored to the wood on both sides by plastic ties. "More security, Gino?" she asked.

"Yes, but not against theft. The San Andreas Fault runs right through this area. The bins are bolted to the walls and floor. Those O-rings and ties keep the bottles from leaving home without me."

Her eyes opened wide. "Oh God, what an earthquake could do here. It would be horrible." She left the bottles and walked over to one of the recesses to examine the painting hung in its niche. It depicted a fisherman preparing to load his nets onto his boat. The man's face was deeply lined and roughened by the salty wind and sun. His hands were strong, but workworn, and his clothes were patched and threadbare in places. "The skill to show such detail," she said. "I can almost see the waves moving."

"My grandfather painted it," Gino said. "He painted all of these. They were a wedding gift to my parents."

"The *vendetta* grandfather?"

"Uh huh. One and the same. They don't belong to me until I'm forty-five. A long time away." He sliced through the plastic ties on two bottles and lifted them from their bins. He handed one to Francesca and led the way back upstairs. "My grandfather knew of my shortcomings a long time ago. Be careful on the stairs. Don't trip. Pretty soon you'll be trotting up and down them as if you were to the manor born."

"I think it takes practice. But I'm game." She tucked the bottle in the crook of her left arm and took a serious hold on the banister.

"I've got your backside, and it's a nice view. Maybe I'll let you get a few steps ahead of me—just in case."

"I know exactly why you're giving me room and it's got nothing to do with my safety or yours," she shot back. "Well, nothing wrong with that. Just don't you get so distracted that *you* fall."

Gino sighed. "Later. I keep telling myself later. It's not working, but I guess we don't have much choice. Let's see what Carla's gotten herself into this time," he said. "One good thing," he added, "the guest house is across the driveway. We'll still have the house to ourselves after she's retired for the evening, and I predict that will be early."

"I wasn't worried," Francesca said. "A resourceful man like you covers all the bases."

"That's my plan exactly," Gino said.

CHAPTER SIXTEEN

Dark Mountain

"Before you even get started, Carla, this is not a good time to hit me up for money. I've got problems of my own, and they're more than enough. Trust me. You want advice. Fine. I'll give it to you. You want a shoulder to cry on. I'm here. I'll listen to whatever you have to say, but money is out of the question."

They were back on the deck, where Gino was laying down the law, and Carla was taking offense. Francesca had walked to the railing and was watching a deer browsing at the edge of the meadow.

Carla's eyes widened. "Jesus, Gino, what the hell's wrong? You ain't never talked like this before. You in trouble or something?"

"Something." He took his gaze from Carla and examined the bottle he was uncorking.

"Jesus, Mary, and Joseph!" Carla rapidly crossed herself. "What the hell you gone and done now, Gino?"

He set down the bottle with care but then slammed his fists on the table. "Dammit, Carla, I am not going to get into this tonight." He shoved a chair out of his way. "Let it go. Just let it go." He turned and headed for the door. "I'm going to defrost some steaks."

Carla raised an eyebrow to Francesca. "I ain't never seen him like this before. He's all worked up and that ain't good for his blood pressure. He'll come around though. He's got a short fuse, but it don't last long." She settled back in the chair and crossed her legs. "We just got to give him time to wind down. So, where'd he pick you up?"

"Airplane. Coming back from JFK. I'd been giving him the brush off. The last thing I wanted out of the trip home was another guy and another problem, but he kept trying. And then finally, he wore me down. And he was funny. I couldn't hold out any longer. We were stuck in a holding pattern and things just kind of progressed from there. You know. Drinks, dinner, picnic. Pumpkin."

"Pumpkin? That what you call it?"

Francesca laughed. "No."

"Okay. But, yeah. He can be persistent when he wants to be. Takes him a while to get his nerve up sometimes, but that's only when he really cares about something." Carla drummed her fingers on the patio table. "Or somebody. Something's on his mind, and you," she tilted her head in Francesca's direction, "are the only one who's going to be able to find out. He sure as hell won't tell me." She clicked her tongue against the back of her teeth and folded her arms across her chest.

"Maybe I'll go help with dinner." Francesca's eyes traveled toward the kitchen window, where Gino was visible, moving about. "I could make a salad or something," she said.

"Good idea. I'll stay here out of the way, while you do what you do. Once we find out the real problem, we can work it out. Ain't nothin' this side of the grave that can't be fixed," Carla said, lifting her glass in a toast. She picked up the newspaper. "I'll just keep busy here. Don't worry about me."

Francesca marched off, head held high and resolve in every step, but she struck out. Gino wasn't talking, and when she returned to the deck with the salad, she shrugged at Carla, whose eyes narrowed in reply. It was only after the third bottle of wine had been opened and dinner was well underway, that the conversation took a different direction.

"They say confession is good for the soul," Francesca said, staring into the depths of her glass, which had just been refilled. "Yeah, we're big on confession," Carla said. "Of course there's penance and all that shit, but you get a clean slate to fuck up again. Works good." She resumed stuffing her mouth with pasta.

Gino glanced at Carla, grunted, and then looked at Francesca, waiting for the rest of it.

"Uh huh," Francesca said, setting down her fork. "I mean everybody's got secrets, right?"

"You don't know the half of it," Carla said with a weary sigh. "Who don't?" She pushed her plate away and gave Gino and Francesca a calculated look. "How about we play 'you show me yours, I'll show you mine'?" She smiled. "I'm talkin' about a *real* pissin' contest. You game?"

"Why the hell not," Gino said. "Ladies first."

"Okay. I brought this up" Francesca said, "and I'll start." Her face reddened. "Gino's already heard this, so I'll see if telling it gets any easier the second time around. I found out my boss was cooking the books and padding his expense account, and he found out that I found out. He made deposits to my bank account so it would look like I was on the take, and then he fired me." Her hands shook as she reached for her glass. "I didn't get downsized. I got axed. Now I don't have a job, can't get a reference, and if I get audited, they'll find the money, and I'm screwed. Even if I blow the whistle, I still look guilty as sin. But I haven't touched a penny of that money, and I won't."

"Good one," Carla said, nodding approval. "So, in the best of all worlds, how would you want this to end?"

"I buy the company, fire him, return the money, and find a computer geek to clean up my records." Francesca's eyes lit up at the thought. "That would be justice. Anything he said would sound like sour grapes. Yeah, I'd like that."

"Okay, my turn," Carla said. "Uh, Gino, what did you tell her about me?" She cocked her head at her cousin.

"Carla, there aren't enough words in the language to begin to tell Francesca about you. Just jump right in, and we'll try to keep up."

"Wise ass," she said. "Okay. I'm a dancer."

"A dancer," Gino said, snorting. "And Capone was an altar boy."

"If you're going to interrupt, this is gonna take a real long time." She cleared her throat. "Anyhow," she continued, "it's been tough waiting for my big break. And I almost had one. I coulda got a chorus line gig at the

Schubert until Tony beat me up. The bastard." She lowered her voice, looked at Francesca, and confided, "I'm an exotic dancer." She made it sound like principal ballerina in the Bolshoi. "Of course, there ain't benefits or nothin' and you gotta do what the boss says. That's the part I got tired of. I mean a girl's gotta watch her assets, if you catch my drift, and I sure as hell didn't want to get into that whole sideline full time."

"Yeah. You sure as hell wouldn't want to lose your focus or anything," Gino mumbled into his glass.

Carla shot him a look and he shut up. "So, there ain't much more. I...quit."

"That's all?" Francesca asked.

"Pretty much," Carla said, swirling the wine in her glass. "Uh...Pretty much." Gino gave Carla a skeptical look and waited, but she was finished. "All right," he said. "Let's pretend there isn't anything more. For now. What's your take on happily ever after?"

"This is good wine." She offered him her glass, and he splashed some more into it. She took a delicate sip and seemed to retreat to some distant place, and when she spoke, her voice had lost the hard edges. "Miss Carla's School of the Dance," she said. "I always liked the sound of that. I wanna be *her*." She stuck out her chin like a defiant child. "That's my happily ever after."

Francesca reached over and patted her hand. "It's a good ending. And it could come true. You can have your happy ending." She turned to Gino. "Okay. Your turn."

He inhaled deeply and let his breath out in a rush. His shoulders dropped as if he'd been deflated. "All right. Francesca's already heard this. As you can tell, we've already had some serious conversation, but here's the down and dirty version. I'm into the Grand Casino in Monte Carlo for five-hundred thousand. I'm five-hundred thousand short. I can't pay it. I've gone over and over the books, and I can't wring another cent out of the operation. There's just no more to take out. It costs money to finance a vineyard and the bottling operation." He ran his fingers through his hair and then locked them behind his head. "Basically, I'm screwed. I won't have enough to make the loan payments, and I'll lose the vineyard, the house. Everything."

Francesca looked about her. From the deck she could see the lights of Monterey sixty miles in the distance. Shimmering in the evening air, the lights danced and flickered. The stars were out now, and overhead, a small plane made its lonely transit of the night sky, its wing lights flashing like twin beacons adrift on a black ocean. She stood and walked to the railing. The deck wrapped around the southern side of the house, and just off to her right, stairs led from the deck to the terraced hillside where the vineyard was planted in neat rows across the leveled slope. Everything spoke of order and meticulous care. She felt a stab of anger that Gino had risked it all at the casino. Carla whistled and Francesca turned around.

"You win. No doubt about it. You sure know how to fuck up, Gino."

"Yeah, I'm the master. I could give lessons."

"So, don't stop there," Francesca said, now back in her chair. "How would you fix it if you could?"

"That doesn't take much to figure out. I'd pay off the casino, pay off the mortgage on the vineyard, swear off gambling forever—maybe join Gamblers Anonymous—and make Dark Mountain the best small winery in California. Might as well dream big, if I'm dreaming," he said and gave a bitter laugh. "Are we all supposed to feel better now?"

"I think I do," Francesca said. "I want to be honest with you. I've got to be, if we're going to make anything of this." Her eyes searched Gino's face.

"Yeah, well…" Gino's voice trailed off. "I've got nothing to bring to a relationship. You'd be a fool to take up with me." He hesitated, and then said, "There's more."

"Oh for Christ's sake," Carla said. "Listen to you. You're talkin' like you're dead and buried. You got potential, Gino. You just ain't used it yet. You're spoiled. That's the problem. And all this self-help shit you keep falling for's just a cover up. You got to get some self-confidence. That's another problem."

"You should talk about self-confidence," he shot back. "Why the hell did you throw your life away? You could have been that *Miss Carla*, if you hadn't married that loser, Al."

"Okay. Point taken. This is now. That was then. I was in love. I was sixteen. I was all alone. What the hell did I know?"

Francesca's head was spinning. "Stop!" She raised her hands to her ears.

"Who's Al?" She dropped her hands.

"My ex," Carla said. "Or whatever you call him. He's dead, thank God, may he rest in peace. I had to do something to support myself. I wasn't in the rich part of the family." She tilted her head in Gino's direction.

"You didn't have to go to work at the strip joint," Gino said. "You could have done anything else."

"Maybe. They paid good though. What did I know? I was only seventeen. After Al got hit by the crop duster, I wasn't thinking right."

"Crop duster?" Francesca choked on a mouthful of wine. Gino patted her back while she waved her arms trying to breathe.

"Yeah." Carla chewed her lower lip. "It was quick, though. One minute he's driving down the interstate and the next, he slams into a crop duster that's stalled on the highway. He was a trucker like my old man, and just about as lucky. Propellers and carburetors all over the road. Bad scene. No insurance, either. But," she said, "when it's your time, it's your time. Weird, though. And now maybe I got Morrie. I think he's got serious potential." She looked up. "He was my ride to California. Him and Jeffrey, his brother. He's stable and everything. Well, he ain't got a job now, but that'll change real soon. He's a contractor. They always get work."

Francesca had regained her breathing and now turned from Carla to Gino, back to Carla, and then back to Gino again. "That's a lot to take in. All right. We were talking, I think. Yes. About that 'there's more'?" she said, her eyes fixed on Gino.

Gino shoved his plate off to the side and stood. "The 'more' isn't all about me. Well, it is, and it isn't. Anybody want any more?" he asked, clearing the empties off the table.

"Sure," Carla said.

"Why not?" Francesca said. "*In vino veritas.*"

"I'll be back in a minute," he said. "One more bottle. I saved the best for last." "Don't fall down the stairs," Carla yelled at his back as he made his way through the door. "Or up, either," she added, with a grin.

****

"This may be a bit young," Gino said. "It's a 2011 Pinot from the vineyard south of Dark Mountain, and I've been saving it. But I think it's time. We'll see." He settled himself in his chair and laced his fingers together behind his head. "Carla, how much do you know about *papa*?"

"That some kind of trick question or something?" "No, it's not. What do you know about him?"

Carla looked at Gino as if he had a screw loose. "You got to admit, that's a real weird question. Okay, what do I know about him? Well, he's loaded, and he's old. What else is there to know?"

"He's an art forger," Gino said. "That's where all the money came from." He sat back and waited for her response. He didn't have to wait long.

"No shit." She let out a howl of laughter. "And here I thought he was a straight arrow. Just goes to show."

"What?" Gino asked. "Show what?"

"Just show," Carla said. "Nobody's a hundred percent honest. Look at your Uncle Manny. Why he was barely out of the joint when…"

"As I was saying," Gino cut Carla off mid-sentence. "*Papa* sent for me last week. That's where this part of the story begins. They figured he was dying, and so I was called in to pay my final respects. But he gave me a job to do before he passes on. He gave me some money to help with expenses, but the problem is, I don't have a clue how to begin, and I think the job is going to cost a lot more than he gave me."

"You owe him, Gino. Whatever he asked you to do for him don't matter. He raised you."

"He sent me to school," Gino said. "There's a difference." "Maybe. But he took care of you. You never needed nothing."

"I suppose," Gino said. "He didn't know what to do with me, so he shipped me off to school. I only saw him maybe half a dozen times between the time I was six and when I graduated from university."

"He paid the bills," Carla said. "You gotta give him that."

"Yeah, he did. I don't blame him. What would he do with a kid hanging around getting in the way? He was a famous man. Rich as Midas, too. So I didn't mind going back when I got the message." He rested his lips on the rim of his wine glass.

"Don't stop now," Carla said.

"Go on," Francesca said. "Tell her the rest."

Gino rubbed his face and covered his eyes. He lowered his hands and looked at Francesca, and then at Carla. "Francesca already knows the story, but *papa* painted many works signed by Angelo DeMontana, known to the art world as The Master. Now they're being stolen and *papa* believes DeMontana's widow is behind it all. She wants to get all of *papa's* works out of circulation before the truth is discovered and DeMontana is exposed as a fraud. That would hurt her fortune big time.

"DeMontana's worth has been skyrocketing since his death. The truth would rock the art world. You see," he said, "*papa* signed each one before he turned it over to DeMontana. Or rather, he painted his initials into every painting and there's a diary that proves his story is true. It lists every painting and *papa* has a paper that tells where his initials are in those paintings."

"Smart thinking," Carla said. "He wasn't taking no chances. Kind of like an insurance policy in case DeMontana screwed him over."

Francesca considered this. "You know, I've been thinking. Why not just use the diary to squelch DeMontana's widow and set the record straight? You could give an interview to an art critic and spill the goods. Or you could plant some rumors on the internet. That's a piece of cake. Then it will take off and do the work for you. You just sit back and let nature take its course."

"It's not that easy," Gino said. "Bianca DeMontana has the diary."

"Bummer," Carla looked up from her nails. "You'll have to get the diary then." "That's the problem," Gino said. "I have to steal the diary—find it first, of

course. Then I have to find some of the stolen art in the DeMontana house, providing there's any art there to find. After that, if I'm still alive, I need to use the diary to decode the art and show the world that Emiliano Esposito is the true genius, The Master, and not DeMontana. That will give *papa* what he wants—his legacy and the fame he's decided that he deserves."

"Cool!" Carla said.

"Fantastic!" Francesca added.

"Impossible," Gino said.

"You can do this, Gino," Carla said. "We can do this. It all fits together. Don't you see?"

"Uh uh," Gino said. "See what?"

"For Christ's sake, Gino," Carla said. "Think! If you pull this off, you'll have all the money you could ever want. Enough to pay everything off. You get your life back. Plus, you give your grandfather what he wants. It's a win-win situation. You can't lose."

"Assuming you're right, and I'm not convinced you are, there's still the slight problem of getting into the DeMontana mansion, finding the diary, getting the stolen art, and getting out without getting arrested or killed. Yeah, sounds easy to me."

"Hold on a minute. Something just clicked." Carla bolted out of her chair, knocking it over in the process. She left it where it fell and ran into the house, emerging with the rest of the newspaper clutched in her hand, waving it in the air as if conjuring up some helpful spirits. "You know, I thought that DeMontana name rang a bell," she said, whipping through the pages of the Arts and Society section. "Here!" she said. "Look at the headline. 'Gala Event at DeMontana Mansion Opens the Art Season'. We could go and scope out the house. Get the lay of the land before we break in and steal stuff."

"Let me see that," Gino said, grabbing the paper and scanning the story. "This is tomorrow night," he said, looking up from the article.

"Yep," Carla said. "It's gonna be a big party. Lots of people there. We could be there, too."

"They're not going to let us in," Gino said. "There'll be checks for invitations at the door. We couldn't get past the valet parking. And what do you mean *we*?" He glowered at her.

"There's a way," Francesca said, tapping her chin with her index finger. "There's always a way." She brightened. "Got it! I'll need a computer and a printer."

"You don't know what the invitations look like. They'll spot a phony right away," Gino said.

"I'm not going to make an invitation," Francesca said. "Something much better. Show me your computer."

"Okay. Whatever you say. But this isn't going to work."

"Don't be so negative. Just let me do this and then judge for yourself," Francesca said.

Overpowered, Gino gave up and led Francesca back into the house to his office. When they returned twenty minutes later, they were both smiling. Gino was sporting a badge that said PRESS and identified him as Arts and Society reporter for the *San Francisco Bay Reporter*.

"Access accomplished," Francesca said. "Gino's in. These people," she tilted her head at the article, "live for publicity. All they want is for you to spell their names right."

"So we're going?" Carla asked.

"I'm going," Gino said. "You're staying here."

"The hell I am," Carla said. "Without me you would never have seen that article. I'm going too. I can be somebody. Who can I be?" "Photographer," Francesca said. "Me, too. We can be your photographers. We're all going."

"This is gonna be a blast," Carla said.

"Yeah," Gino said. "A blast." He choked down the remains of his wine.

CHAPTER SEVENTEEN

San Francisco

"Can you believe this? Parking spaces aren't easy to come by and here's one just two doors down from my place." Francesca reached for her purse and fished around for her house keys. "Here, Gino. You pull in here, and I'll back my car out of the garage. Then pull out and park in the garage and I'll grab the space."

"Sounds like a lot of trouble. Why don't Gino just park here and stay here?" Carla was craning her neck to check out the neighborhood. Waller Street, deep in the heart of The Haight, was an eclectic mix of restored Victorians—the "Painted Ladies"—and homes waiting for gentrification, corner grocery stores, and bistros.

"No can do," Francesca said. "There's a two-hour limit and you *will* get ticketed. I've got a residential parking permit. As long as I move the car every seventy-two hours, I'm good."

"Still sounds like a pain in the ass," Carla said as Gino parked.

"It's the City," Francesca said, as if that explained it all. "San Francisco. But it's one of the best cities in the world. I wouldn't live anywhere else." She frowned. "I sure hope I don't have to live anywhere else. At least the rent is paid up through the end of next month. Something will happen. It's got to."

"Kinda crowded. Makes New Haven look like the burbs," Carla said, eyeing Francesca's house, one of the restored Victorians painted a light blue with violet trim. It was wedged between two other houses, all so close together there wasn't room to slip a piece of paper between their side walls. "This whole thing is your place?" she said.

"It's an old neighborhood. The house belongs to a family friend. They've owned it since forever," Francesca said, "and my apartment is on the third floor. It's tiny, but it's comfy. The garage is one of the best features. It was the only perk I got when I rented. My father made sure of it. People would kill for a garage. I have to warn you. It's not overly roomy, but your car will fit if you're careful. You've got a little wiggle room. Your car's pretty much the same height and width as the Bug. You're just longer by about three and a half feet." She grinned. "That leaves you about sixteen inches to spare. Back in a jiff."

Carla and Gino watched her sprint up the outside stairs of the house. A few minutes later, the garage door lifted. Francesca backed out in a 1967 orange Volkswagen Bug and idled just behind them, waiting to slip into the space.

"Cool!" Carla said.

"Very nice," Gino added, after finessing the Maserati into the garage, but he was looking at Francesca, not the Beetle.

Francesca was waiting for them on the sidewalk. "If you turn sideways as you get out of the car you'll have an easier time getting out of there," she called. "Just hold the car door so it doesn't bang against the wall while you do. There's so much auto paint on that wall I'm thinking about putting a frame around it and calling it modern art." She looked at Gino. "Think your grandfather would approve?"

"Modern art wasn't his area of expertise, I'm afraid," Gino said. "He was more a post-Romantic."

"It is kinda colorful," Carla said. "Don't see any orange, though."

"Not yet, anyway," Francesca said. "I'm really careful with the Bug. Come on. I'll show you Headquarters for The Esposito Caper."

Gino grimaced. "I'm still not liking this at all. You make it sound like child's play."

"You ever watch kids play? I mean really? It's serious stuff." She led the way up the flights of stairs to her apartment. tossed her purse onto a table by the front door and her coat onto the sofa. "It's not a really big headquarters, but it *is* centrally located and we can come and go without attracting anybody's attention. I mean," she looked at Gino, "if we're going to be breaking and entering and stealing and such, we need a safe place as a center of operations. Also, I can work on your credentials here—put them in one of those convention sleeves and jazz up the printing a bit so you look really official. I'll do one for me and for you, too," she said to Carla. "We can both be staff photographers. We'll take turns. How does that sound?"

"Sounds fine," Carla said, walking to the window. "Where's San Francisco Bay? I always wanted to see the Golden Gate Bridge. When I get my dance studio, I'm gonna have a view of that bridge."

"You can't see it from here. Getting an unobstructed view of the bridge costs money and lots of it. But who knows? That could be in your future."

"Let's leave the future for the future. Right now, we've got work to do," Gino said, taking his grandfather's scrapbook out of a leather shoulder bag. "If we're going to do this right, we need to do our homework." He set the scrapbook on the table alongside the computer.

"I'll make coffee," Francesca said.

"While you two are getting set up, I'm gonna take a walk," Carla said. "Just for a couple of minutes down the block. I ain't never seen San Francisco before and I don't want to waste a minute. I'll be right back. Don't start without me."

"It's not the starting that concerns me," Gino said. "It's the finish."

****

At seven-thirty that evening, an orange Volkswagen Beetle found a tiny parking space on Webster around the corner from the DeMontana mansion. Gino, Francesca, and Carla exited the car and joined the milling crowd outside the home.

The early Italian immigrants had settled in the North Beach area, but Angelo DeMontana was no ordinary immigrant. He'd gone straight from Florence, Italy, to Pacific Heights, San Francisco, and he'd bought one of the pricier mansions on Washington Street. Built during the twenties, it was a classic Italianate three-story affair with enough windows and height to qualify as top rate. It also had a generous setback from the street, and tonight the circular drive was lined with some classy pieces of foreign automotive engineering. The interior of the mansion was in high-wattage mode, and outside, *candelaria* illuminated the walk paths. The driveway, also awash in light, curved to the right after passing by the front door. Following the natural contour of the land, it took a slight dip before ending at the garage, the former carriage house.

On the east side of the home, a brick walkway traced a path through a rose garden and led to a wrought iron gate that opened onto the formal herb gardens in the rear. Tonight the backyard was deserted except for a couple of smokers stealing a few puffs in the marginal shelter of the pavilion.

Inside, everyone was in the ballroom, guzzling high end liquor and fruity martinis. A waiter was circulating with a tray of drinks and Carla helped herself to a glass of champagne. "Confidence booster," she said to Gino, who scowled at her. He scowled again as she fondled the fluted crystal, downed the drink, and slipped the empty glass into her shoulder bag.

"Put that back," he said through clenched teeth, grabbing her elbow and squeezing hard. "*Miss Carla.*" He waited while her hand lingered on the glass stem.

"Right." She sighed but returned the glass to a tray strategically placed next to the bar and burdened with empties. "This Miss Carla thing ain't gonna be easy."

"And stay with me. Now where did Francesca go? I knew this was a mistake. You two were supposed to be taking turns. I can't ride herd on both of you at the same time."

Carla pointed to a small group of women gathered by the hors d'oeuvres where Francesca was taking head shots.

"All right. All right. Don't go wandering off by yourself. I don't want to have to go looking for you when it's time to get out of here. It would have helped if you'd worn something more professional."

Carla looked down at her little purple dress with the plunging neckline and hem that just barely covered her rear. "This is my professional dress. My best one. And I accessorized. Francesca gave me these pearls to class it up. What the hell's wrong with it? Do I look fat or something?"

"You look like you're working the party, not working for the newspaper." He clenched his teeth. "Come on. Time's wasting." He turned and headed into the crowd.

Carla stuck out her tongue at his retreating back and tottered after him on her four-inch heels. She took Francesca's digital camera out of its case, hung the strap around her neck, and joined Gino, now standing with a threesome discussing the dubious future of endowments for the arts.

A tall man with sparse hair combed centurion-style over his scalp leaned into Gino's badge. "The Foundation hasn't had a decent article in months. What do we have to do to drum up some interest?"

Gino pulled a small spiral notebook and pen out of his pocket and prepared to take notes. "I'm here. Tell me a story, mister."

"Schuyler, Cameron Schuyler. President and CEO, Bank of the Golden State." The centurion cleared his throat. "Philanthropy is dead." He bobbed his head aggressively. "You can use that. It makes a good title. Got to grab the reader."

"Cam, you're a pompous ass." The second man in the group, a short, pudgy man wearing glasses with lenses so thick his eyes looked like distant specks, snapped his retort. "And you can use that." He winked at Gino. "Philanthropy isn't dead. Wounded, yes. It will snap back. Always does. Right now, everyone's tightening belts."

Gino made furious scribbles in his notebook. "Right. And you are?"

"Lorenzo Mondani, CFO, Bank of the Golden State." He chuckled and the sound was deeper than Gino would have expected in a small man. "I keep an eye on Cam."

Gino looked up from his notepad at the third man and raised a quizzical eyebrow.

"Bruce Morgenstern. USMC Retired. I'm just with them to keep an eye on my money."

Gino gave Morgenstern a serious look. "So you keep an eye on them?'

"That's my way of thinking."

"Quite an assortment here, it appears," Gino said, closing his notebook and looking around the room. "I haven't spotted the *grande dame* yet."

"Bianca? She's holding court over there." Lorenzo tossed his head in the direction of the bay windows on the far side of the room. "She's the blonde in the gold dress conversing with the gent in the brown suit."

Carla had been snapping pictures of the trio as Gino interviewed them. She turned to get a shot of Bianca DeMontana and the man she was talking to. She got the picture and as it processed on the digital, their features sharpened and a cold chill sweep over her. She tugged at Gino's sleeve but he swept her hand away as if she'd been a mosquito.

"You'll have to take a number if you want to talk with her," Lorenzo continued. "You'll have more luck connecting with her nephew. That's Michael DeMontana over there by the piano."

Carla pulled on Gino's cuff, harder this time. "Much obliged," he said. "I'll go have a chat." He turned to Carla. "What?" he asked, but she was gone. He looked around but she had vanished. He looked around once more and gave it up. She probably had to use the bathroom. He forgot about her as he scoped out Bianca DiCicco DeMontana. She wasn't much past fifty, and her body was slim and toned.

"That's one society blonde for sure," Francesca's voice came from behind his shoulder.

"Have you seen Carla?"

"She's in the car. Said she didn't feel good and asked me to let you know where she was. She said you told her to let you know when she went anywhere. She doesn't look very good. But I've got the camera." She patted the digital.

Gino's eyes narrowed. "Was she drunk? I told her to stop sampling the champagne."

"No, I don't think so. She just seemed edgy. Maybe the crowd was too much for her. She'll be fine. Anyhow, as I was saying, our Bianca is quite a knockout." She nodded in Bianca's direction. "That's a Kim Song."

"A what?" Gino backed up to avoid being sideswiped by a waiter with a tray of fresh drinks.

"What she's wearing. That over the shoulder yellow gown with the empire waist. Very nice, and very, very expensive. Goes perfectly with her society blonde hair. Good blunt cut that angles towards her chin." Francesca nodded approval. "Kim Song is one of the up-and-coming San Francisco designers. Her name was all over Fashion Week. That's her right now, walking up to Bianca."

Gino studied Bianca's face, matching it with the photo in the scrapbook. No doubt that Bianca was living well. With any luck, they could change that.

Bianca whispered something to her companion, the silver-haired man in the brown suit, while she let her fingers run lightly down his jacket lapel. She kissed him on the cheek and crushed out her cigarette in a crystal ash tray before leaving him with Song. Apparently she was the only one permitted to smoke on the premises. The man tossed back the remainder of his champagne and wiped his mouth with the back of his jacket sleeve.

Francesca pursed her lips. "Money can buy fashion but it can't buy class. That guy just doesn't fit in. Wonder who he is?"

"There's something familiar about him. Like I've seen him somewhere, but I can't put my finger on it." Gino turned back to Francesca. "He's not important."

Francesca nudged him and jerked her head in Bianca's direction. "She's looking for somebody," she said, "and I think she's found him."

A tall, dark-haired man in his early thirties came out of the crowd to stand by Bianca's side.

"That's her nephew, Michael DeMontana," Gino said. "He's a real player. I've seen him at the tables in Monte Carlo. He's a high roller and wins more often than not. Something," Gino said, "that I've never experienced. I've never played at his table. He's definitely out of my league."

Francesca squeezed his hand. "We're going to win this one. Just have some faith."

Bianca and her nephew spoke together for a minute or so and then separated. She made her way through the guests, stopping to exchange a few words here and there. When she reached the library door at the far side of the great hall, Michael was waiting. He followed Bianca into the room and shut the door behind them.

"I'm ready for action," Francesca said, checking the camera. "Carla got most of the downstairs, but I don't think she did much on the second floor.

I'll wander upstairs and shoot some pictures there for our reconnaissance. If we're going to B&E, it can't hurt to have all the info we'll need."

"I'll go check out the perimeter," Gino said. "See if I can overhear anything between Bianca and her nephew in the library. Meet you back at the car in fifteen minutes." "Righto, Chief," Francesca saluted. "I'll just snap a few more shots and make sure we've got enough photos to do the whole layout when we get back to the house."

Gino strolled through the foyer and let himself out. The place was so big he didn't have a clue where the diary would be. In a drawer, in a closet, on a shelf, in a safe. The possibilities were nearly endless, and he was discouraged. He kicked at a loose paver and added "under a rock" to his list of hiding places. The damn thing could be right under his nose and he wouldn't know it.

The landscaping didn't provide much in the way of concealment, but he eased his way between the rose bushes and the ivy, positioning himself by the library window where he could get a narrow view of the room inside. Keeping to the side, he could see bookshelves lining two walls of the library with the third wall taken over by a stone fireplace that backed up against its twin in the ballroom. Two overstuffed armchairs were to either side of the casement window. There was a baby grand piano in the far corner and a leather couch with two end tables across from the fireplace. He couldn't hear what Bianca and Michael were saying, but he got an eyeful, nonetheless.

Michael DeMontana leaned against the mantel, martini in one hand and a crowbar in the other. He raised his glass in a toast and Bianca, seated in the chair to the left of the window, raised her own glass in response. Michael tapped his finger on the crowbar. She extracted the pink plastic toothpick from her drink and nibbled at an olive.

Michael stepped back from the fireplace and drained the last of his martini. He set the empty glass down on the mantel and then pulled on a pair of surgical gloves. He turned to face the mantel and reached up to the painting hanging on the wall above. His hands midway on the gold frame, he hesitated and looked back to Bianca who motioned him to go on. He lifted the picture from its hooks, laid it on the rug, and pulled it from the frame. He rolled the canvas and handed it to Bianca, who carried the painting to the wall on the left of the fireplace, pressed the spine of a volume on the third shelf from the ceiling and waited for the bookcase to swing out, revealing the vault behind. Then, Michael returned to the window, opened it, and tossed the crowbar onto the ground below.

Gino attempted to flatten himself against the side of the house when he saw Michael coming his way, but he tripped over an ivy root and fell directly beneath the window instead where he couldn't escape the eighteen pound piece of steel as it came out the window and grazed his head on its way to the ground. The jolt would have sent him to his knees if he hadn't already been there. He heard the window being closed and the lock snapping into place. None of it made any sense. His head hurt like hell and his thoughts were fuzzy. What the hell was the business with the crowbar? He picked up the tool and turned it over in his hands. These people were crazy. Gino used the crowbar to help himself to standing and when he looked through the window again, Michael had gone but Bianca was still there. She was seated at the library table, making a notation in a small book. Gino squinted, and he realized he was looking at the diary. He dropped the crowbar on his foot and stifled a yelp.

Bianca closed the diary, turned off the table lamp, and left the library, the diary still in her hand. Gino backed away from the window. He pushed through the hedges and returned to the garden path. Except for the main floor, the mansion was dark, but within a minute a light came on in a room on the second floor. It wasn't on for long, perhaps less than thirty seconds, and then it went out.

He could end this thing tonight. The diary was in that room on the second floor. How many places could there be to search in one lousy room? He'd just wait for the right moment. His thinking had cleared and now thoughts of every crime show he'd ever seen raced through his mind. He took the blue silk display handkerchief from his lapel pocket and retraced his steps. He gave the crowbar an industrious wipe down, then tossed it aside tossed and jammed the handkerchief into his pants pocket. Time to return to the Bug and debrief.

"What the hell happened to you?" Carla's mouth fell open, as Gino limped down the walk and climbed into the front seat. "I just left you half an hour ago and you didn't look like this."

"Gino?" Francesca asked. "Are you all right?"

"I'm fine," he said through clenched teeth. "It's just a bump." He felt the small egg on his forehead and winced. "It feels worse than it looks." For once, Carla didn't jump down his throat demanding to know what he'd found. In fact, she was suspiciously quiet. He exchanged a look with Francesca, who shook her head. Something was wrong, but Carla wasn't talking.

"What time you got?" Francesca asked him.

"Almost eight forty-five. The party should be getting ready to pull up stakes and head for the next stop on the night's agenda. That would be the Italian Consulate. The paper said that affair begins at nine."

"They won't leave until after nine," Francesca said. "Nobody wants to be the first one there. It's all about appearance. There won't be anybody to see them arrive."

"Well, they can't all be last," Carla piped in from the back seat. "I mean how stupid can you get. Somebody's got to be first."

"Nobody said they were bright, just rich," Francesca said.

"Guess they don't want to get the good food before it's gone," Carla said. "I bet they put out a good spread at the Italian Consulate. Nothing cheesy like ravioli or pizza."

"I'm getting hungry," Gino said. "They'd better get moving soon." Almost on cue, the valets began retrieving cars and the first wave of party goers emerged from the house. It took half an hour to clear the place with Bianca and Michael being the last to leave.

Gino left the Bug and returned to his position by the wall behind the rose bush. He looked at his watch. Ten minutes had passed since everyone had left. He gave it an extra five for insurance, but as he was about to make his move, a black Mercedes came back up the drive. Gino cursed and retreated farther back into the hedges.

Michael DeMontana left the motor running, got out of the car, ran around the front of the house to the pathway, passing within inches of Gino, who tried to merge with the wall. At the library window, Michael put on the pair of surgical gloves, picked up the crowbar, jimmied open the window, tossed down the crowbar, raced back to his car, and drove away. Instantly an ear-shattering alarm sounded. Gino startled and cursed again. It would be only a matter of minutes until the police arrived. He straightened and fled back around the corner to Francesca and Carla, waiting in the Bug.

"What's with the alarm?" Carla asked. "What did you do, Gino?" "I didn't do anything. It was the guy—Bianca's nephew."

Carla raised an eyebrow. "The alarm, Gino. Why's the alarm going off?"

And suddenly it all made sense. A broad smile broke across Gino's face. The painting. The diary. The crowbar. "Because the DeMontanas just burgled their own house. I know where they're keeping the stolen art. And I think I know where the diary is."

CHAPTER EIGHTEEN

San Francisco

"What's that?" Francesca squinted and leaned over the steering wheel. They'd just crossed Octavia, and she'd spied something in the middle of the street ahead.

"What's what?" Gino, eyes closed, had his head on the headrest, listening to the pounding in his brain.

"Looks like a pile of clothes," Carla said. "Sweet Mother Mary. It ain't clothes. It's a body!"

Francesca hit the brakes, pulled over, and jumped out of the car with Gino and Carla right behind her. Beside the body, a woman in a heavy black overcoat was in hysterics, crying and pulling at her hair. A crumpled shopping cart lay on its side next to her, its contents strewn across the pavement.

"He didn't stop! He didn't stop!" The woman wailed, continuing to pull at her clothes and her hair. "Bobby! Bobby! He killed you, Bobby!"

It didn't take a medical examiner to prove the woman right. Bobby wasn't going to get up again. Francesca tried to put her arm around the woman's shoulders, but she shrank from the touch, shaking her head and making guttural sounds deep in her throat. She moaned and then pointed at something off in the distance. "Devil car," she almost whispered the words. "Devil man." Then she looked down and moaned again.

"I'll call the police," Francesca said, crossing the street back to the car.

Carla knelt by the woman. "What's your name, honey?" The woman stopped keening and looked at Carla, her eyes vacant and confused. She moved her lips but said nothing. Finally, she turned her face away and began to pick up the scattered bits of clothing one at a time and pat each one against her chest before folding it and placing it at her companion's side.

"That's okay," Carla said. "You just keep folding. It'll help."

The woman returned to her task. Carla watched her work. Her motions were almost mechanical. Hard to tell the woman's age. Her life was etched in the lines of her face and she could have been anywhere from thirty to sixty. Her skin was taught over high cheekbones, and her eyes were wide set and large. She had a small, straight nose that turned up slightly at the tip. Her hair was a lifeless brown and straggled out from beneath the scarf she'd tied around her head. Once she might have been beautiful, but that must have been a long time ago. Now her skin was sallow, and a deep scar ran from her left eyebrow to the corner of her mouth. Her hands trembled. Whether from shock or fear or drugs, it was impossible to tell.

When the police arrived, Francesca told them all she knew and admitted it wasn't much. They'd been driving and had found the victim lying in the street. They hadn't seen the accident. Officer Peter Walsh took their statements, and then he and his partner turned their attention to the woman, but she wasn't offering much help either. "The devil man killed Bobby. The black devil car killed Bobby." And she began to wail again. Finally, they gave up. They took pictures of the crime scene. The ambulance came and collected the body and somebody dragged the shopping cart over to the sidewalk.

"What about her?" Francesca asked Officer Walsh.

"She doesn't know anything, or she's too wasted to remember if she did." He closed his book.

"No, I mean what's going to happen to her?"

"Happen? We're not taking her in, if that's what you mean. She's free to go wherever she wants."

"But you can't just leave her here. She's in no condition to take care of herself.

There's got to be something you can do," Francesca said. "Look, lady, I'd love to help her. Really, I would. But there's nothing I can do. She's got *rights*. And if I step on those *rights,* it's my ass that's in the slinger. Sorry.

That's just the way it is." He opened the door of the patrol car and hesitated. "I could call Social Services. Maybe they'll send somebody out to check on her, if she's still here. That's the best I can do."

Gino, Francesca, and Carla watched the squad car leave. Francesca handed the keys to Gino. "You drive," she said.

They piled back in to the VW and started for home. "At least he didn't tell us to 'have a nice day'," Carla said.

They'd gone three blocks in silence when Gino slammed his hands on the steering wheel, cursed, and made a left turn, heading back towards Octavia. Carla patted Francesca's hand. "Son of a bitch," was all Gino said, but he said it with feeling, and Francesca put her arm around his shoulders and hugged him.

The woman was standing in the gutter, staring into the street to the place where Bobby had died, the stack of neatly folded clothes in her arms. Gino parked the car.

"I'll go," said Francesca.

"Francesca and I can scrunch into the back seat," Carla said. "She can have the front. She probably don't like being cooped up. Where we takin' her?"

"If she'll let us," Gino said, "St. Vincent de Paul's on Fifth. They'll get her a bed for the night and a shower and a hot meal. Maybe some clean clothes. Tomorrow, I don't know, but at least for tonight, she'll be off the streets."

The woman allowed Francesca to lead her to the car. Gino told her where they'd take her, if she would like to go there. Without a word, she took her seat. Ten minutes later, at the homeless center, her stack of folded clothes held tightly to her chest, she paused by the front door and said in a soft, clear voice, "Mary. My name is Mary." Then she went inside.

****

"That son of a bitch," Gino said. "Black car. Speeding. It was DeMontana." Back in the VW, they were headed home.

"You can't prove it," Francesca said. "We didn't see anything, and the woman doesn't remember anything."

"The cops'll never find him," Gino said. "A black car. That's all she knows. They'll never find him."

"Not without help, they won't," Carla spoke up from the back seat. "But that car'll have some front-end damage for sure. You can't do that and not mess up your ride. I say we check out the next party stop, look for the car, cop the plate, and then figure out what to do next."

"You've got a devious mind, you know that?" Francesca said. "I like the way it works. The Italian Consulate's only a few blocks away. Can't hurt to do a little investigation on our own. What do you say, Gino?"

"What I say is this whole adventure doesn't seem to be working along the lines we'd planned out. By now the police are at the DeMontana house so going back there isn't an option. Might as well see what we can find. If it was DeMontana, the car shouldn't be that hard to check out. We're looking for a black Mercedes sedan."

The Italian Consulate, on the corner of Webster and Broadway, took up most of the block. It was a massive building, built in the Palazzo style. The word 'palace' described it well. White marble blocks formed the façade and reinforced a solid look of permanency. It was built to endure. Tonight the windows spilled their light onto the streets, making golden rectangles along the asphalt. The doors were open, and guests streamed in and out of the entrance hall in a steady procession. For Gino, that meant traffic. Cars coming and going and wedging themselves into miniscule parking places. "Well, that was a less than brilliant idea," Francesca said, surveying both sides of the block lined with black automobiles at the curb.

"There's sure a shitload of 'em," Carla agreed, nodding at Broadway which was also overwhelmed with black.

"Is that some kind of Italian thing?" Francesca asked.

"More like some kind of rich thing," Gino said. "Black is classy."

"So's orange," said Francesca, giving the dashboard an affectionate pat. "So what's the plan?" said Carla. "We gotta have some kind of plan."

"Plan. Right." Francesca scanned the street. "First, we have to find someplace to park the Bug. I might be able to squeeze into that little space at the corner. Nobody's going to be ticketing these folks tonight. Maybe we'll be okay for a little while." She finessed the car into the postage stamp-sized space.

"You're only sticking out a foot or so beyond the corner," Gino said. "It'll have to do. Let's be quick. We don't fit in with the surroundings. I'll take this side of the street and the cross. Francesca, you take Broadway southbound. Carla, you take Broadway going north. If you see anything, give a call." He held up his cell.

"Thanks, Gino," Carla said, making a face. "If I'd a known I was gonna be going up and down a hill the size of a mountain, I woulda worn hiking boots." She frowned at her purple stiletto heels and then took them off and slung them onto the floor of the back seat. "No point in ruining a good pair of stockings either," she said, wriggling out of her panty hose.

"If you're done undressing, can we get on with this?" Gino said. "I'm taking Webster Street in case DeMontana decides to leave early."

"Suppose he does?" Francesca said. "Then what?"

"I don't know. Then there won't be a car here with front end damage. That won't tell us anything. All we've got is now. Let's get moving."

****

"I got something." Francesca was halfway down the block on the east side when she called Gino and Carla. "It's black. Big wow there. But it's got a broken left headlight, the fender is smushed, and there are scratches along the driver's side. I think we've got our car." She disconnected and used her phone to take some pictures of the damage and the license plate.

"Smushed?" Gino asked.

"Yeah, well." Francesca was standing vigil on the sidewalk by the car as they walked up. Gino was massaging the bump on his head and limping from the crowbar insult to his foot, and Carla was out of breath from trudging back up the hill. It wasn't hard to spot the damage.

"Looks smushed to me," Carla said. "Now what?"

"Beats me," Gino said. "We've got a lot of pieces that aren't fitting together yet. And one of them, if I may remind you, is the diary we don't have. We're on the outside looking in."

"Time," Francesca said. "Give it time. It'll all fall together." She winked at him. "Trust me."

CHAPTER NINETEEN

SFPD Central Division Headquarters

"I got a theory about crime," said Inspector Steve Cranston, mulling over the offerings of The Lucky Dragon's takeout menu. It was lunch time and his stomach was rumbling.

"You and every other cop." Inspector Elizabeth "Liz" Paone was shuffling through the reports on her desk, a pencil gripped between her teeth, and an intent expression on her face. "It's here somewhere." A stale cup of coffee teetered on the mouse pad, threatening to take out her keyboard, and she grabbed the handle just as it was about to make its fatal move.

The SFPD's Art Theft Division had an impressive name and no budget. It operated under the umbrella of property theft, consisted solely of Paone and Cranston, and was housed in the Hall of Justice building on Bryant Street in the area called SoMa or South of Market. The building was old and the office crowded. Those were the good points.

"It's the lunar effect," Steve continued. "You know the word *lunatic* comes from the Latin word for moon, don't you? There's always a crime spike when there's a full moon. That's a scientific fact."

Liz spit out the pencil. "Yeah, just like earthquake weather. After the fact, everybody says they knew it was coming. They could tell by the weather." She picked up the pencil and jammed it into a cracked mug that used to be her favorite until she'd dropped it on the tile floor.

"You scoff, but there's enough evidence out there to prove it."

"Maybe." Liz straightened one pile of papers, stuffed it into a file box, and started in on another. "There it is. I knew it was in here somewhere."

"What?"

"Another DeMontana got lifted last night. That's the third one in the past three months. And this," she waved a sheet of paper over her head, "is the latest from Interpol on two taken from a museum in Paris. Tonight's take is close to home. Getting bold. Hit a house this time."

"That's Northern's jurisdiction," Cranston said. "They're not going to have the paperwork done for hours."

"I know, but it won't hurt to stop by and see what they have. I need some air, and it's as good a time as any to check out the scene. See what Northern's got before we add the DeMontanas to our victim list and do the interviews. We can pick up something along the way." She looked at the menu. "You want Chinese? Or, I think I got a coupon for Mexican here somewhere." She considered the pile of paper she'd shoved to the back of the drawer.

"I want some real food. Steak. Loaded baked potatoes. Biscuits and gravy. Chicken fried steak." Cranston sighed. He tossed her the menu, picked up a carrot stick, and stuck it in his mouth. "I've got to lose twenty pounds."

"Twenty?" Paone gave the menu a last glance. "More like forty."

"Yeah, well, twenty's a start."

"You should drink green tea. It's got a lot of health benefits."

"It looks like panther piss," Cranston said.

She tossed the menu onto his desk. "You choose. I'll drive."

CHAPTER TWENTY

San Francisco

The kitchen table in Francesca's apartment was piled high with coffee cups, empty chip bags, soda bottles, and gum wrappers. Francesca surveyed the mess, hands on her hips, and shook her head. "This is not acceptable. How are we going to think clearly if we're eating garbage? We need brain food, not sugar and salt and grease." She opened the fridge and studied the contents, finally deciding on some fruit. She rinsed some grapes in the sink while Carla sliced some apples and got the peanut butter out of the cupboard.

"Try this," Francesca said, offering Gino an apple slice dipped in peanut butter.

"What the hell is this?"

"It's called food, and it's got nutritive value unlike the rest of the crap we've been ingesting. Every cop movie I've ever seen, the criminals eat junk food. If we have a higher purpose, we need to eat better."

"Yeah, maybe," Carla said. "But I seen Sal and the rest of them guys eating pretty good. And you don't get higher up in the Mob than that. Of course, Rico don't eat too good, and Tony's a pig, so you could be on to something." She shook the colander and lifted the grapes onto a paper towel to soak up the remaining water.

Gino accepted the plate of fruit as he wadded up the fifth stick of spearmint he'd been chewing into a ball and shot it toward the waste basket. His aim was wide and Carla ripped off a piece of the paper towel from under the grapes and used it to pick up the gum. "You didn't even come close. That's another reason you'd be a lousy basketball player."

"What? Short guys can't jump? Sorry, Carla. In my next life I'll ask to be taller." He returned to studying the society pages and making notations on a calendar he'd requisitioned from Francesca's desk.

"Maybe I don't want to know anything more than I already do," Francesca said. She was examining the photos they'd taken of the black Mercedes at the Consulate. Carla was poring over the photos she'd taken at the gala, arranging them by room.

"I got some good shots of the upstairs," Carla said, fanning out the photos like a card hand. "Waited until the john downstairs was busy and went looking for the can upstairs. Figured I had a good excuse if I got caught. But I didn't. And the ones you took are good too."

"That Bianca is one cold number," Francesca said, looking at a group shot. "That face doesn't have a line on it." She set the photo down. "How'd you like to have a face like that?"

"Not me," Carla said. "There ain't nothing there but makeup. Sure it costs money, but you can just do so much with it. Makeup don't cover up evil. And she can't cover up those evil eyes. They give me the heebie jeebies." She shuddered. "She's one stone cold bitch."

"I don't think I'd want to spend a whole lot of time with her. That's the God's truth," Francesca said. "Here's one more of her that I took. She seems real cozy with the guy next to her. He sure doesn't look like her type. He doesn't have that society look. And judging by that overdone 'in the know' smile he's beaming around the room, he's out of his league and out of the loop. I wish I could place him." She dropped the photo onto the table. When she turned away Carla put her coffee cup on it.

"I think we might be in that same category. Out of our league, that is. We're amateurs, and these people are pros at what they're doing," Gino said. "They've been at this a long time. And messing with the Mafia is not on my usual list of stuff I need to do before I die. If you two have finished with the character analysis, I could use some help here. I'm stumped. The next chance to get the diary is Monday, when the DeMontanas are at the opening of the Picasso Festival at the Hunter Museum of Fine Art downtown. *Purely*

Picasso is the name of the exhibit. After that, I don't know. It could be never."

"All right," Carla said. "Monday, it is."

"Just like that, Miss Chipper?" Gino said.

"Well, we've got an event planner right here. Jacking the diary is an event. So it looks like a no brainer to me. Turn it over to Francesca." She caught Francesca's eye and winked.

"Why not?" Gino said, tossing down the pencil. "I sure don't have anything to contribute."

"Yes, well." Francesca sat back in her chair and tapped her lips with her finger. "You're right, Carla. We can do this. It's just something we need to plan, isn't it? Organizing a theft is really no different from organizing anything else. One step at a time. That means lists. We need to make lists."

"Lists," Gino said.

"Yes. Planning is simply a matter of listing tasks, the equipment required to complete each task, and assigning a person to be responsible for the task. Then you brainstorm whatever complications might arise and develop a protocol for either dealing with them as they arise or preventing them from occurring in the first place."

Gino squinted at her as if he could make some sense out of what she was saying if he only had a better focus. He gave it up.

"Like this." She took a legal pad and wrote *Stealing Diary* at the top of the page. Gino grimaced. "Stay with me. It'll all make sense shortly. Let's start with the complications first. What could go wrong?" she asked. "Oh, let's see. We could get caught. Go to jail for the rest of our lives. Get killed somehow. Just about anything you could think of, I guess," he said.

"If you're going to be so negative, this isn't going to be easy," Francesca said, pointing her pencil at his nose.

"Yeah, you could give us bad karma. I don't need no more bad karma. I've got a new life," Carla said. "So you need to be positive."

"I'm positive we could get caught, arrested, or killed," Gino said.

"You know," Francesca said, "I think we need to get some sleep. This is all going to look so much better in the morning." She tossed her pencil down and pushed back her chair. "Carla, guest room is down the hall, last door on the left. Gino, you're with me." She got up, cleared the garbage from the table, and set the coffee maker for seven in the morning. Carla grabbed her pocketbook and headed for her room. Francesca beckoned to Gino with her index finger.

"Yes ma'am," he said. "Whatever you say. Is this going to be a Special Event?"

"Special as you make it," she said, and Carla's laugh reached them from all the way down the hall through the closed door.

CHAPTER TWENTY-ONE

San Francisco

"I think we should skip the complications part for right now," Francesca said, pouring coffee and then checking on the cinnamon buns in the oven. "Looks like about another five minutes." She closed the door and the aroma wafted through the house, an enticing call to breakfast. "I know I said we were going to eat healthy meals, but cinnamon buns have raisins in them. We can fudge a little. And the sugar will give us energy. Anyhow, we were confusing complications with outcomes. We probably should just start with the logistics."

"You're the boss," Carla said and took the juice glasses to the table, setting them next to the plates and silverware. "Where's Gino?" she asked.

"Still shaving. He'll be here in a minute."

"I'm glad he don't do that two-day beard look. I don't get why guys think that's sexy. It just scratches when they kiss you."

"It's all marketing. We're programmed to like things or do things in order to make money for advertisers. Very little of what we think or do is original. It's all been carefully thought out for us."

"I dunno. Maybe. Don't see how not shaving makes anybody money."

"Oh, but they do shave. That look takes a lot of upkeep."

At that moment, Gino, freshly showered and shaved, made his appearance.

"Thanks for shaving, Gino," Francesca said.

"Yeah. Thanks, Gino," Carla added.

Gino took a small step backward. "You're welcome." His look was dubious as he ran his hand across his cheek.

"Buns are ready," Francesca said. "Everybody ready for a working, semi-healthy breakfast? We've got orange juice, too." She picked up her pencil from the legal pad she'd already begun making notes on. "Let's walk through the whole scenario from start to finish. We'll ignore any complications that could occur along the way. For now." She eyed Gino with a firm gaze. "Fine," she said without waiting for a response. "Here it is: One, we need a car. We have one. We can use the Bug. Check. Two, we need a driver. Again, check. Carla can drive. Three, the alarm system will need to be deactivated or something."

She looked up from the list and tapped the pencil against her lips. "I don't know anything about that." She made a notation on the pad. "We'll need to do some research. Four, Gino gets into the house, goes upstairs to Bianca's room, finds the diary, and then retraces his route until he's safely back at the car. And five, we drive away. See? Only five simple steps." She made three horizontal lines at the end of the list and set the pencil neatly along the bottom line. "Now, doesn't that sound doable?"

Gino, with a mouthful of cinnamon bun, could only glare daggers at her. By the time he'd swallowed, Carla had joined the conversation.

"I can help with the alarm system," she said. "Actually, it ain't me. But I know somebody who can do it." Her eyes softened.

"Morrie, I bet?" asked Francesca. "I want to hear more about this guy."

"He's real good at that stuff, being a contractor and all. He does his own electrical. He's real good at everything," she added, smearing some cream cheese onto her cinnamon bun.

"I don't think getting everybody and his uncle involved in this is good for our health," Gino said. "The more people who know, the more chance there is for a leak. A screw up. Somebody blackmailing us. Whatever." He reached for another bun. "No."

"Yes," Carla said. "Gino, I get what you're saying, but if you don't do something about that alarm system, you ain't gonna get three feet inside that house. I know Morrie. You can trust him. He's into all that electronics shit.

Honest. He did all that stuff in the Army. I mean, if you can't trust a soldier, for Christ's sakes, you can't trust nobody." She looked hurt.

"Morrie. Morrie. Who's this Morrie dude you keep bringing up?" Gino asked. "Morrie. Morrie Landow. Weren't you listening when we poured out our hearts

at your place? I drove all the way cross-country with him. That's not important now. You'll see, Gino. We need him."

Gino clenched his teeth. "All right. I'll meet Morrie. But if I don't like him, he's gone. No arguments, *capisce*?"

"Yeah, Gino, *capisce*." Carla beamed at him and pulled out her cell, punched the speed dial, and left the table as the call connected. She spoke for a few minutes and then returned, just in time to snag the last bun. "He'll be here this afternoon," Carla said. "I kinda gave him a rough idea of what we want to talk about, so he'd be prepared. I didn't tell him nothing about no heist, though. Don't worry, Gino. You'll like him. You'll see."

****

And there was a lot to like about Morrie. Standing in the doorway, there wasn't much empty space. He stood about six foot two and weighed in the neighborhood of three hundred pounds, most of which was solid muscle.

"Morrie works out," Carla said, making the introductions with definite pride in her voice. "He works out real regular."

Morrie extended a hand. Gino took it tentatively, but Morrie wasn't the type who needed to show his strength. He shook hands firmly but didn't crush any bones or tendons in the process. Gino's impression of Morrie was made then and there. "We need some information on alarm systems," Gino said, leading the way into the kitchen. "Carla told me a little about what you need. I brought some specs with me for the more popular types of systems." He set his attaché case down on the table and looked around the apartment. "For something this size you don't need too many bells and whistles. I think the homeowner economy package from Burkins will suit your needs. I used it on my last contracting job. Apartment house. Each dwelling had its own system, but they were all wired into the main unit."

"I told you I didn't spill the beans, Gino," Carla said, going over to Morrie and slipping an arm around his waist. "But I knew you'd like him. You do, don't you?" She ran her tongue across dry lips and waited.

Morrie kissed the top of Carla's head. "She's something, isn't she? I've been waiting for somebody like her just about all my life. She's a dancer, you know. A real dancer."

Gino coughed. "Yeah, she sure is something all right. A dancer. You have no idea." He winked at Carla, who let out a big sigh of relief. "Have a seat, Morrie. This is going to take some explaining. Motive is important here, I want you to understand. We're not crooks—well, at least not in the strict meaning of the word. But if you're not comfortable hearing the whole story, tell me now."

Morrie pulled out a chair and stretched out his legs. "If Carla's in on it, then I am too. And this is as comfortable as I get."

Carla settled herself at the kitchen table, stared into the depths of her coffee cup, and hiccupped.

"Go on," Morrie said. "I'm listening."

Gino stood and rested his arms on the back of his chair. "We need to gain entry to a place that has a state-of-the-art alarm system. The sign stuck in the grass outside says it's a Jurgen."

"I know the system," Morrie said. "You want to get past it, is what you're saying." "Yeah. I guess that's it. How do we do it, how long do we have before they notice it's down. Things like that."

Morrie nodded and rummaged through brochures in the attaché case and finally extracted a glossy folder extolling the virtues of the Jurgen. "It's a beauty, all right. It's got thirty-two defensive zones, an anti-cut function for the phone line, battery backup for a power outage." He folded back the cover and handed Gino the page with the specs. "Yep, it's got it all," he said.

"Surveillance cameras?" Gino asked, pausing midway down the page.

"And motion sensors," Morrie said. "They're what activate the cameras, so if you take the sensors down, the cameras aren't a problem. Any pets in the house?"

"Pets?" Gino asked. "I don't know. I didn't see any, but they wouldn't have been out when we were there for the open house."

Morrie laced his fingers behind his head. "Can you find out?" Gino looked up from the brochure. "Maybe. Is it important?"

"Could be helpful. Motion sensors are usually pet immune when the owners have animals. The sensors can be set for a certain height, so the pets can walk around the house without triggering the alarm. Some of the more sophisticated systems forgive an animal up to almost ninety pounds. Those work on body heat and infrared sensors. Kind of complicated, but you get the idea. So, yeah, it would be a good thing to know."

Francesca was back at her list, making notations on the items and adding comments in the margin. "We have to hit the house Monday night," she said. "That gives us two days. Not all that much time. I'll go through all the pictures we took and see if there's anything there that might indicate a pet. I'll also look for the motion sensors. Carla did a good job of getting all the walls downstairs and a few upstairs. I shot a few of the upstairs hall, but I only had time to get one of Bianca's bedroom." She walked to the desk and took a magnifying glass out of the top drawer. "At least I'm assuming it was Bianca's bedroom. It was at the head of the stairs and off to the right. That's where Gino saw the light come on."

Morrie took the brochure from Gino and circled two pictures of motion sensors. "This is what you'll be looking for. I'm guessing they went with wall mounts." He handed Francesca the booklet, and she propped it up against the sugar bowl for a ready reference.

Gino was pacing the confines of the kitchen. "The diary's just the first step. What the hell am I going to do with it if I get it?"

"When, not if," reminded Francesca. "We've had this conversation before." "Yeah, Gino, you gotta think positive. It's gonna all work out. One step at a time. We get the diary and the next step will show itself. Just wait and see. So you need to do something productive while you're waiting."

"I'm going to get some fresh air. I need to think," Gino said. "Somehow I've got to find a way to get the stolen paintings back and prove the DeMontanas are behind the thefts. I'd also sure as hell also love to nail DeMontana for killing that man. Right now all we've got is a photo of his car with front end damage. No witnesses. No evidence. Nothing."

Morrie stopped with his coffee cup halfway to his mouth. "I know I'm just here as a consultant, but you want to get me some clarification on what you just said? The part about the killing thing, if it's not too much trouble?"

CHAPTER TWENTY-TWO

San Francisco

Inspector Liz Paone pushed up her glasses and rubbed her eyes. It was almost quitting time and she was tired. "Hey Cranston," she said, "you making a fresh pot? I'm losing my concentration here."

Steve held up the carafe in response and dumped enough grounds into the filter to wake the dead. "I'm way ahead of you. But I've got heartburn that won't quit. I don't think coffee's going to do me any good."

"If you'd stop eating all that crap you wouldn't have heartburn all the time." "What's eating you? You're wound up tight as a mattress spring. That ex of yours giving you trouble again?"

Liz took off the glasses and stared at the lenses. "No more than usual. He's got Morgan this weekend, and I know what's going to happen when he gets back on Monday. It'll be 'Dad lets me do this' and 'Dad lets me do that' until I'm ready to scream. But I can't say anything. Feels like I'm on a tightrope. I say the wrong thing and the whole week is shot to hell. Jim would love for me to have a meltdown. Then he'd get Morgan for keeps." She reached for a tissue and set to work scouring at a smudge on the outside of the lens.

"It's tough," Steve said, "but if you don't mind an observation, you did the right thing ditching the jerk. You're a good mom. Cut yourself some slack. You got your mom living with you, and she takes good care of Morgan while you're working. You're not gone more than any other working mother, and you spend more time with your kid than most do. You forget,

Morgan's in school most of the time you're at work, so what are we talking about here? A couple of hours a day. That's nothing. A hundred and twenty minutes? Big deal. Give Morgan some credit. He's a smart kid, and he knows more about the situation than you think he does." Steve began rummaging through his desk drawer in search of the antacid tablets. "Kids figure out how to work their parents by the time they're two. It's nothing personal. It's just the way kids are. He doesn't want to lose you any more than you want to lose him."

Liz stopped scrubbing her lenses and put the glasses back on. "I know. I'll survive. Eight more years and he'll be off to college and I'll wonder where the time went. Meanwhile, back at the ranch..." She opened the folder that held her notes from the interviews they'd had with the DeMontanas concerning the break in and theft. "You know, something about this whole thing doesn't smell right. If you asked me what, I couldn't tell you, but still...I don't know. They're too smooth. The whole thing went off like it was choreographed. I mean," she put the file down and looked at her partner. "They leave for the consulate. That's fine. But when I asked Bianca about who was left in the house, she said nobody. I asked about the caterer's cleanup crew, and she said they were scheduled to return early in the morning for that. Bianca didn't want anyone in the house while she was gone. Not your usual SOP, but maybe it's *bona fide*. But wouldn't you be just at least a little bit upset that somebody had broken into your home and taken something that meant something to you? These guys were as cool as a spring day in Sausalito. They said all the right things but..." she stopped there.

"I lost a yo-yo in the fourth grade," Steve said. "Actually Pete Salvatore took it at recess. I was so mad I wanted to punch his lights out. But I was a skinny little kid and there was no way I could fight him."

"What did you do?"

"Oh, I cut his bike tires with a razor blade. Funny thing is he bawled like a baby. I think it was then I realized a bully was just that. He never bothered me again. And I got my yo-yo back. But mad? I was so mad I couldn't think of anything but getting the guy who'd taken my stuff."

"Any theft is a personal violation of space. It's not natural to dismiss it as something inconsequential. Even if you're rich."

"I'm thinking especially if you're rich. That's how they get that way, you know?"

"So, where does that leave us?"

"It's leaving me with heartburn. I don't know about you. I got to find some antacids somewhere. I'll be back." And Cranston left in search of relief, leaving Liz to search through the reports for something that would give her a lead.

Bianca had given her the guest list. She'd made a pointed remark that no one in attendance at the open house could have possibly been involved in the theft of the painting. Many of them, in fact, were generous patrons of the arts. The catering firm was bonded and licensed and had been in business for years. Everyone, simply everyone, used them. It wasn't possible they were the culprits. There were some reporters from the *Examiner* there, of course. After all, it was the opening event of the art season. But everything had been arranged by Jennifer Fabriani, the event planner. She took care of the valet service, the house staff, everything. The police would have to talk with her. As for the theft itself, she really couldn't help any more than she had. After all, she'd been at the consulate with her nephew, hadn't she?

Michael DeMontana hadn't been any more helpful. He didn't know anything. He hadn't seen anything. They'd all left the party for the Italian Consulate somewhere after nine. He had rushed home as soon as he got the call from the security service that the alarm had been tripped. That was about nine-thirty. When he got there, a security guard was waiting for him. They searched the house and found the library window open and the painting that had hung above the fireplace mantel was gone. That's when the police arrived. Liz checked the police report. The responding officer was on scene at ten o'clock. He'd been held up by a fatal hit and run a few blocks from the DeMontana mansion. Liz bit at her upper lip. She made a note to check the hit and run report. Coincidence, perhaps, but DeMontana admitted rushing home. He might have seen something. If he had, why not tell them? A hunch was sometimes a cop's best friend. She made some more notes. A talk with the officer who responded to the hit and run was a priority. She closed her notebook and read down through the names on the guest list. It read like a Who's Who of the rich and famous and when she got down to the latter part of the alphabet, she whistled.

"What?" Steve was back and pouring coffee, balancing the carafe on the edge of the counter while he mopped up some overflow.

"Our friend Bianca didn't do a whole lot of thinking before she released the guest list. Lucky for us. Who do you know whose last name starts with Puglisi? Hmm?"

"Son of a bitch," Steve said. "Curiouser and curiouser. Why do you suppose a nice guy like Sally the Pipe was chumming it up with the lady?"

"Don't know," Liz said, "but I'm going to make it my business to find out." "Sally's been skating on thin ice for a while now," Steve said. "Word is he's about to go down for income tax evasion and some other financial missteps. Maybe he's trying to court favor with the *hoi polloi* to show his softer, more genteel side. Donate to the judge's retirement fund or something."

Liz huffed. "In that case, he picked the wrong party to show up at. He probably cussed a good one when he found out about the theft. Unless, of course, he was there as more than Bianca's date, in which case he'd be 'shocked, shocked that theft is going on' under the nose of organized crime."

"Your Bogart impression needs some work. Or maybe it's Claude Raines. Whatever." "Most of me needs some work. Pull up those Interpol files, will you? It's time to check the MOs of the other thefts against last night's."

"Be quite a feather in our caps to get to the bottom of this one," Steve said. "What do you suppose the odds are of us coming up with nine DeMontanas, two Picassos, and a Monet?"

"Don't know," Liz said, "but my money's on the good guys."

"That would be us," Steve said.

Liz nodded. "That would be us."

CHAPTER TWENTY-THREE

San Francisco

One fortunate consequence of Francesca's unemployment was that she'd shipped all her supplies home, including her paste-up board, and she and Carla used it to tack up every photo they'd taken during the DeMontana open house. They scrutinized each one with the magnifying glass as they put it up and went over all of them one more time for insurance, but they came up short. There was no sign that a cat or dog or cockatiel or even a boa constrictor roamed the premises. No cushions on the floor, no chew sticks or rubber balls peeking out from under the sofa. Nothing.

The women returned to the kitchen table with the bad news, but Morrie was already thinking ahead. "It was just a long shot, but worth a try. Now instead of flying under the radar, so to speak, we're going to have to jam the signal at its source."

Gino looked up from the scrapbook he'd been studying. "You mean the control panel," he said. "It's got to be somewhere by the main entrance for convenience. You don't want to have to sprint through the house after arming the system."

Morrie agreed. "Usually they're right next to the front door. Many folks put them in the hall closet, if they've got one. That way the panel is out of sight but still easy to get to."

"That's it then. There's a coat closet in the foyer to the left of the door, and Bianca and her nephew weren't more than a few seconds behind the last guests, when they left for the consulate," Gino said.

Morrie consulted the Jurgen brochure again. "We'll need a universal remote for starters and some other supplies. I need to make a run to the electronics shop and the hardware store," he said. "I'll be back in a bit. I'll get the remote done this afternoon."

"I'm coming too," Carla said. "I like hardware stores."

Morrie smiled. "She's one in a million."

"That's the God's truth," Gino said, returning to the scrapbook.

It was a cold day with no sun. Overnight the warmth of autumn had vanished into the damp chill of winter. The skies were leaden and threatened rain, but the electronics shop was just down the block and the hardware store was only a couple of places down from that, so they walked.

Carla slipped her arm through Morrie's and rested her head against his shoulder. "You talk good. You know that, Morrie? I mean you don't cuss and all that, but there's more. You got a way of putting words together that sounds good." She raised her head and skipped a half step to match his pace. He slowed to throw her off. She punched his arm. "I like you Morrie. You know something? I'm thinking Gino might not be all wrong about the self-improvement shit he does. He's always reading about how to make himself better or taking a course about that kind of stuff."

"You going somewhere with this, Carla?" Morrie said. "I think you're just fine the way you are."

"No. I need improving. I mean, how's it gonna be when I open my dance studio if I don't talk like classy people. Nobody's gonna take lessons from somebody who can't talk good. They'll think I'm stupid." She sighed. "Will you teach me how to talk right? I'm a good listener, and I'll try real hard. I figure if I work on one improvement a day, within a week I'll be pretty good and in a month, I'll be close to damn perfect."

"If that's what you want, it's fine with me." Morrie said. "When do we start?" "Now," she said. "I don't got time to wait to get classy. What do I do? I need like homework or something."

"Well, let me think for a minute. I've never taught anybody anything like this before."

"No shit?" Carla said.

"That's as good a place as any to start," Morrie said. "Taking that word out of your vocabulary. From now on you're going shitless."

Carla furrowed her brow. "Huh? Oh. Shit. That's a really useful word, you know. I can do this, but I'm gonna need a substitute. Maybe more than one. I need to cover a whole lot of conditions and situations." She concentrated on matching his pace. "This ain't gonna be easy. But you know, this is one of those turning points life throws at you. You can decide to change at the turning point, or you can go on doing what you do and nothing changes. I'm not gonna throw this chance away." She looked at Morrie. "A week ago, I wasn't going nowhere and now," she spread her arms wide, "I am." She dropped her arms and her pace slowed. "There's one thing you need to know. I mean about me. We got to talk, Morrie. About some serious sh-stuff."

"Once I get the jamming device made," Morrie said, "we'll have all day tomorrow. Let's take a ride and scout some real estate for the dance studio and we can talk all you want. I promise I'll listen to whatever you have to say."

"You're sh....oops." Carla hesitated and then her expression cleared. "I mean,

that will be... wonderful," she said, and whispered into Morrie's ear. "Did you catch that? I didn't say it. I thought it, but I didn't say it." She beamed. "This new kind of talking high class ain't gonna be so fuckin' hard after all."

CHAPTER TWENTY-FOUR

San Francisco

Inspector Steve Cranston was searching through his computer database, his efforts punctuated by occasional sounds of disapproval and frequent notations on a legal-size notepad. An hour and a half of plowing through old wants and warrants produced nothing.

"Turn up anything?" Liz was involved in a database search of her own, although hers was taking a different tack. The Art Loss Register and the National Stolen Art File index, along with what she'd downloaded from Interpol and Scotland Yard, were giving her a pretty good sense of current events in the underworld of art crime.

"Making a start," Steve said, holding up the printout. "Moving on to priors. You?"

"Hardly making a dent, but I'm getting an education. Art theft is a multi-billion dollar business, and most of it disappears into private collections. Theft for hire, in a lot of cases. At least that's the way it is in Europe. In the States, art isn't usually the objective. It's just something else that's boosted during a burglary along with the jewelry, money, and anything else that can be fenced. That's what makes the DeMontana case different. It's got a European flavor." She put her glasses on the desk and rubbed her eyes. "You know, I'm thinking this could be part of something bigger. The burglar only wanted the painting. He walked right past some valuable antiques and rare books. I mean there was a Remington on the mantel. He left that. That in itself is weird, but there were also bookshelves crammed with first editions of some rare books. Again, not one taken. It was just about the painting. So, where's the painting now? Hmm?" "That's what we're working on, my friend," Cranston said. "You're making progress already. You've determined the theft was just about the painting. Think of all the potential suspects you've eliminated from the get go."

"Right. But if we had a budget, just think what we could do. We could travel the world, visit exotic places, eat haute cuisine—something you'd appreciate—and we could make some righteous collars in the process. But, no. What's our budget this year? Two hundred bucks for ink and file folders with an occasional pen and pencil thrown in?"

"Don't be bitter. It doesn't become you. Think of the perks we get. All the stale coffee we can drink, our own parking spaces, Benny's Bagelry down on the corner. Shall I go on?"

"No." She picked up her glasses and twirled them by an earpiece. "You know what I think? I think it's an inside job. I keep coming back to that. It's too neat. And I think the theft, the hit and run, our less than concerned victims, and Salvatore Puglisi are somehow all connected in a not-so-neat-and-tidy little package. That's what I think. Proving it," she pointed her glasses at Steve, "is going to be the tough part."

"You like a challenge," he said.

"Mmmm." Liz put her glasses back on. "Why do you suppose Puglisi's moved to the Left Coast? His operations are all back in New Haven and Providence. If he's coming up on racketeering and income tax evasion charges, you'd think he'd want to be stoking the home fires."

"My guess is he's left town during a minor cleanup operation. NHPD pulled a couple of bodies out of Beaver Pond last week. Both of them were connected with Sal's operation." Steve rummaged through the papers on his desk. "The *Register* consigned it to page two under the fold. Anthony Milano—a bouncer at Sal's strip joint—and a Rico Bonelli—bartender at same. They'd both been worked over and then sent on to the next world with a single slug to the back of the head."

"So Puglisi's elsewhere with a rock solid alibi, even captured on film and splashed over the front page of the Society section of the *Examiner*. What a nice guy. A real pillar of the community."

"I'm also interested in the pillarette."

"You mean Bianca?"

"Operating on the 'where there's smoke' principle, I'm going to do some digging on her background, as well. Michael, Bianca, and Salvatore."

"Have fun, the four of you." Liz stood and took her jacket off the coat rack. "I'm going to talk with Ms. Jennifer Fabriani, the event planner. She'll have names, if nothing else. We'll see if there're any other shining lights of organized crime among the *hoi polloi*. Speaking of events, you want I should bring you back some nutritional items? Some carrot juice maybe or a nice salad?"

Steve leaned back in his chair and laced his fingers behind his head. "Pizza. No anchovies. Lots of pepperoni. Extra cheese. And a diet root beer."

"Shame. Shame. What happened to your diet?"

"Same thing that happened to my ex-wife. Gone for good. Sometimes it's best just to accept your reality. I'd rather die with a full stomach than a starved one. Besides, I can't think when I'm hungry, and I need to do some serious thinking about this unholy trinity. And I *did* specifically request a diet root beer." He opened his side desk drawer and took out the antacid tablets. "I bought a new bottle. Just getting prepared," he said, giving Liz a determined look. "Oh, and get a packet of those hot peppers to sprinkle on the top, will you?" He reached for his wallet. "Here's a twenty."

"I shouldn't do this, you know. I'm enabling you." She took the money and waved the bill in his face.

"And you do it very well," Steve said, returning his attention to the computer. "Go. Bring food."

Liz stuffed the twenty in her wallet and scribbled Fabriani's address in her notebook. She left Steve with a final threat. "If they've got diet pepperoni, I'm getting it."

"Hey Liz, hang on a second. Come here. Look at this. It gets better and better." Steve's printer was cranking out the paper as he spoke. "Birth records."

"When you decide to start at the beginning, you're not kidding," Liz said, peering over his shoulder at the multiple windows Steve was working.

He minimized all but one and pointed at an entry. "I don't see what you're pointing to," she said, squinting at the screen.

"Put your damn glasses on and look. You're squinting so hard you're going to scare the pixels." Steve was nearly bouncing in his chair, a triumphant grin on his face. "I love these genealogy websites. If it's anywhere, they've found it. Look here." He took a ruler and held it up against the computer screen to isolate one line of text.

Liz grabbed her glasses from her purse and then leaned in, her lips moving as she read the line. "Donna Puglisi married Victorio DiCicco in 1957. They had three children: Victorio, Paolo, and Bianca." She straightened. "Puglisi. Small world. The same Puglisi?"

"Same family," Steve said, moving down the screen with the ruler. "This will make it easier to see." He opened a new tab and a graphic of the Puglisi family tree appeared. "Here's the connection: Sal Puglisi's grandfather and Donna's grandfather were brothers. That makes Sal Bianca's second cousin. It's a family affair."

Liz whistled. "So that cozy scene with the two of them wasn't *amour*, but family affection?"

"Maybe, maybe not. But that little art heist is beginning to look more and more like family business. It's going to make checking priors a hell of a lot easier."

Liz straightened and rubbed at a kink in her neck. "Nice work, Steve," she said. "You know, you deserve that pizza, and in your honor, I'm going to forget the diet pepperoni." She slipped her glasses back in her purse and buttoned her coat. "Hope I'm half as successful with Ms. Fabriani. Why don't you check her records while you're at it? Maybe she's a kissing cousin too."

****

Liz returned with the pizza and her interview notes with Fabriani to find Steve shuffling papers from his desk to a card table he'd appropriated from the break room. So far he'd created three short stacks from one tall, lopsided one that threatened to topple over and shed its load onto the floor.

Something that looked like a dry sponge was jammed under one of the table's legs and Liz eyed it with suspicion.

"Where did you get that?" she asked, pointing to the sponge. "It doesn't look healthy."

"The john. Damn table wouldn't hold still. The back leg's warped or something." He looked up. "Don't worry. I'll put it back when we're done."

"That's not what worries me. You don't know where that thing has been." She slapped his hand as he reached for a slice of pizza. "Here. Use this." She pulled a bottle of hand sanitizer from her purse. "I honestly don't know how you've survived as long as you have."

"I'm immune," he said, slathering on the sanitizer and rubbing his hands on his trousers.

"You're something. That goes without saying." She cleared a space on her desk, opened the pizza box, and set out the napkins and pepper packets. "Root beer or ginger ale?"

"Whatever. Root beer. At least it's half right." He grinned. "And I've been an industrious worker bee while you were out and about." He waved a slice of pizza over the card table and a glob of mozzarella spilled over the edge and slopped onto the top paper of the smallest stack. "Damn. That's the one I need." He scraped off the cheese and popped it in his mouth.

Liz blotted at the grease stain with a paper towel. It was a futile effort and she only succeeded in smearing the ink. She held the paper up to the light. "You can see right through it now. How does grease do that? Anyway," she set the paper back on the pile, "what did you find?"

Steve pulled his desk chair over to the card table and settled in. "The problem is that motives for art theft are essentially the same as for any other theft. A chance at a quick profit probably ranks high on the list if not *numero uno*. If it's work for hire, it's going to disappear into somebody's private collection after a healthy payoff to the thief. With that in mind, I've divided the last ten year's worth of reported thefts into three broad categories: probable inside jobs, work for hire, and crimes of opportunity." Steve tapped his forehead. "Good thinking, eh?"

"Superior." Liz munched thoughtfully on a crust. "I'm guessing the biggest stack is crimes of opportunity."

"And your guess would be correct. The element of intensive planning is generally absent. Somebody sees something he likes and decides it would look nice in the parlor and packs it off after work. Or somebody who doesn't think jacking the general office supplies—paperclips and pens—is a big deal, and then spots the corporate art on the wall and figures, 'What the heck,' and adds those to the take. That's why I'm discounting the obvious opportunity thefts for now and focusing on the other two." He ripped open a hot pepper packet and sprinkled the entire contents on the rest of his slice of pizza.

Liz raised an eyebrow. "Want some pizza with your pepper?"

"Cayenne is good for you." He pried the slice free with his pocket knife. Liz winced. "When was the last time you washed that knife? It's got stuff stuck to it."

"Washed? You don't wash pocket knives. You wipe them." He demonstrated by wiping the blade with a paper napkin. "See? Perfectly clean." He bit off a generous portion of pizza and chewed with relish. "Anyhow," he continued between mouthfuls, "some of this is hard to believe. And I don't know whether to call them crimes of opportunity or inside jobs. Sometimes they're related. Like this one." He picked up the summary he'd printed out and read an excerpt. "A secretary at a leading financial institution sold the painting in the reception area online and replaced it with a bad copy from a consignment store." Steve turned to Liz. "Turns out it was a Chagall and the boss was a collector. He was browsing online through the art offerings and found the stolen painting advertised. He clicked on 'Buy it now' and started an email correspondence with her using a fictitious name. She divulged her whereabouts—probably thinking he had romantic potential—and he notified the police who made the collar when she went to mail the painting at the local post office. That's the beauty of online commerce. You can be anybody. Pick your name and nobody has to know who you really are."

"I take it she's no longer employed there."

"Or anywhere else, unless you count the license plate factory," Steve said. "This one," he continued, glancing at the second paper in the stack, "was local. That's what caught my interest, but it crapped out. The butler, like our secretary, replaced the original with a copy. This time he'd simply taken a photo of the original and had it enlarged. Took the owner all of twenty-four hours to discover the switch." He looked at Liz. "Don't even say it."

Liz groaned. "And this one." She lifted the third sheet off the pile and scanned it. "The guy who installed the security system at the art gallery? Nice touch."

"He left his pocket knife behind, after he sliced the Rembrandt out of the frame."

Liz pursed her lips. "And I suppose he wiped it on a napkin when he was done? I've never understood that. I mean the slicing thing. You'd think the painting would be worth less with part of the canvas gone. They've got to reframe it. And if it gets cut again, it gets smaller. And smaller. Sooner or later, you don't have much left."

Steve looked up from the report. "Only you would think of that." He took the short stack off the card table and set it on the floor by the desk. "These thefts are all random. A Chagall, a Rembrandt, and a Renoir. Each one a single theft by a specific individual for a purpose—economic gain, love of art, revenge, whatever. And these cases are also solved." Steve took a sip of root beer. "Also, the thieves weren't especially bright."

Liz nodded. "Creative, though. You have to give them that. Inside jobs and crimes of opportunity. Seems like opportunity is the key here—that and a tendency toward larceny. So that leaves us with work for hire as our motive. Unless some of these thefts cross over into inside jobs." She leafed through the stack. "And there's always the possibility of a copycat crime. Someone reading a newspaper account of a theft may decide to copy the MO. Fifteen thefts." She looked up. "Could our thief be in this pile? That is the question."

"Art theft has been big business from the beginning," Steve said, "but for our purposes I've narrowed the search to thefts that included DeMontanas. And I've found something interesting." He sat back in his chair. "Crowbars. Two of these heists, three counting the current theft, used a crowbar to gain entrance through a window in a private residence. In all cases, the crowbar was left behind. No prints. Two more paintings were taken from small galleries that had minimal security." He turned to Liz. "All it took was a walk through to locate the painting and then a return trip at night. Simple alarm system that could be jammed with a cell phone. Hell, my own grandmother could have done it, for all I know. And the last four showed no signs of forced entry. It was as if they had the keys to the house. Since the maids or housekeepers were at the home in their own quarters, and the owners were coming and going at odd hours, the owners hadn't bothered to set the alarm."

Liz wiped her lips with a napkin and took a final drink of ginger ale. "Crowbars, cell phones, and house keys. That's a diverse pool of tools. The criminal mind never ceases to amaze me." She gathered up the remains of their

dinner and held up the last piece. "Last chance."

"No thanks," Steve said. "I'm on a diet."

Leaving Steve to his paperwork, Liz began the process of entering her interview notes with Jennifer Fabriani into the computer. Fabriani ran a full-service agency through her list of vendors, providing valets, caterers, coat room attendants, bartenders, servers, bussers, and cleanup crew. The number of people who had access to the DeMontana mansion on the night of the theft was daunting. Probably upwards of twenty, maybe thirty. Add the hundred or so guests to the mix, and it seemed as if half the population of San Francisco could have made off with the painting.

Chalet's Valets had overseen the parking arrangements. She tapped a fingernail on her wireless mouse. Valets made minimum wage and relied heavily on tips. Supplementing their income would be high priority. Their job was simple enough—park and retrieve cars for people attending events. They needed car keys to do that. Most people left their keys in the ignition and left the motor running when they got out of their vehicles at a classy event. Not everyone took the time, or had the foresight, to remove their car keys from their key rings and pocket their other keys. Somebody interested in getting access to an exclusive venue could play the odds and, if they scored, could make copies of house keys left on the ring for future use. They could find everything they needed to know from the registration and insurance papers in the glove box.

Once she'd started on the house key angle, Liz found more fertile ground. Chalet's Valets also provided indoor valet services, checking hats and coats and other items for guests. Liz rolled her pencil against her cheek. Someone checking coats and purses would have access to whatever was inside them. Once the items were stowed in the closet and the owners had gone off to the festivities, it would be easy to search a wallet or a purse to get credit card numbers and a host of other personal information. With an impression of the house keys taken from keys inside the purse or pocket, an enterprising thief would have carte blanche to gain entry to the home or start piling up some serious credit card debt before the victim even knew anything was awry. Sounded like a scheme well-suited to the Mob.

Society moved in small circles and someone interested in lifting some items from a home could be fairly confident in knowing when the home would be empty. The indoor and outdoor valets could be in cahoots. All they'd need to do would be to consult the Society pages of the local paper and discover when the next must-attend event would be held. Then they could stage their own version of an open house.

"Hey Steve, I may be onto something," she said. "Ever heard of Chalet's Valets?"

"Catchy name. That's part of Fabriani's outfit. I did what you asked, but there wasn't much to find. A few parking tickets. Minor fender bender back in 2010, but other than that, she's clean. She did move here from Palermo about five years ago, but that's all I could find on the quick."

"Still, there could be a connection. Might be something. Could be nothing," she said, rising from her chair and walking to the card table. She sorted through the files and took the house key theft files back to her computer.

****

"Well, found something interesting here," Liz said fifteen minutes later. "The other victims all used the services of Jennifer Fabriani or Chalet's Valets at some point. Not necessarily at the time they'd been hit, but within a year's timeframe of the theft." There was a lot more digging to do on

Fabriani but it could wait until tomorrow. Liz was tired. She stretched and yawned. "Time to wrap it up for tonight, kemosabe." She shut down the computer and took her purse out of the bottom desk drawer. "I'm outta here. You coming?"

"In a minute. I'm right behind you. Just looking for the antacid tablets." "Cranston, you're going down a one-way street the wrong way and you're accelerating into the curves. Time to hit the brakes. That's the last pizza I'm buying for you. From now on, it's bean sprouts and tofu."

"I'd rather die."

"You keep on this way, you will. And it's not going to happen on my watch. Tomorrow," Liz raised an index finger, "I'm bringing fruit and veggies, and you're going to find a whole new world of dining pleasure."

Steve mumbled something unintelligible and Liz stopped at the door. "I'm not kidding Cranston. I want to keep you as a partner, and if it means shoving bean curd down your gullet, goddammit, I'm going to do it." She held the door open as Steve shuffled through it, a man on his way to the gallows. "Oh, cut the crap, Cranston. You have no idea how good food can taste. It's fuel, not a substitute for your sorry excuse for a sex life. Believe me, I know."

"Whatever. My sex life isn't a shitload better than yours, far as I can tell. Don't see how the hell food is going to make any kind of a difference."

Liz paused, hand on doorknob. "Ouch. That was cruel, but point taken. All right. But Steve," she paused, searching for the right answer but came up empty.

"I like food. I like sex too, but that's not as easy to come by. Food is good." He winked at her. "So is sex." "Oh, Steve," she said. "When the hell did life get so damn complicated?"

He put a hand on her shoulder. "Sometime around the sixth grade, I think. And it accelerates from there. Why do you think cops have the highest divorce rate out of a gazillion or so professions? We're married to the job. We relate to our buddies. We hang out, talk, socialize, drink, whatever, with our buddies. You're worried about your kid. You're worried about what your ex is telling your kid. You've got nobody to talk to because you rush home to try to be Supermom. Liz, Morgan will grow up in spite of you. But what about you? Don't you want somebody to be with who understands the job? Somebody who knows when to talk and when to shut the hell up? You've got to leave yourself some room for options." Steve buttoned his jacket and straightened his tie. "Took me two years after Maggie left me to realize I wasn't a flawed person. Fat maybe, but not morally flawed. Give yourself the same slack. Find somebody who thinks you're ok. He's out there. But if you're going to find him you need to start looking."

"You're too young to have so much wisdom," she said. "But you're right. I need to get out more." She lifted her chin. "Okay, I will get out more. I'm not going trolling, but I'll be open. Regardless, I'm still bringing fruit and veggies for lunch tomorrow. And you will eat them."

"I'll do that if you'll do that," Steve said, and they parted company at the parking lot.

CHAPTER TWENTY-FIVE

The Streets of San Francisco

The rain that had threatened since Saturday made its appearance in force, just as Gino and his posse set out to reclaim the diary. Urged on by a fierce westerly wind that drove the rain sideways, the drops pelted the orange VW's windshield, and the wipers beat a furious rhythm as they pushed their burden left and right. Traffic was light, and the few pedestrians out and about were bent into their umbrellas, using them like battering rams against the driving rain.

"It's an omen," grumbled Gino, hunkered down in the passenger seat and straining to see the road ahead.

"It's rain," said Francesca. "Just rain. There's nothing ominous about it. It's supposed to be raining in San Francisco. It happens. Not often this time of year, but it happens, and I repeat, it's not ominous."

"Ominous," chimed in Carla, wedged into the back seat with Morrie. "That's one of them words I need to add to my lingo. Ominous. Ommmminus. It's got a high class sound, don't it? I'm gonna start a list." She rummaged through her pocketbook until she located a small notepad and a pen. She looked up. "How do you spell it?"

"T-r-o-u-b-l-e," said Gino.

Carla sighed and put the notebook and pen back in her bag. "Maybe this ain't such a good time for improving myself."

Morrie pressed his fingers on the newly programmed universal remote, safely out of the elements in a zipped plastic sandwich bag that rested on his knees. "Let's go over the plan one more time, just to be sure we're all on the same page. We can't afford to make any mistakes." "Good idea," Gino said. "All right. My cell is fully charged and set on vibrate. When it goes off, it means the alarm has been jammed and I'm safe to enter the house."

"If, and I stress *if,* the cell vibrates again, that means somebody is coming back to the house and I've turned off the remote," Morrie said. "That means the alarm is back on and functioning. You need to either get out, or if you can't, get down and get still someplace safe."

"That's the part I'm not liking too much," Gino said. "What if I can't get out? If I get caught in the house, it's all over."

"You have to think positively," Francesca said. "A positive attitude will produce positive results. We've gone over this and thought about every eventuality. We're prepared for anything and everything." She took her right hand off the steering wheel and patted Gino's knee. "Have faith."

"And," Morrie said, "when your cell vibrates again, that means somebody has entered the house and deactivated the alarm. You'll have enough time, hopefully, to find a way out of the house before you're seen. The library window is still your best means of ingress and egress if you're on the ground floor. You're hidden from the street by the shrubbery and far enough from the front door to give you some breathing room. Upstairs, it depends where you are. Find a room with a window big enough to get out. You've got the rope ladder. Hang it from the sill and bail."

"Suppose the cell doesn't vibrate that third time," Gino said. "What then?"

Morrie frowned. "Good point. Let me think about that." He looked out the rain-

streaked side windows and rubbed his lower lip with his thumb. "Okay. If that person coming up the walk doesn't enter the house, I'll call your cell, hang up, and call again. That'll be the signal that the alarm wasn't activated and you can go on with the search. The first vibrate means go, the second means no go. If your cell vibrates, stops, and then starts again, that's a go." Gino ticked off all the starts and stops on his fingers and finally threw up his hands. "Whatever. It will work. It's got to. Everybody's got their assignments. Francesca stays with the Bug, ready for the getaway. Morrie's on the remote, and Carla's on standby as lookout." Gino inhaled and let his breath out in small measured puffs. What could go wrong? The VW splashed through the streets, its headlights punching out circles in the darkness and its tires sending out streams of water that mounted the curb and broke over onto the sidewalk, miniature waves crashing on a rocky shore.

****

"This is du juvo all over again," Carla said.

"What?" Gino was adjusting his gloves.

"Du juvo. You know. When you do something but you know you've done it before."

"That's déjà vu. Jesus, Carla."

"Whatever."

She was looking out the car window, checking the street for pedestrians and traffic. "Here he comes again going the other way." She pointed at an elderly man walking a miniature Schnauzer. The dog was as bundled up as the old man with a scarf and a raincoat and even a cap with a rain visor.

"That don't look right. If I was a dog I'd be embarrassed," Carla said. "You better wait until he's gone, Gino. Old folks sometimes got good memories." The old man and his dog moved on down the sidewalk, oblivious to everything around them, intent on getting home and dry and warm.

And indeed it was like *déjà vu* all over again, Gino thought now, crouching under the library window. He was sheltered from most of the rain but still getting damp, waiting for Michael and Bianca to finish whatever had brought them into the room. Repairs hadn't been made on the jimmied window yet, and it was stuck open a couple of inches. Snatches of conversation or, more accurately, argument drifted out through the open window from the library. Gino inched up until he could see into the room. Michael was pacing while Bianca was seated in the same chair she'd occupied the night they stole the painting.

"We're pushing our luck, Bianca." Michael paused in front of her chair. "Nobody's luck holds out forever. We've got a good haul, and it's time to get out while we still can. I'm done. The cops aren't stupid. Did you see the way that Inspector was sizing us up? I tell you, she's on to us. And Sal isn't going to be in any position to help out. You been reading the news? He's a liability. I don't care if he is family. I do care if the cops can tie him to us. Whatever he's done to assist in our little venture isn't worth it anymore. It's time to cut our losses before this all goes bad. And I've got to get my car out of here soon before the cops come snooping around again and find something."

Bianca crossed her legs and smoothed her skirt over her knees. "The police don't know anything. Nobody knows anything, Michael, and you're done when I say you're done. Or have you forgotten the details of this arrangement?"

"I haven't forgotten anything. But I know when a good thing runs its course." "So do I, but we're in no danger. Just do what you're told and everything will work out fine. There are five more paintings to take, and we're not quitting until we're done."

"I don't like it, Bianca. I've got a bad feeling. And, again, what about the car? I've got to get it repaired. I can't drive it. I can't take it to a body shop. They keep records. What am I going to do? I can't leave it in the garage. What the hell am I going to do with it?"

"That's your problem, Michael. I don't have anything to do with your stupidity." She stood. "You're sure no one saw you?"

"Just that bag woman, but she was so wasted she can't identify me or the car. No worries there."

"Incompetence."

Michael raised his hand in a fist and shook it in her face. "I wasn't incompetent when I offed that bitch that was screwing your husband. I don't remember any complaints then. You were all sweetness and light and said that was the last thing I'd need to do to get on the gravy train."

Bianca pushed his hand away. "That was then. This is now. Besides, accidents happen all the time on the ski slopes."

"That accident was more carefully arranged than your so-called marriage and you know it. You ordered it, and I delivered. I kept my end of the deal.

But traffic accidents happen and that's what this was. I didn't set out to kill anybody."

"The results are the same, aren't they? You think you're making some sort of moral distinction? You killed them both. She's dead, and the man you hit with your car is dead." She waved her hand dismissively. "But the dead don't talk. You've got nothing to worry about."

"I'm telling you, Bianca. I'm finished."

"The subject is closed. You're finished when I say you are, Michael," she said, getting up from her chair and striding to the door of the library where she stopped and turned to face her nephew. "And right now, I say you're coming with me to opening night for the Picasso exhibit. Get dressed. I don't want to have to wait for you. And Michael, lay off the booze. This event is important for us. I don't want a scene. If Fabriani's group gets the keys we need, it means at least two more DeMontanas will be off the market before the month is out. I want everyone's memory of us to be as cultured patrons of the arts. That means you will stay sober." She took a cigarette from the pack on the table by the door and lit up as she left the room.

He cursed her but followed along behind. Gino gulped and slid down the outside wall until his rear end connected with the cold, wet ground. Who the hell were these people? Michael had confessed to the hit and run and to another murder as well. His grandfather's scrapbook with the image of the woman on the ski slopes in Grenoble flashed before him. Donna something or other. Bianca had had Michael kill her. "What the hell have I gotten into?" he asked himself. Theft was one thing. He hadn't bargained on murder. His cell vibrated and he retrieved it from his pants pocket.

"They're at the front door. He's arming the alarm now with his cell. Stand by," Morrie said. "All right. They're in the car. I'm going to jam the signal. Good luck. Disconnecting."

Gino took a deep breath, put on his latex gloves, and forced the window open enough to allow him entry. Once inside, he switched on his flashlight and froze, waiting, but no alarm sounded. So far, so good. Piece of cake. He worried too much. He walked through the library, into the hall, and up the stairs to Bianca's bedroom suite. The door was open.

You could tell a lot about a woman from her bedroom, Gino thought, surveying Bianca's suite. The room had all the warmth of a magazine layout or a display room at a furniture dealership. Heavy draperies in a geometric gold brocade hung stiffly at the window. Gold pillows in assorted sizes nearly obscured the gold duvet that covered the bed. His feet sank into the plush carpet, again gold. A portrait of Bianca above the bed presided over the room with Bianca displaying a regal gaze. Mirrors were everywhere, on the walls, on the dresser, on the vanity. He looked up at the ceiling half expecting to see one there as well, but there was nothing except a crystal chandelier, its diamond pendants suspended on gold stands. And there was the pet they'd been looking for. On the vanity, a goldfish swam around and around inside a fish bowl going nowhere but crazy inside its glass prison.

Where was the diary? Bianca hadn't been upstairs more than a couple of minutes the night of the open house, so the diary was most likely not locked away in a wall safe or hidden behind some secret partition that took time to open. He was looking for a drawer or a shelf. Maybe a box or a cupboard. There was a writing desk, a dresser, a vanity, and a nightstand—all with drawers. There was a closet with a shelf, and there was a small bookcase—actually just two shelves beneath the window seat. He flexed his fingers and cracked his knuckles. All he needed was time. The glimpse he'd gotten when Bianca had carried it from the room told him the diary was small and black. It could fit almost anywhere. He felt himself starting to perspire and his stomach muscles were tightening. Time to get moving.

He started with the vanity to the left of the door. The vanity was a dark wood with a gold-flecked marble top. A gold-backed hand mirror and hairbrush were laid diagonally across the marble parallel to each other with a cluster of perfume atomizers to the left and a small gilt-edged jewelry box to the right. The center drawer was crammed with creams and lotions. The side drawers were stuffed with lingerie. The nightstand held a small clock positioned so its time display was visible from the bed. Gino glanced at the time. He'd been in the room three minutes.

The writing desk held a quill pen and ink set, a gold desk lamp with a pull chain, and a small blotter with burgundy leather corners. The drawers were full of tabloid magazines. Bianca was neat on the surface, but the real story was here, in the jumbled contents of the dresser and the desk drawers. She was all about show. Basically, she was a slob.

The bookshelves were crammed with hardcover editions of current best sellers aligned along the front edge of the shelf, except the first one on the left which jutted out half an inch or so, as if someone had taken it out and replaced it quickly. He removed the volume, but the space behind it was empty. He ran his hand along the space behind the rest of the books on the shelf, checking to see if maybe she'd stuffed it there. Nothing. He replaced the book. Where else could she have put the diary?

The drawers of the writing desk, vanity, and nightstand all proved equally fruitless. Fruitless, except for the .38 special in the top nightstand drawer. He lifted the duvet and looked under the bed. Not even a dust bunny. The maid did good work.

And then the phone in his pocket vibrated. The alarm was back on, and he froze in place. Somebody must be coming up the walk. It was too soon. Nobody was supposed to be back for at least a couple of hours. Beads of perspiration broke out on his forehead and he resisted the impulse to wipe them away. Seconds passed like hours. His words came back to haunt him. *Piece of cake.* It wasn't good to tempt fate. He ought to run like hell. Drop the rope ladder out the bathroom window and get out. But he didn't. He couldn't. He stayed put, frozen in place, and waited. These people had killed somebody. Two somebodies, actually. That didn't bode well for his future if they found him in the house. A minute or so later, the phone vibrated again. Perfect. Just terrific. Somebody was now in the house and the alarm system had been turned off. Nowhere to run now. Still, the diary had to be in here some place. Some place easy to get to. Gino's eyes traveled around the room and locked on the door to the bathroom. An exit—he could get out the bathroom window. He moved cautiously through the door.

More gold. So much gold it just looked cheap. The same gold-veined marble from the vanity repeated itself on the countertops and the floor. Gold fixtures, gold throw rugs, and a gold filigree frame around the mirror above the sink. A white wicker stand held gold bath towels rolled and stacked in the space beneath the recessed top shelf, where a hammered tin box with ornate cutouts was filled with decorative soaps. A gold pillar candle sat on a tall, rectangular stand decorated with inlaid mosaic, a crystal vase of tapers next to it. The candle wasn't centered and looked about ready to topple off the stand. He wondered. The stand was probably twelve by sixteen inches. That would be about right. Just a hunch, but it was all he had.

In the silence, the sound of the bedroom door closing was magnified until it sounded to Gino like the gates of hell snapping shut behind him. Bianca was in the bedroom. No time now. There was no time to get out the window. He could hide in the Jacuzzi and hope she wouldn't see him, an idea he dismissed as soon as it popped into his head. There was no shower curtain, and she'd have to be blind not to see him hiding in plain sight. He could bolt through the door and maybe get away, but the diary would be lost forever. And she'd see him. She'd find out who he was and the Mob would track him down. He knew that for a fact. It was all over. But it was all he had and just as he'd made up his mind to make a run for it, the doorbell rang downstairs. It didn't just ring once. It rang and stopped and then rang again and again. Bianca swore and he heard the bedroom door slam.

Gino moved fast. He set the candle aside and searched the stand until his fingers found a small depression on the back. He pushed down and the side fell away, clattering on the marble floor. He reached inside and there it was, no bigger than one of those address books you buy at the drugstore. The soft black leather cover was faded to brown in a few places and the edges were worn as if the book had been carried in a pants pocket for a number of years. That's exactly where he put the diary now.

He surveyed his prison. The bathroom window was way too small. He'd never get through it. The only way out was through the tall bedroom windows that opened onto a small balcony framed in some flimsy decorative wrought iron. What's the worst that could happen, he asked himself. He could fall. It was only the second floor. Second story man. That was him. Maybe he'd land okay. Maybe he'd break his legs and die of gangrene. He shot one more glance at the door and went for the window. There was no place to hook the ladder over the sill. The damn wrought iron dipped and flipped and didn't leave a level four inches let alone the dozen he needed to set the ladder in place.

"Don't look down!" Carla's voice came up in a stage whisper.

"How the hell am I supposed to get down if I don't look down?" he said. "Good point." She paused. "Don't look down too much. And don't fall on your head or anything important."

"How'd you know I'd be here?" he asked.

"We've been watching the flashlight move around the room. Then it went out. So you had to be here. You really need to work on your burgling skills. They stink," she said.

"Climb over the rail and dangle. I'll get your feet." Morrie's voice was a welcome intrusion into Carla's babbling.

"Hurry up, Gino, she'll be back any minute," Carla said. "Pretty clever, huh? We couldn't leave you trapped in there, so I thought if I leaned on the doorbell she'd have to go see what was going on. It worked, but you'd better get your ass off that balcony pronto."

Gino tossed the rope ladder over the balcony, and it collapsed into a tangled mess on the ground. "It doesn't look all that strong," Gino said, giving the railing a push with his hand and being rewarded with a noticeable wobble, but Morrie reached up and guided him down, taking the brunt of Gino's weight as he let go of the railing. They ended up in the sodden dirt that cushioned their impact.

"Did you get it? Did you get it?" Francesca had joined the group.

"I got it and a whole lot more I hadn't bargained for," Gino said. "I wish I could see Bianca's face when she finds out the diary's gone and she realizes it's the beginning of the end. So far, so good. Let's get out of here."

CHAPTER TWENTY-SIX

San Francisco

The orange Bug sped away from the DeMontana mansion with Francesca at the wheel, intent on avoiding the larger puddles and checking the rear view mirror at frequent intervals for signs of pursuit. The storm was nearly over. It was just drizzling now, and the tires threw out a trail of mist as most of the water had drained from the streets and now rushed down the gutters and through the grated entrances to the storm sewers.

"It's murder," Gino said, through chattering teeth. His clothes were damp and the adrenaline rush had passed, leaving him chilled and shaking. His hands trembled as he clutched the diary. "They've gotten away with murder. Both of them. A stolen diary is one thing, stolen art is something else, but murder is not where I want to go." He looked at the diary. "I don't care what this book tells us. It's not worth it."

"Murder makes it worth it," Francesca said. "You mean the hit and run. Are you sure?"

"Oh yeah. Make that two murders. I was butt up against the window, and Bianca and her nephew were having a real row. She's got a voice like a rusty saw when she's mad and she was way past mad. She was giving him the riot act, and he wasn't having any luck getting her to back down.

"Bianca had Michael kill DeMontana's mistress—you know, the one in the newspaper clippings that died in that accident on the ski slope in Grenoble. It was no accident. And now Michael wants out of the whole scene, but Bianca's holding that murder over his head. She wants to keep boosting *papa's* works, and she's using him for that too. And yes," he added, "Michael did the hit and run. He admitted it to Bianca. She ran him over the coals for that one. They're a real pair of sweethearts and I, for one, don't relish being next on their victim list."

"We knew they weren't model citizens, Gino," Francesca said. "They, or rather, Bianca, is dangerous because she's the brains of the operation. And she's got the Mob to back her up. That makes her doubly dangerous. And Michael is dangerous because he's weak. But his biggest danger is to her and she knows it. That rant you're talking about sounds like she's getting scared. Frightened people screw up. The diary is worth all of it, Gino. It's the first step in restoring your grandfather's legacy."

"Frightened people don't think straight. That could mean she'll do anything. Even come looking for us if she can. And may I remind you that my grandfather's legacy is that of the world's most successful art forger? He's not what you'd call a model citizen either," Gino said.

"Yeah, but he's family," Carla said. "That means something. You can't quit now, Gino. You owe him."

"You need a hot shower and a change of clothes. Maybe a stiff drink," Francesca said. "We'll go back to my place. You'll feel better once you've warmed up."

"I don't think I'm going to warm up to murder," Gino said.

"Don't think about what they did. Think about what you're going to do," Morrie said, adding his voice to the conversation. "You can warm up to justice. If they've gotten away with murder, we can make sure they don't continue that way. And if we happen to break a few laws along the way, it's all for a good cause. We just need to think this thing out. There's always a way."

"And don't forget Mary," Carla said. "It don't seem fair. She was a nice old lady, and she didn't deserve to lose her Bobby like that. Now she don't got anybody." Carla's face fell. "Being all alone has got to hurt. I wish we could do something about it."

"Maybe we can," Francesca said, careening around a corner and sending all of them shifting to the left. "After all, look what we've done so far! We've got the diary!"

An hour and a half later Gino felt human again. He'd stood in the shower until he'd drained the hot water tank and was now wrapped in a terrycloth robe. Granted the robe was a rosy shade of pink with red sateen hearts sewn onto the pockets, but he was willing to overlook the fashion statement in exchange for warmth.

"You look adorable," Francesca said. "I might have some bunny slippers in the closet, if your feet are cold."

"Don't," Gino said. "Just don't." He glared at Carla and Morrie. "Not one word from either of you."

Carla sniggered and Morrie covered his mouth with a large hand.

"You're taking this like a trooper," Francesca said, "and it won't be long now. The washer's done and your clothes are in the dryer. You'll be back to normal in no time."

"I don't think I'm ever going to be normal again," Gino said, "if this is any indication of the way my life is headed."

"Normal is highly overrated," Francesca said. "It's also extremely boring. Anybody ready for something bracing and restorative?"

"I'll be bartender," Morrie said, after Francesca showed him the liquor cupboard. "I'm taking orders." He took the bottle out of the cupboard and set it on the counter with a flourish. "You can have anything you want as long as it's Scotch. Scotch rocks. Scotch with a splash. Scotch neat. Just name your poison."

Gino groaned. "Yet another way to die."

****

"Oh, no," Gino said. "No. No. NO. So far, I've broken into a house, stolen a book, interrupted an entire neighborhood's communication signals, which is probably a felony to add to the other felonies. I'm not doing anything else. No." Dressed once again in his own clothes, he was feeling more in control and less like a leftover from a Valentine's Day party.

Francesca and Carla exchanged looks. Morrie waited. He was stretched out on the recliner, fully extended, relishing the comfortable room after being confined in the VW.

"Two wrongs don't make a right," Gino said, horizontal on the sofa, his Scotch with a splash resting on his stomach.

"Yeah," Carla said, "Sometimes it takes three or four. You know, it wouldn't be hard. All we gotta do is frame them for something bad. Something that'll make the cops take a real close look at them and what they've been doing. Then we step back and let nature take its course, so to speak. Settin' up a frame is easy. They do it all the time on television."

"Are you even listening to me?" Gino asked.

"No," Carla and Francesca spoke at once. Morrie grinned and took a healthy swallow of Scotch.

"Goals and Objectives," Francesca said. "That's what we need to establish first. What's our goal? That's easy," she said, answering her own question. "We actually have two, and they're not mutually exclusive. We want to retrieve the stolen art, and we want to bring the thieves and murderers to justice."

"Don't you like the way she talks?" Carla said, from her seat next to Francesca at the kitchen table. "That's how I'm gonna talk when I get to be high class. I'm already not using bad language. I think I'm almost ready for the next part."

Gino looked at her as if she had more than the usual number of screws loose.

Francesca was too absorbed in creating her lists to notice.

"As I said, objectives," Francesca said. "What do we need?" She steepled her hands on the notepad. "We need the police to find the car. That's easy. We do an anonymous tip. But it's got to be a credible tip, one that will get them a warrant. Then, how about if when they find it, they find a little something extra as well? It wouldn't be hard to plant something small that will nudge their investigation to the next level. Gino's already got experience with B&E. He could get into the garage easily."

"Getting out is what concerns me," Gino said, getting up off the sofa and joining the women at the table. "And what exactly are you thinking of planting in the car? Another body? You want me to kill somebody? No problem." He closed his eyes. "I've got two suggestions and I'm sitting next to one of them."

Francesca swatted him and Carla sniffed.

"Seems like the perfect plan to me," Morrie said. "There's no statute of limitations on murder, after all. We nail them for Bobby's hit and run and get the police to reopen the investigation into the murder on the ski slopes. Sounds like a great idea. From what you said, it won't take much for DeMontana to start singing if he thinks it'll save him some hard time."

Gino opened one eye and used it on Morrie. "Fine. Whatever. Just you all come see me in the Big House on visiting day. I should be there for about a hundred years. If I don't get killed first."

"Something small, hmmm?" Francesca was leafing through the newspaper. "You know, sometimes fate works on your side. Okay. This is small," she said, showing Gino a photo spread about an exhibit opening at the Yerba Buena Art Gallery.

"What's small?"

"This Rembrandt. It's one of his early sketches. Worth a fortune, I should imagine. But it's small." She set the paper down and beamed at Gino. "It's perfect." "It's insane," Gino said.

"Just listen," Francesca said. "It won't be difficult. It just takes planning. Look what we've already accomplished." She sat back, hands folded in her lap, looking composed and in control. "Just a couple of days ago, you thought the diary was impossible to get. And now we have it. Of course, we don't have a whole lot of time to plan for the next part. Like we've got tonight. We should do a walk through tomorrow, just to make sure we've got the bugs worked out."

"Bugs? We don't know shit from bugs. What are you talking about?" Gino said.

"That sounds good," Carla said. "I enjoy culture. I'll do the walk through. And Gino, please clean up your language."

"We are not doing any walk through, and we aren't stealing a Rembrandt. Period. End of discussion. What did you say, Carla?"

"Please clean up your language. What could it hurt just to case the joint? I mean, do a walk through? I like that. Sounds high class," she said.

"Most art galleries can't afford high-tech security," Francesca said. "That's why you see all those people in white shirts and dark pants or skirts standing around the various rooms. They watch who goes in and comes out. They're more of a visual deterrent than anything else. Even the cameras usually only spot the traffic areas. That means we'll need a distraction. A diversion." Francesca was back making notes as she spoke. "We'll also need a nondescript car with bogus plates."

"No problem on that last part," Morrie said. "I can get one from the property room."

Gino blanched. "Who are you?"

Morrie winked at Carla. "My brother's got a friend who's a collector. He's local. Well, Campbell. That's close enough to qualify as local. He's got a buddy who has a connection. I can have him get me a back plate. Need anything else in that department?"

"The nondescript car," Francesca said.

"On it," Morrie said and got up from his chair and made a call. "Done," he said, resuming his seat. "I've always enjoyed procurement. Smooth as silk, so far."

Francesca checked off two more items on the list and then set down her pen. "Yes, it all revolves around planning. Careful, methodical planning. All right. The distraction. It can't be too big or too small. Sort of like Goldilocks. It needs to be just right. Believable is the main thing." She brightened. "Yvonne!" she squeaked.

"Who's Yvonne? Carla asked, beating Gino to the question.

"My grandmother," Francesca said. "She'll be perfect."

"Is there anybody in the state of California who won't be in on this?" Gino asked. "And what about your grandmother?"

"To answer the first question, don't be silly. We need a team if we're going to do this right. We've got a team now," Francesca said but then frowned. "We need someone to drive the getaway car."

"That'll be Jeffrey," Morrie said, looking at Gino. "My brother."

"Of course," Gino said.

"Great!" Francesca said. "We've got Gino and Carla, Morrie, me, Yvonne, and Jeffrey. Six is a good number."

"Six comes between *shit* and *sorry* in the dictionary," Gino mumbled.

"Language, Gino," Carla repeated.

"Actually, if you count everyone in the Yerba Buena Women's Club, the number is closer to twenty-six, but of course they won't all be in on the heist."

Gino's expression had gone way beyond pained to something approaching sheer terror.

"Yvonne and one or two of her friends—maybe Frances and Nellie—but that's it. The rest of them will be there for volume—to fill up the room so that other visitors bypass it until the Club has moved on to the next stop on the program. Believe me, with all their accessories, they can create quite a logistics problem for anyone trying to get in their way or hurry them up." Francesca smiled encouragement at Gino. "Yvonne will organize their appearance. She's very good at delegating and putting events together. I think my talents come from her. Anyway," she continued, "all the ladies are elderly. I think Frances is the youngest, and she's seventy-eight. Some of them use canes and a few use walkers. I don't remember if anyone uses a wheelchair, but Josephine might after having broken her hip. They're a delightful group of women, Gino. You'll love them."

"Of course," Gino said. "Naturally. Sure."

"Relax, Gino," Carla said. "Nothing's gonna go wrong. We got an event planner."

Francesca straightened and patted herself on the shoulder. "First things first. I'll explain the diversion factor after we've committed the layout of the art museum to memory."

While Carla cleared off the table, Francesca disappeared into her office bedroom, returning with a roll of butcher paper, a yardstick, some colored markers, photographs, and a brochure for the museum. She covered the table with the paper, taping down the edges and corners. "There's software that will do this but I don't have it, and we don't have time to get it. This will have to do. Before there was high-tech, there was low-tech. We're going low."

She took the yardstick and drew a vertical line, dividing the paper into two work areas. She lined out Van Ness and the cross streets for several blocks above and below the art museum in one section, drawing arrows to indicate one way streets. "There's the template," she said. "Now we add stop lights, stop signs, through alleys, and anything else that may become useful during the getaway." She glanced at Gino. "I mean the return trip." She pointed to the markers. "Gino, you and Morrie can work on that."

Carla was peering over Francesca's shoulder. "What do we do?" she asked. "You and I are going to dissect the museum." Francesca took the brochure and opened it to the diagram of the interior, pressing the pages down so they lay flat. "I picked one up last time I was in there. Didn't think I'd have use for it again." She smiled. "Guess I was wrong."

"It's just a big box," Carla said, "kind of like a present all wrapped up just for us."

"I know what you mean," Francesca said. "Okay. Here's the layout to copy onto the bigger paper. I'll draw in rooms, doors, and hallways. Here are the photos of the artwork in the room we'll be targeting. Some of the photos in the brochure include people visiting the gallery. Just cut them out," she said, handing Carla scissors. "Make the pictures as small as you can. Then tape them to the walls, positioning them according to the lead photo in the newspaper. The Rembrandt is on the north wall just to the left of where the guard will be standing. He could touch it, he's that close. You sketch in the front entrance doors and the route to the target room. Let's put in the bathrooms too. You never know if they'll be necessary."

Carla nodded, selecting a marker. "Damn straight." She flinched. "I mean, that's right." She reached for the scissors and cut away a group of society types gathered in front of a painting. She was clipping along the edge when she caught her breath and dropped the scissors on the table.

"S'matter?" Francesca said, holding a marker between her teeth as she reached for the tape to mend a tear in the paper.

Carla had picked up the picture and was staring at the caption. The Yerba Buena ladies weren't the only ones sporting canes. The fine print read "Bianca DeMontana accepts donation to the Arts Guild from Connecticut businessman Salvatore Puglisi." Sal had his arm around her waist and was planting a kiss on her cheek. She had her arm around his back and looked like she was reeling him in. It didn't take a genius to realize they were more than fellow patrons of the arts. Carla whistled. "Damn. Damn. Damn. I knew it. It was him. I knew it. I didn't want to believe it. But shit. Small world," she muttered, cutting Sal away from the art and crumpling him between her hands. She tossed him into the wastebasket.

Two hours later they had a fair approximation of the museum on the paper. "Time for food," Francesca said. "Working dinner tonight."

"Maybe pizza wasn't the best choice," Francesca said an hour later, surveying the grease spots that obliterated some essential marks on the butcher paper.

"Good though," Morrie said, reaching for his fourth piece.

"I can rework those lines with the black marker. They'll just look funky. After tonight we won't need them anymore anyhow. We'll have to burn this paper," Francesca said, looking about the room as if a fireplace would materialize if she concentrated.

"The sink," Carla said. "I burn a lot of stuff in the sink."

"Yeah?" Gino asked. "What kind of stuff?"

"You know. Stuff." She poured some wine. "Sometimes you don't want people going through your trash. They do that with famous people you know. Make a whole lot of money off their garbage."

Gino shook his head. "They make paper shredders," he said. "You might think about one of those instead of setting your kitchen on fire."

Carla looked at Gino as if he'd lost his senses. "Somebody who really wanted to could put those pieces of paper back together again. I seen it on television."

Morrie nodded. "They can do some amazing stuff with paper," he said.

Gino put his hands up to his throbbing temples. "Speaking of paper, we've got everything laid out on the butcher paper. Now what do we do? How do we work it?"

Francesca smiled. "With these," she said, holding up a bag filled with toy cars and miniature people to fit into them. "Toys of the trade. Choose yourself first, and then we'll fill in the crowds, people on the sidewalks, crossing streets, driving— everything. This isn't going to happen in a vacuum."

"What about cameras at street corners?" Morrie asked. "You know the ones designed to catch red light runners or idiots blocking the box?"

"That's where the bogus plates come in and the nondescript car. You'll all be wearing hats and dark glasses. That brings up another point. We're going to hit the gallery in the late afternoon. It closes at four-thirty, so the ladies will make their entrance about four. I'll be with my grandmother. By four-twenty-five, women will be scattered around the room with the Rembrandt, and everyone on staff will be wanting to hurry them along. Guards will be tired. At four-twenty-seven, Yvonne will begin an argument with Mildred and threaten her with her cane. Nellie will join them. That will bring the guard over to intervene. I'll lift the painting, and we'll all exit the building at precisely four-thirty. Oh, that reminds me." She scribbled on the note pad. "I'll sew a pocket into my big, boxy jacket today. It'll be big enough to contain the Rembrandt, and I'll line it so the painting won't move about and get bent or creased.

"Outside, traffic will be picking up—that could be good or bad for us— and more people will be on the streets—also either good or bad. At the end of the work day people are tired and thinking mostly about getting home. They can't always rely on their memories, if they're asked to recall a certain event. Even if they see something, they may not remember it or may not think it's important. Anyhow, I'll walk out the main entrance, and then leave Yvonne and the other women and get into the waiting car. We'll drive back to Gino's vineyard." She paused for breath. "After that, well, I haven't gotten that far yet." She looked around the room at her co-conspirators.

Morrie was at the living room window, watching the cars go by, his hands clasped behind his back. He turned to Francesca. "The inside part sounds good, but the outside part—the getaway—I'm not sure about. Timing is as important outside as it is in." He walked over to the table and moved one of the toy cars out of position so that it was double-parked. Then he moved the rest of the vehicles until he had a double row that spanned the entire block. "That's it," he said. "Not one getaway car, but about a dozen, all lined up and ready to move at the signal."

Francesca's brow furrowed and she tilted her head, studying the new arrangement on the traffic grid. "I give," she said. "Wait! I know what that is. Morrie, you're a genius." She clapped him on the back. "It's brilliant!"

"Yep. Car show on the road," Morrie said. "Gino said you would be organizing a car show, and that got me thinking. There's nothing a classic car enthusiast loves more than taking the car on a drive, and there's a whole group of Roadmaster fanatics in Santa Clara County.

"We'll use my buddy's '54 Roadmaster for the job. He'll schedule an impromptu drive to the city, calling in as many cars as he can. We'll have them assemble along the block in front of the art gallery and drive from there to Golden Gate Park." He chuckled.

"Jeffrey can take care of arrivals and departures. Nobody's going to be watching you, Francesca. No offense, but these cars will have everybody strolling by for a look. We'll drive away as soon as you're in the '54. I'll be at the wheel with Carla as shotgun. When we get to Golden Gate Park, Francesca gets out of the Buick and into Gino's car, and they drive back to the vineyard. Even if the police stop by, there's absolutely nothing to link us with the Rembrandt."

Gino shook his head. "You know what bothers me the most about all of this?" He didn't wait for an answer and fixed each one of them with an accusing stare. "That you all are having no trouble whatsoever becoming criminals. This can't be a good thing."

Carla smiled, Francesca hummed, and Morrie cleared his throat. You couldn't argue with that kind of logic.

CHAPTER TWENTY-SEVEN

San Francisco, earlier that night

Michael and Bianca's earlier argument made for a silent drive to the art museum, and they parted company as soon as they surrendered the car to the waiting valet. Michael, blatantly ignoring Bianca's directive not to drink, vacated the driver seat and drew a bead on the no-host bar to chat up the local talent. Bianca made her way to a small group of patrons assembled by the hors d'oeuvres buffet, grazing among the offerings.

The gnawing ache behind her right eye that had troubled her most of the afternoon was now impossible to ignore, and even the recessed lighting in the gallery was painful. She considered a small plate of crudités, but her stomach felt uncertain, and she was forced to accept that a full-blown migraine would hit her before the evening was over. She made a few polite comments and plastered an interested smile on her face, but engaging in small talk sapped the rest of her energy. Within the hour, she excused herself and made her way back through the crowd to the front of the gallery. She debated calling for a cab but decided by the time it arrived she could already be home. Instead, she summoned the hatcheck girl and requested the keys from Michael's coat. The girl obliged without any questions. Once outside, Bianca signaled for the valet and left Michael to fend for himself. Undoubtedly, he was already involved with a female and his plans didn't include returning to Pacific Heights that night anyway. If he did, he could get a cab or walk. She didn't care.

Once in the car, a glance in the rear view mirror reflected a face pale as death and she felt worse than she looked. She grimaced and concentrated on the road ahead. Arriving at home, she pulled into the garage and pressed the code to open the door from the garage into the house. She deactivated the alarm at the front door and kicked off her heels. They scudded up against the door of the hall closet. Stepping around them, she paused at the foot of the stairs, her hand on the newel post, steadying herself before the climb to the second floor. In her bedroom, she bypassed the light switch and made her way in the dimness to the windows, reaching for the cord to pull the draperies closed to block the glare from the streetlight on the corner.

She tossed the extra bed pillows onto the floor and was pulling at the duvet when the doorbell sent a stab of pain through her head. She pressed her hand against her forehead and cursed. Damn Michael. The one night he'd decide to come back to the house instead of bedding down elsewhere. She thought about leaving him standing on the doorstep, but the bell rang again and continued without stopping. She cursed again. If she didn't feel so shitty, she'd rake him up one side and down the next, but she'd already done that once tonight with no apparent effect. She left the bedroom and went back down the stairs to let him in.

Jerking the door open, she prepared to let him have a piece of her mind before she went back to bed, but he wasn't there. No one was there. She frowned and called his name. No response. She looked about her and down the walk. A chill swept over her, and she retreated into the house, set the lock, and waited. A moment later the doorbell rang again. This time she didn't answer, but instead pulled the venetian blind aside and peered out into the darkness. There was nobody on the front step. Perhaps the doorbell had an electrical problem. A short or something. Her thoughts were muddy and she stood, wondering what to do. She waited a full five minutes, but the bell didn't ring again. Finally, she climbed the stairs back to her room. If it rang again, she'd call the police. For now, all she wanted was some heavy drugs from the medicine chest in her bathroom and then to fall into bed and sleep. There was no way around it. To find the sedatives she needed, she'd have to turn on the bathroom light. She closed her eyes and flipped on the switch. Even behind her eyelids, the glare hurt, and she was determined not to open them until she was standing in front of the medicine chest with the cabinet door open. Her plan failed when she stubbed her toe on something hard. Her eyes flew open and the pain seared. She'd stumbled into the glass vase that held the tapers for the pillar candle. Puzzled, she turned to see the candle on the floor and the stand on its side, its secret compartment open and empty. The migraine retreated to some distant place beyond sense and feeling, replaced by something that felt like a sucker punch.

Bianca stood helpless, absorbing the magnitude of what had happened. She wanted to scream, and it took all her will power to stay calm. Back and forth her thoughts played havoc with her. There was nothing to be done. The diary was gone. She'd been a fool. No. She hadn't been a fool. Nobody knew she'd hidden it in the pillar stand. But obviously somebody had. Who could have known the diary was here? She should have taken better precautions. But nobody could have seen her hide the diary. Nobody had access to her boudoir. The maid? No. She'd not been in the house since yesterday. And she would have left the room just as she'd found it. She'd never leave the vase or the candle on the floor. The woman bordered on compulsive. She couldn't have done it. But someone had. How did they know? She'd been watched. When? Who'd been watching her? She'd been careful. It wasn't her fault. It was her fault. Two sides of the argument struggled against each other in her mind, but regardless, it was all irrelevant now. What to do next was the main concern. She picked up a towel that had fallen from the rack and refolded it, all the while her thoughts racing. She closed the compartment of the pillar stand, replaced it on the table, and repositioned the candle.

Everything was back in place. Everything was as it should be, except for the diary. The diary. Where was the diary? Another cold chill swept over her. The doorbell. That was the distraction. She'd been played. Stupid. If not for the damn headache, she'd have known what was happening. She wasn't supposed to be home. Who knew she'd be gone? Who knew she'd returned and needed to get her out of the way? Bianca grabbed her robe hanging on the hook on the back of the bathroom door and tied the sash around her waist, giving the knot a tug, just as the doorbell rang again. She strode to her nightstand, retrieved the .38 special from the top drawer and proceeded downstairs for the second time that night.

Her dressing gown trailing along the risers and the .38 in her left hand, she paused at the landing to assure herself no one had entered the house. The doorbell continued to chime, and she moved forward, approaching the door from the side. Peering through the leaded glass, she discovered the source of the noise. Michael was on the front step, leaning against the doorframe, his thumb firmly holding down the button on the doorbell. Bianca relaxed her grip on the revolver and unlocked the door.

"It's about time you decided to let me in. I've been standing out here for half an hour," he said. "What the hell were you thinking? You might at least have told me you were taking the car. I had a hellofa time getting anything coherent out of the valet. They acted like I was trying to steal the car. Which wasn't there, I might add." His eyes were bloodshot and his words slurred.

Bianca studied his face. Michael was definitely drunk but his anger was genuine. He wouldn't be coming back to the house if he'd taken the diary. It took time to get this shit-faced. So if not Michael, who? She stifled the sudden urge to unburden herself and tell him what had happened. No. Better for her if he didn't know. It might be all he needed to bail on her. She frowned, stepped away from the door, and allowed him in, watching as he wove an uncertain path up the stairs and down the hall to his room. She locked the front door and returned to her room, replacing the .38 in the drawer before she picked up the phone and placed a call. Up until now, she'd done it all on her own. Except, of course, for Michael, but he did what he was told and didn't contribute in any meaningful way to the planning of the operation. She had to get the diary back, and soon. It was the key to everything. She lay back on the bed and pressed her palm to her eyes, waiting for Sal to answer the phone.

CHAPTER TWENTY-EIGHT

San Francisco

Salvatore Puglisi was reflecting on his life as he left a gala function at the DeYoung to answer Bianca's summons. Wherever he went, women caused him nothing but trouble. It was worse when they were family since you were stuck with them. Bianca's sideline had been profitable, but her idea of security was the cookie jar. And what did she mean by, "It's more than just the diary?" Was Fabriani wanting more of a cut? She was expendable at this point. There were other ways to get access. He clenched his jaw and drove on.

All the lights were on at the DeMontana mansion, and Bianca was pacing the living room floor, pausing periodically to peer out the window at the passing traffic. Her stomach was upset and she felt like crap. She wasn't even sure how to tell Sal what had happened. She heard the sound of a car engine shutting down in the driveway. She straightened her shoulders and went to answer the door.

Sal pushed past her without so much as a glance. She followed him into the kitchen, away from the street and any prying eyes. He pointed to a chair. "Sit," he said, "and tell me what the hell is going on. What have you done?"

What had she done? She'd made them both a hell of a lot of money. That's what she'd done. And now it was all coming back on her. She felt the first stirrings of righteous anger and when she faced Sal, her voice was steady.

"Someone broke into the house while we were away at opening night for the museum. I came back early because I had a migraine, or I expect they would have taken more than the diary. But they knew exactly where to look for it, and that means it had to have been someone who had been in the house or who had watched me from the street. I don't know." She rubbed her temples with her fingers. "I'd hidden it in the candle stand in my bathroom. Nobody could have seen me put it there. The only logical answer is that somebody knew about the diary, knew it was in the house, and waited until I'd gone to look for it. Unfortunately," she paused, "they were successful."

Sal took a seat across from Bianca, his face a mask. He tapped his thumb against his chin. The diary was gone. Things could be worse. They'd taken nearly a third of the Espositos off the market, but any one of the paintings still out there could be enough to destroy what they'd worked for if somebody either by chance or by design started looking closely. If the diary had been stolen for ransom, they'd be getting a phone call or an email soon enough. It could easily cost them five hundred thousand, maybe a million. Maybe more. But if it was being held for ransom, he could deal with it. The cleanup wouldn't be much. Who'd have the balls to take that tack?

Bianca interrupted his train of thought. "At first I thought it was Michael. He's been wanting to get out of this." She shrugged. "But he came home later, plastered and angry that I'd taken the car. He's asleep upstairs. You want me to get him?"

"Later. He'll keep." Sal waved away the offer. "He's not going anywhere." Michael was the first one he'd thought of. It would be like him, the sniveling sorry excuse for a nephew. But not even Michael would be that stupid. He didn't have that much initiative. Or enough brains to carry it out. Maybe somebody put him up to it? But who? All he cared about were skirts, and the kind he associated with didn't have any brains either. Nix Michael. But that Fabriani dame. She had brains, and Michael could have talked to her. Fabriani would be easy. He'd check her out first. Who else?

There was Esposito. Esposito knew, but he was a dying old man. He should be making his peace with the Almighty. There was an American grandson, though. Esposito could have told him the story and convinced him to get the diary. That would be like the old man. Conniving old bastard. What was that kid's name? Gino. That was it. If the kid was anywhere nearby, he'd be a good bet. At least he'd better be a good bet. Nobody else knew the diary even existed. The kid was a vintner like his grandfather, and he lived in California. That meant either the Napa Valley or the mountains. Finding him wouldn't be all that hard. A vintner grows grapes and sells wine. Simple enough to find out where he was.

Sal dialed information on his cell. No listing for a Gino Esposito in Napa, but there was one with a Los Gatos number. He had the number dialed and let it ring until the answering machine picked up with a detailed greeting and instructions for leaving a message. He disconnected and jammed the phone back in his pocket. He'd check out Dark Mountain Vineyard in the morning. He turned his attention back to Bianca.

"You said there was more." He stroked his cane and waited.

Bianca fiddled with the sash on her dressing gown, avoiding Sal's eyes. "I made entries in the diary," she said. "You know. Separate entries. I had to. Getting the Espositos off the market was one part but the other part, you know, whenever we'd take another painting, I'd add that in the back with the title and the date we took it. And if we sold it, who we sold it to and for how much. It was a way of keeping track. Sort of an inventory. It was logical. We needed some way of keeping track. After all, they're two different operations, but they meshed very well together." She touched his arm, trying to press her case.

"Getting the Espositos off the market is one part. If we don't get that done before somebody discovers that my dearly departed didn't paint them all or even all that many of them, I can kiss my wealth goodbye. That's not acceptable. But the other part of our business arrangement has been quite lucrative for both of us, if I might remind you. I'm your *entrée* to that world of cultivated tastes. Without me, you'd have no chance in hell of getting access or even finding out what to take, for that matter. You don't know art. You need a cultured palate for that. You can't muscle your way into art appreciation. But we're a partnership. You find the buyers, and I provide access to the merchandise. It comes in and it goes out quickly. Most of it anyway, unless I take a fancy to it or you decide it's something you like. Just like placing your order at the drive-thru. And I've never let you down. The last entry was for the Renoir. You know I'm right." She closed her eyes and waited. If Sal were going to kill her, this would be the time.

The color drained from Sal's face, and he slammed his cane on the table. Bianca tensed. Her hands shook as she listened to him curse her for the rest of this life and on into eternity. His face was mottled red and spittle had formed at the corners of his mouth. She wondered if he might be on the verge of a stroke or a coronary. That wouldn't be a bad thing. Eventually, however, he wound down and wiped his perspiring forehead with his sleeve.

"Fabriani," he said.

"What about her?" Bianca said.

"Does she know about the diary?"

"Of course not. She has no need to know. She furnishes us with keys and gets her cut. That's all."

"Unless somebody told her. Is she in the diary too?"

Bianca nodded.

"You've got the whole damn operation written down in a book. One book. One very small missing book. Am I hearing you right?"

"Sal, I thought..."

"You thought. You thought. You thought you'd keep all the Espositos on ice here until you were ready to move the lot of them back to Palermo. Great idea. You don't have a thought in your head. And where did all this thinking get you?"

"I know. But..." He held up a hand for silence and then stood. "Get me Fabriani's address. How much art did she decide she liked? Tell me. How much does she have that belongs to me? Get me the goddamn address. I'm going to handle this my way."

CHAPTER TWENTY-NINE

San Francisco

When the doorbell rang at nine-thirty the next morning, Gino and Francesca were barely out of the shower. "D-day," Francesca said, tossing him a towel and reaching for her terrycloth robe. By the time he'd dried off, shaved, and dressed, Francesca had the coffee ready and the table set for three. A diminutive elderly version of Francesca was seated at the kitchen table, considering the offerings of a bakery box crammed with donuts. She settled on a chocolate with sprinkles and set it on the plate next to her coffee.

"Grandmama, this is Gino," Francesca said, also examining the contents of the bakery box. "Gino, Grandmama Yvonne." She selected a jelly donut. "Don't worry. There are plenty left. Grandmama believes in a hearty breakfast." She took a dainty bite and dabbed at the powdered sugar on her chin. The strawberry jam oozed onto the plate, forming a fragrant puddle.

"You are Italian," Yvonne said, blowing on her coffee to cool it.

Gino looked from Yvonne to Francesca, who smiled encouragement. "Yes, ma'am," he said. "Sicilian."

Yvonne set down her coffee. "Call me Yvonne. Italian is good. Family is important, and Italians respect family. Sicilians especially. So do Asians." She regarded the crumbs on her plate and turned her attention back to the box. "Although I don't approve of the current trend to lump all Asians together. A practice I am guilty of myself, at times, I'm afraid. I am Korean. And French. The French I am not so sure of," she gave a Gallic shrug, "but the Koreans believe strongly in family. And that," she looked up from her search in the box, "is why I have agreed to help." She motioned for Gino to sit. "Eat. And then we will talk of today's matters. But first, I want to hear about your grandfather." She chose two old fashioneds for her second course. "Tell me about him and his life."

Gino relaxed. All grandmothers were the same. Food before anything else. He poured himself a cup of coffee and grabbed the first donut his hand connected with, a bear claw. His grandfather. Where to begin? What could he tell Yvonne? If she were going to play a part in this production, she deserved to know the whole story. If he screwed up, something that happened on a regular basis these days, it seemed, Francesca would be in real trouble. And so he told Yvonne everything, beginning with how his grandfather had taken him in after the accident that had killed his parents. He told her about his vineyard in the Santa Cruz Mountains. She regarded him with a steady gaze as he told her of his gambling debt and his desperate need to pay it off, straighten out his life, save the vineyard, and respect his grandfather's dying wishes. Finally he told her he loved Francesca. And then he drank his coffee, waiting for the verdict, as if he'd been a career criminal going up for parole for the last time. A small, old woman he'd met only half an hour ago held his future in her hands.

****

Yvonne nodded. "All right," she said. "I understand. I understand you have made mistakes. That goes with youth. But I also understand your intention to make corrections in your life and your need to do what your grandfather has asked. I have to tell you, I'm excited." Her cheeks were flushed and her eyes twinkled. "It's been quite some time since I've been involved in anything on such a scale." She looked up. "I was young once, of course." She smiled at him. "I wasn't always so boring. That's the downside to being ancient. One tends to lose a sense of spontaneity. However, when I was a girl, I sowed a few wild oats—nothing quite so daring as this—but I've had my share of adventure. And now this. It's a fitting way to round out a life, I think. I was pleased Francesca thought of me." "There is risk," Gino said, doubt beginning to eat at the confidence he'd felt earlier. "If we don't succeed..." He threw his hands in the air and left the sentence unfinished.

"Don't be foolish," Yvonne said. "Of course, we must succeed. I have no intention of having Francesca arrested." She tilted her head and looked at him out of the corner of her eye. "Or myself either. You, I don't know that well yet, but if Francesca loves you, and she says she does, and if you love her, as you say you do, then I do not intend for you to be arrested either. So that is that." She took a sip of coffee and excused herself to make a trip to the bathroom.

"Grandmama doesn't pull any punches," Francesca said. "She likes you, Gino."

"How can you tell? Seemed like a rather weak endorsement." "Nonsense, she likes you. Believe me, you'd know if she didn't."

Francesca refilled the coffee cups and cleared the table. Yvonne returned to the table where she produced a three-ring binder from the satchel she'd placed on the floor by her chair.

"Names and addresses of all the women in the Yerba Buena Ladies Club," she said. "And also the calendar of events for the year. I've taken the liberty of retyping the schedule so it appears the trip to the museum has been on the books since January." She looked up. "Just in case anyone should ask, I thought it best to prepare. Anyhow, I often change things around. Nobody else has the master schedule. Events come up on short notice, and it's important to be flexible. Details like that are important when you're planning an event such as the one we're about to conduct." She closed the notebook. "I send out emails to remind the girls where and when to assemble. Most of them are quite competent with the computer, but I always call them as a reminder that morning. I've already done that. There will be some carpooling and some will drive themselves. Others will be dropped off by family. I will be coming with Francesca.

"Mildred and Josephine know what to do. They don't know the whole story. That's for their protection, of course, but they do know it's important and for a good cause. And they love to participate in anything the least bit theatrical. Mildred did theater in her youth and was quite good, I'm told. Josephine can do amazing feats with that wheelchair. She was a marathon runner in her younger days, and she's itching to get back on her treadmill. In the meantime, she's gotten quite adept at maneuvering that thing." Yvonne sat back and folded her hands on the cover. "This will be quite interesting."

Of that, Gino had no doubt.

****

At three-thirty that afternoon, the first five members of the Yerba Buena Ladies Club were dropped off by their rides and strolled at a leisurely pace through the front door of the art museum just as the first two Buick Roadmasters from the Santa Clara contingent pulled up and double-parked on the east side of Van Ness Avenue.

By four o'clock, the ladies' numbers had increased to twenty-eight and the cars to fifteen. Morrie stood curbside, distributing newly printed temporary parking permits to each driver. Taped to the driver side window, the permits allowed the vehicles the privilege of assembling along the entire length of the 200 block. Already, the cars were drawing a crowd of admirers and the sidewalk was soon packed with enthusiasts and curious pedestrians.

Jeffrey had fastened a banner across the grille of the first car in line. The banner proclaimed *Annual Ride to the Park.*

"A tradition has to start somewhere," he said.

"True," Morrie said.

"So, now's as good a time as any, and I've been itching to drive one of these beauties."

"They've got style, that's for damn sure."

Inside the museum, the ladies traveled as a group from one room to the next, a formidable entourage with their canes and walkers and, in Susan's case, a portable oxygen tank that bumped along beside her on two mismatched wheels, the result of a quick repair after she'd run over the frame with the Bentley. Francesca pushed Josephine's wheelchair and served as guide and interpreter as they moved along.

At precisely twenty-five minutes past four, Yvonne and Mildred began a heated discussion of the artistic merits of a Degas on the wall opposite the elderly guard, who was now taking frequent and not-so-subtle glances at his wristwatch. Francesca slipped away from her position by the wheelchair and moved to the other side of the room as Mildred raised her cane above her head and began swinging it as if it were a baton and she a twirler in a high school marching band. All the ladies were now involved, and the noise level was escalating rapidly as the women chose sides. Alarmed, the guard pushed through the crowd of women to separate the potential combatants, restore order, and usher the lot of them out of the room.

Before he could get to the scene of the argument, however, Josephine moved into his way and blocked his path, causing him to trip and land on her lap. She slapped him, a healthy swack that jarred his dentures loose and sent them sailing through the air, landing on Sara's arm, which caused her to let out a bloodcurdling scream as she grabbed the offending pearlies and flung them away from her. They dashed against a marble pillar where they separated at the third bicuspid.

Josephine's slap had caused her purse to slip down her arm and while it dangled from her wrist by one strap, the contents cascaded to the floor and among the fallout were eleven butter pats she'd stolen from the Early Bird Special at the Carriage House. The butter pats, shedding their protective paper coats, turned the hardwood floor into the equivalent of a skating rink in a few spots, minus the benefit of skates. Thus, as the women slipped about the room, careening off each other and into the walls, and the guard was occupied with freeing himself from Josephine and reclaiming his teeth, Francesca removed the Rembrandt from the wall and tucked it into the newly fashioned inside breast pocket of her navy blue blazer. She returned to her post by Josephine and winked at her. Josephine patted her hand and smiled.

As abruptly as it had begun, the argument wound down, the guard collected his busted dentures, and Yvonne gave the high sign. The Yerba Buena Ladies Club took their leave, ushered out by the harried guard who didn't look back as he moved the women out of the room, down the hall, and out the door to their waiting transportation, which would deliver them to Yvonne's home, where they would sip sherry and review the day's events.

At the door of the museum, Francesca paused to take in the spectacle playing out on the street. She turned the wheelchair over to Yvonne and wove through the admiring crowd of spectators chatting with the drivers of the Buicks. Several cars had their hoods up to showcase the engines underneath. Francesca made for the red and white Buick Special third in line. Once seated inside Morrie's Roadmaster, she pulled a bright pink headscarf out of the glove box and tied it under her chin, sitting up as straight as she could to keep the contents of her pocket from bending.

Seeing Francesca in the passenger seat, Morrie left the group he was chatting with and returned to the car. He honked the horn and the drivers closed the hoods and returned to their vehicles. One more toot on the horn and the procession moved out at a stately pace headed for Golden Gate Park.

****

At the museum, the guard was wiping his perspiring forehead with a handkerchief and examining his ruined dentures with disgust. He picked up the extension phone and called for the janitor to clean up the buttery mess on the floor and it was then, as he was pointing out to the janitor where the pats had fallen, that he noticed the empty space on the wall beneath one of the recessed lights. Curious. Something had been there. Something had to have been there. Damned if he could remember what it was, though. He frowned. Had it been like that all day? Nobody had told him any of the paintings had been taken down for cleaning. Surely he would have noticed the empty space earlier in his shift.

Realization dawned and with a sickening feeling, the guard turned and fled down the hall to the office to report the theft. The office was closed and locked. Everyone had left for the day. His first thought was that he'd be blamed. It had happened on his watch. That was not going to happen. He considered his options and decided to follow the most logical course of action. He left. When the theft was reported, he'd be shocked. Yes, that was it. Shock. He could do that. He knew nothing, after all. Why should he be the one to take the blame? For all he knew, the painting could have gone missing anytime during the day. Probably on that annoying woman's shift.

He wasn't responsible. And with that comforting thought Horace Finkelstein, guard, left for home.

****

Meanwhile, the Roadmasters turned left onto Grove, right onto Franklin, and then left again onto Fulton, which gave them a straight shot to Golden Gate Park. Crossing Fillmore, Morrie picked up the first faint notes of a siren and checked the rear view mirror. The sound grew louder and within half a minute he made out a police car, moving fast and closing rapidly. He clenched his teeth and prepared to move over. Damn it all to hell. What had he done wrong? Everything had gone on schedule and according to plan. What had he missed? He cursed under his breath. This was his idea. He'd convinced the rest of them it would work. Ahead and behind, the Roadmasters made room for the oncoming squad car which sailed on by on its way to a call somewhere else. Morrie's hands gripped the wheel so tightly his knuckles whitened. Francesca let out the breath she'd been holding, looked at Morrie, and burst out laughing. After a second, he joined in and, the tension relieved, they moved back out into the flow of traffic.

Inside the Park, Gino and Carla were waiting on JFK Drive by three open parking slots Jeffrey had opened up courtesy of the orange traffic cones he'd appropriated from another project elsewhere in the Park. Francesca exited the Roadmaster and walked to the orange Bug, removing her pink headscarf and handing it over to Carla, who tied it under her chin and walked over to the Roadmaster. Morrie unscrewed the temporary license plates and replaced them with the originals. He slipped the fake plates into a paper bag which he handed to Jeffrey.

The line of Roadmasters made the driving loop through the park and then headed for the Golden Gate Bridge, after which they would conclude their day at a restaurant in Sausalito.

****

Gino and Francesca and the Bug continued along JFK drive, eventually merging onto MLK Drive and then Route 35, which led down the coast to home. Once safely on the highway, Francesca took the sketch out of her blazer pocket and laid it in her lap. It wasn't any bigger than a Christmas card. She reached around to the back seat and got the shirt box she'd put there before they'd left the house. She folded tissue paper gently around the art and laid it carefully in the box, replaced the lid, and returned the box to the back seat. "We did it," she said, touching Gino's shoulder.

"We did," Gino said. "Two down, one to go. When we get back to the house, I'm going to spend some serious time with the diary. So far, all I did was flip through the pages, but it's crammed full of notes, and there's a bunch of stuff in the back that looks like it was written in a different hand. Time. I need time."

CHAPTER THIRTY

San Francisco

"Here we go," Liz said, waving a printout in the air. "Hot off the press. We've got another theft right down the street. Grab your coat, or in your case, turn around, and we'll head out while the trail is maybe still warm. And what's the matter with you? You walk like you've been run over by a street sweeper." It was eight A.M. and she'd gotten to the office a half hour early to play catch up with the files. She was on her third cup of coffee and looking for a fourth.

Steve Cranston was indeed moving as if each body part had its own complaint. He took a slurp of coffee from the cup he was holding and mumbled something into the lid.

"Did I hear that right?" Liz said, reaching for her jacket. "I must have gotten it wrong. It's not possible."

Steve looked up from the coffee. "I went to the gym last night after work. It's not a good place to be. People sweat there." He resumed working on the coffee. "I hurt and I need food."

"Let's go, Charles Atlas. We'll pick up the cops' breakfast of champions on our way."

"Finally. Something is going right," Steve said, following Liz out the door. "What's missing this time?"

"A Rembrandt. Worth a bloody fortune and the museum isn't insured. I wouldn't want to be the one in charge of that place."

Five minutes later they were on the road. Rush hour traffic had settled into a slow crawl, something like an Olympic swimmer doing laps. The more aggressive drivers swerved and merged, passed the slower cars, and cut them off with nothing to spare, forcing the more cautious drivers to hug the curb lane.

"If I were still on patrol, I could make my quota in half an hour," Steve said, looking out the window at the mess outside.

"There's no quota, remember?" Liz said. "There's only enforcement."

"Yeah. Right. You've gone over to the dark side, my friend," he said. "You forget what it was like on the streets."

"No, I remember. I also remember that I enforced very well." Liz grinned as she cut across two lanes and hung a left onto Van Ness. She pulled into the yellow zone outside the Yerba Buena Art Museum, and Steve tossed the SFPD placard onto the dash.

The museum director, Jonathan Watrous, was in a state and spoke in short bursts punctuated by frequent throat clearing and a strange habit of moving his lips as if he were mouthing some internal dialogue. He met them at the door and preceded them through the entrance hall and into the office. He was short, about five foot four, heavy set, and walked like a sailor facing a stiff wind. Steve was mesmerized by his gait and looked up only after Liz had given him a sharp elbow in the ribs.

Watrous began his recitation. The theft had been discovered during the morning's cleaning. The janitor had been checking the light bulbs over the paintings and noticed a light with nothing underneath. He'd reported to the front desk and the manager, Ms. Jocelyn Furtando, had checked for herself and made a complete report which would be available for them.

Ms. Furtando had consulted the collection listings and discovered the missing painting was an 11 x 6 inch sketch, "The Judgment" by Rembrandt. She called the police to notify them of the theft. She'd already taken the liberty of calling all the security personnel who had been on duty yesterday and asked them to report to her office. She hadn't told them why they had been summoned. "It's one of the procedures in our Operations Manual," she said, indicating a small binder on her desk.

Watrous led Liz and Steve to the room where the sketch had hung. "That's where it was," he said, pointing out a small space on the wall near the door that led into the main hall. "The painting wasn't insured," he said. "In fact, none of our paintings are. We can't afford the premiums."

"You mentioned security personnel," Steve said. "What is the extent of the security for the museum?"

"Well," Watrous began, "the security personnel. That's it. They make their rounds at irregular intervals—that's to keep people from discovering a pattern— and when there are crowds in a room, especially young people, the guards keep them from touching the art. Fingerprints can cause irreparable damage to the oils. People just can't seem to help themselves. They have to touch everything." He cleared his throat again.

"This time somebody did a bit more than touch," Liz said. "What about nighttime? Motion detectors? Cameras? Anything of that nature?"

Watrous brightened. "Yes, we have motion detectors in the halls and at the entrance." Then his face fell. "They didn't go off," he said. "What does that mean?"

"That's what we're going to try to find out," Steve said. "Let's start with the names of the security personnel."

"Ms. Furtando has all of that laid out for you," Watrous said. "I've put the workroom right next to her office at your disposal. I'll have the files brought in there." He hunched his shoulders. "I'm afraid I don't know their names. I don't pay attention to that sort of thing," he said and turned to lead them back to the front office.

"What do you suppose he does pay attention to?" Liz asked Cranston under her breath. "If there were ever a place begging to be hit, this is it."

Steve grunted. "Who provides your janitorial service?" he asked.

Watrous stopped and turned. "Ms. Furtando will have that information," he said.

"Of course," Liz said.

Watrous left them in the capable hands of Ms. Furtando who already had the personnel files neatly laid out on the table in the workroom along with a pitcher of ice water and two glasses. "Janitorial service? We use Jennifer Fabriani as our vendor. That way we don't have to bother with the details. She provides whatever we require. When the guards arrive, I'll send them in," she said and closed the door, leaving Liz and Steve contemplating short rations and one page files.

"Fabriani, again," Liz said. "She keeps turning up like a bad penny. What do you think about Watrous?" she asked Steve, pouring them both a glass of water. "Cheers." She took a sip and set the glass down.

"Either he puts on a really good show or he is the most clueless person I've met in a long time," Steve said. "My gut tells me he's not involved."

"I'll go with that for now," Liz said.

****

Sylvia Brownley was first. A former art teacher, she volunteered at the museum three days a week. As a frequent visitor, she never expected one day she'd be working at the museum. When they'd asked her if she'd be interested in becoming a security guard, she'd laughed until she realized they were serious. *They*, apparently, was Ms. Furtando. Sylvia was seventy-five years old. She had a keen intelligence and didn't waste time after the introductions.

"I expect there's been a robbery. Or I should probably say burglary, since no one seems to have been held up at the point of a gun or knife," she began. "It's not all that surprising, given that there's so little actual attention paid to security. I mean, look at me. And I'm better than the other two you'll meet shortly. This is a nice supplement to my pension and social security, if you're wondering why I do this. More importantly, I get to see people and be among them every day. And to answer the question you haven't asked yet, no, I didn't take whatever is missing. It wouldn't make any sense, would it? I mean, all this is mine already." She looked from Liz to Steve and opened her arms wide. "I have all of this every day. It wouldn't make any sense for me to take anything. It would diminish my world." She folded her hands in her lap and waited.

Liz smiled. "I understand," she said. "But perhaps you saw something that didn't seem quite right or that didn't register right away?" She waited as Sylvia considered this.

"Well," Sylvia said, "I wish I could be of help. There's nothing more exciting than being of value to the police, but for the life of me, I can't remember anything out of whack. I walked my rounds during my four-hour shift, stopping to sit a bit when the rooms were empty." She looked apologetic. "Sometimes when there are big groups, it can get tiring, making sure everyone has their questions answered and making sure they don't touch anything." She leaned forward confidingly. "Mr. Watrous stresses the importance of people not touching the paintings. He's very precise about that."

And so it went for the rest of Sylvia's interview. The second guard, Miles Manning, was eighty and wore glasses thicker than the lens on the Hubbell telescope. He was not all that interested in art, but he was actively looking for the fourth Mrs. Manning and wanted a woman with cultivated tastes. So far, he hadn't found Mrs. Right but was hopeful. He sure would like to help but didn't know what he had to offer.

Last was Horace Finkelstein. Finkelstein was a slack-jawed man of about seventy and went on the defensive the moment he entered the work room. "I don't know anything about anything," he said, his hand on the doorknob. "Is that all?" He turned to leave.

"Just a moment, Mr. Finkelstein," Liz said. "Come in. Have a seat." She pointed to the empty chair across the table, from which Mr. Finkelstein would have an excellent view of the door that would open for him when she decided it would open and not until.

Finkelstein walked to the chair and yanked it around so he could straddle it, arms folded and resting on the chair back which provided a weak but symbolic barrier against the onslaught of impending questions from the law.

Steve began. "Thank you for coming in on your day off, Mr. Finkelstein. We appreciate any help you can give in our investigation."

Finkelstein looked from Liz to Steve and then back to Steve again. Finkelstein reminded Steve of one of those hovering, annoying, whining little bugs that plague you when you're outdoors. Not dangerous, not venomous, just annoying.

"As I said before, I don't know anything."

"About what?" Liz said.

"Anything."

"That's amazing, isn't it, Steve?" she said. "I've never known anybody who didn't know anything about anything. Remarkable."

Finkelstein's brow furrowed and his eyes narrowed into slits. "I don't like people making fun of me," he said.

Liz leaned forward and spoke into his face. "Then straighten up and give your memory a jog. What happened yesterday during your shift? And don't leave anything out. That's when it happened, isn't it? It will be better if you tell us the whole story now."

Finkelstein shifted in his seat, not an easy task given his posture. He pulled on his earlobe and then clasped his hands behind his neck and rotated his shoulders, the audible crack causing Steve to wince. "I didn't do anything wrong," he whined. "It wasn't my fault."

Liz fixed him with an even gaze, but God, he was a spineless weasel. No, that was wrong. Weasels were good. This guy was worthless. He was a rat, even smelled like one. Didn't appear to have bathed in recent memory. She wrinkled her nose but kept her calm.

"No one is saying you did anything wrong, Mr. Finkelstein," Steve said. "Just tell us what happened, and we'll take it from there."

Finkelstein nodded. He looked at Steve. "It was those women. The whole bunch of them. Cackling hens. All gussied up like floozies. Makeup and jewelry. Rich bitches, all of them. Looking down on people who have to earn money any way they can. Treating you like a schmuck. Treating you like you're just a piece of dirt to be stepped on."

"I know what it's like to work for a living, Mr. Finkelstein, and I can understand how difficult it can be dealing with the public," Steve said.

You have no idea, Liz thought, but she ventured in now that they had Finkelstein talking. "What women were there yesterday during your shift?"

Finkelstein took his attention from Steve and focused on Liz. These cops were like him. They worked too. They didn't think he'd stolen the painting. It was those women. He had to make those women pay for what they'd done to him. It wasn't fair. It wasn't right. "All of them," he said. "There had to have been thirty of them." He nodded. "The whole group.

They come through the museum couple, three times a year. Sometimes more. Always the same thing. Bumping into you with their walkers. Tripping you with their wheelchairs. And that woman with the oxygen tank is the worst. She's probably the one who took it." He sat back, satisfied. The police would take it from there.

Liz stared at Finkelstein, incredulous. "The women are elderly, that's what you're saying? And they're wealthy? And they visit the museum on a routine basis?"

"That's what I said. They call them patrons but I don't see anything patriotic about them. They're useless." Finkelstein was done.

"Thank you, Mr. Finkelstein," Liz said. "We appreciate your time. We'll be in touch if we need any additional information." She looked at Steve, who crossed his eyes. Finkelstein jumped back from his chair and fled the room.

"Well," Steve said, "that was less than useful." He rubbed his face and stifled a yawn. "What next?"

"Beats the heck out of me," Liz said. "Furtando gave us the list of the regulars and the Yerba Buena Ladies Club is not only on the regular list but endow the museum to more figures than I can count. Most of the women have the museum named as beneficiary in their wills. Just not the type to pull a heist like this. I don't know. What do you think?"

Steve raised one of the glasses provided with the ice water and examined it. He rubbed at something stuck on the rim. "Nobody is beyond suspicion, but if I had to make a wager, I'd bet on Finkelstein before I dropped a buck on the ladies. Think we need to do a bit of checking on him before we bust the golden girls."

CHAPTER THIRTY-ONE

Dark Mountain Vineyard

Gino lay on the sofa in the great room, waiting for a Great Idea, the diary on his chest and a notepad by his side. His head made a soft impression in the down throw pillow, his eyes were closed, and his thoughts were scattered. The notebook was blank as he hadn't had a brilliant idea all morning.

Last night's adrenaline rush was long gone, replaced by fatigue and a restless nervousness. The nervousness was not lessened by the knowledge that there was only one positive outcome and numerous less than favorable potential outcomes to this whole affair. But all they needed was one brilliant idea. Even a not so brilliant idea would work. Breaking and entering wasn't as easy as you'd think. And they didn't even want to take anything. They wanted to leave something. It shouldn't be this hard.

The room was quiet. He watched Francesca drinking coffee with her eye on the clock. The shirt box with the Rembrandt inside was on the dining room table next to the sugar bowl and between the candle sticks. At ten o'clock, he heard a car pull up outside. Gino hoisted himself off the sofa, stuffing the diary in his pants pocket and leaving the empty notepad behind. He walked to the door. Carla and Morrie stood on the step, arms full of groceries. "You don't never lock the door, Gino," she said. "But that's probably a good plan, considering. Anyhow, I'll make lunch before we drive to the city to finish up." She made it sound like a weeding project that just needed the walks swept and the sprinklers turned on. He took two grocery bags from her and deposited them on the counter in the kitchen. Morrie brought in the last three and then poured himself a cup of coffee which he took out to the back deck. "What's in all these?" Gino asked, surveying the crammed counter.

"Just the essentials. I'm thinking we need some serious nourishment before we tackle the last part of this." Carla tucked her hair behind her ears and emptied the bags, arranging the groceries in neat rows on the counter. Francesca rose from her seat and examined the offerings.

"Pasta. It'll give us energy for tonight. We stopped at the fish store on the way down from Sausalito. Those Buick car people sure know how to have a good time. When I get my dance studio, I'm gonna have one of them cars. Anyhow, we dropped it off at Morrie's friend's place in Campbell and picked up the truck. But as I was saying, they had some killer clams." She looked at Francesca. "You like clams, right? I'm thinking linguine with red clam sauce. We got some baguettes and salad stuff to round out the meal."

Francesca nodded. "I love fresh seafood. You can't get that anywhere but on the coast." She unpacked the rest of the groceries. "You like to cook."

"Yeah, well New Haven ain't known for its fresh seafood," Carla said. "You gotta consider the sewage factor." Francesca made a face but Carla continued. "They've got the water going out into the Sound better than they used to but you still gotta be careful. But yeah. I like to cook. All Italian women cook. It's how we control our men. Oh, and a nice red wine," she added. "Gino can get the wine. That will give him and Morrie something to do while we're cooking. Gino can spend half an hour talking about wine. Me, I just like to drink it." She grinned.

"You know, you were really good yesterday," Carla continued, opening a can of tomato paste. "I mean it. It was just like you'd been doing this all your life." She gave Francesca a critical look. "It was your first time, right?"

"Yes, and the last, I hope."

"You can get used to it. Once you've taken something, the next time ain't such a big deal. Not that I do this on a regular basis, you understand." She opened one of the produce bags, selected half a dozen tomatoes and took them to the sink to wash. "You wanna get me one of them big pots in the pantry? The sauce takes a couple hours to simmer down." Carla was examining the spice cabinet, handing Francesca the oregano and basil. "Just set them down on the counter. I'll work on the garlic. You can put the salad together."

For the next two hours, Carla and Francesca labored in the kitchen while Gino and Morrie discussed the merits of a particular Zin they'd taken from the wine cellar and other safe topics, deliberately not discussing the one topic that weighed on their minds. At two o'clock, they sat down to dine. It was a feast. Fresh bread, crisp salad, and Carla's linguine. Gino had just filled his plate when the doorbell rang. Francesca ran to the Great Room, grabbed the shirt box, and fled to the office, Carla right behind her. With the door opened a crack and their heads together, the women watched Gino get up and answer the door.

"Who is it?" Francesca whispered.

"Dunno. I can't see shit," Carla said. "Oh, oh. This ain't good."

"Let me see," Francesca said, opening the door a little more before Carla closed it quietly and firmly in her face.

"No, trust me on this," Carla said, her mind racing. "Gino got a gun anywhere in here?" she asked.

"No. Maybe. I don't know. What's going on?" Francesca said. "Who's there?"

"Sal," Carla said. "Sal Puglisi. And it ain't no social call. Check the desk drawers. But be real quiet. We gotta find some kind of advantage or we're all dead."

"Sal's the mobster in those newspaper photos," Francesca said. "What does he want with us? Oh, shit. You suppose he saw me take the Rembrandt? And Gino's got the diary in his pocket. Oh, this is bad." She tiptoed to the nightstand and opened the top drawer, pawing through the contents. A bottle of aspirin, a Swiss Army knife, and some coins. No gun. Where else to look? She straightened and pressed her palms to her temples. Gun. Gino told her he kept a gun for rattlesnakes when he went into the vineyards. Where did he keep it? Her eyes traveled around the room, searching. *The kitchen.* The gun was in the kitchen in the drawer of the planning center where it would be close at hand when Gino left the house. It might as well be in Outer Mongolia for all the good it would do them now. The voices in the great room were growing louder. She looked at Carla and slowly turned the door handle, opening the door just a crack.

"What are they saying?" Carla said. "Can you hear what they're saying?" She was trying to see around Francesca but not having any luck.

"I can't make out the words, but the tone isn't good. It's low, so nobody's shouting, but that might not be a good thing either." She moved away from the door and jerked her head in the direction of the French doors that opened onto the deck.

"I'm with you," Carla said, joining her on the deck. "Now what?"

Francesca was peeking around the corner at the end of the deck and looking toward the front door which was shut. There was a shovel leaning against the side of the house, and she grabbed it by the handle but then she saw the pumpkin at the same time Carla did and nodded.

"It's going to take both of us. How good an arm do you have?"

"Not as strong as my legs, but strong enough."

They crept along the front of the house below the windowsills of the two front windows to the left of the door.

"On three," Francesca whispered.

They squatted and locked arms under the pumpkin, raising it to waist level. Carrying the mega pumpkin from Half Moon Bay between them they continued on up the three steps to the first portion of the side deck and set their burden down outside the sliding glass door that led into the Great Room. Sal was standing with his back to the deck door, holding a gun on Gino and Morrie. Carla waved her hands over her head until she caught Gino's eye. She held up three fingers and Gino blinked twice in reply. Then she and Francesca lifted the pumpkin. With two practice swings to get up momentum, they put all their strength into the final swing and hurled the pumpkin through the glass door. Sal whipped around at the crash and Gino dove at Sal's feet while Morrie rammed his head into Sal's gut. The gun went off, and Sal crumpled.

Francesca and Carla stepped in through the shattered door, stepping around glass shards and pumpkin pulp and giving Sal a wide berth. "At least he ain't bleeding on the good rug," Carla said. "He didn't watch many cop shows. You don't never expose your back."

Morrie bent over Sal's inert form and listened for a pulse. He shook his head and stood. "Right through the heart. He's gone."

"Was he alone?" Francesca asked.

Gino nodded. "He came for the diary. He said he knew we had it and we were going to give it to him or he'd kill us. I believed him. He'd looked at the dining room table and had just asked where the rest of our dinner party was when you two showed up at the window. Good thinking and good timing."

"I liked that pumpkin," said Francesca, surveying the mess on the floor.

"That pumpkin saved our lives," Gino said.

"That's a lucky pumpkin," Carla said. "You oughta scoop up some seeds and plant some junior pumpkins for luck."

Gino looked at Sal and then at the dinner they'd never gotten to eat. "*Vendetta,*" he said. "Please tell me this is going to end sometime soon. Now what the hell are we going to do about him? Calling the police is probably not the best course of action. I'm all thought out." "That makes two more things to do," Francesca said, frowning. "We've got to get rid of the body and the car." She looked at Gino. "We're not making much progress lately. Our To Do list keeps getting longer and time is the only thing that's getting shorter." She ran her tongue across her lips and looked out the window at the car parked at the edge of the drive. "Usually I like lists. I can cross off what I've done. This one isn't working the way it's supposed to. It's like one step forward, two steps back." She sighed. "Some event planner I am." She looked down and stuck out her tongue at Sal's corpse. "I hate you," she said.

"Feel better?" Gino asked.

"Actually, yes. I do." She straightened. "All right," she said, squaring her shoulders and turning from the window. "If we've got two more things to do besides planting the art and getting the police to find DeMontana's car, then we'll do two more things. That makes four things." A cloud crossed in front of the late afternoon sun, sending the room into shadow. Francesca shuddered. "Four is unlucky. We've got to get busy and whittle that number down to zero pronto."

Morrie was standing by the broken door, looking out at the hillside, hands on his hips. "There is a way to get rid of him and never have to worry about him ever again." He looked at Gino. "Do you know any property up here that's sold recently?"

"The way today has been going that question almost makes sense," Gino said, but seeing Morrie was serious, he gave it some thought. "Wainright's place, down the road a few miles or so. It sold but the new people haven't moved in yet. Why?"

Morrie's expression was hard to read. "It's simple, really. And simple is always best. You got an old truck on this place? Good. Get some gloves and round

up a tarp. We'll take Sal for a ride."

"You ain't gonna leave Sal in the house for the new people, are you?" Carla said. "Are you out of your freakin' mind? Some kind of welcome present Sal is." "Nope. They'll never know he's there. And after a little while, he won't be," Morrie said. "That's the wonder of a septic tank. Before a house sells, the tank has to be pumped. It won't be pumped again for years. And even if it is, there won't be anything left but teeth and a few bone fragments, and that'll all get scooped up and mixed in the honey wagon. Nobody's going to be looking for him and nobody is going to find him. Sal is gone for good."

"I'll get the tarp," Gino said.

"I'll clean up," Francesca said, and she went for the broom and dustpan.

"I'll take care of dinner," Carla said. "You're gonna work up an appetite. We'll eat when you get back." And she kissed Morrie. "Ain't he somethin'?" she said, turning to Francesca who smiled back at her and tossed her head in Gino's direction.

"*This* was in the back seat." Morrie had just gone out the door but returned from the car and stood on the porch, his extended arms offering a sullen black poodle like a small burnt offering. The dog snarled, or more precisely, did its best impression of a snarl, which revealed an overshot lower jaw and some crooked tiny teeth. He set the dog on the floor in the front hall, and it lifted a leg and wet down the nearest table leg. A small rivulet dripped onto the hardwood floor and shimmered in the sunlight. Gino looked at the dog and then at Morrie.

"What is that?"

Carla looked down at the defiant animal and then bent to look at the license tag. "Maximus? What the hell kind of a name is Maximus? It don't sound right. Who calls a little dog Maximus?" She looked down at the small black dog who met her gaze. "No wonder you got an attitude. You been disrespected. That Sal worked his shit everywhere." She made little kissing sounds with her lips and picked up the poodle who responded by licking her cheek. "You got a new life, and you need a new name." She held the dog at arm's length and assessed his features. "Pierre." She looked at Gino. "That's a classy name for a dog. And him being a French poodle and all, it fits. I know about poodles. They got them fancy hairdos. Just like Pierre." She set Pierre down on the rug and removed his license tag. "We'll get you a new one. I promise." He looked up at her, adoration in his eyes, then trotted to the door and looked back. "You gotta pee, dontcha?" she said, patting him on the head as she reached for the doorknob. "He don't want to go in the house no more. He knows when he's being respected. Just like people." She raised an index finger and pointed to the sky. "Respect." She followed the dog outside and closed the door behind her.

"Women and dogs," Gino said. "What is it?"

Francesca smiled. "It's who we are."

****

Two hours later Gino and Morrie were back, minus Sal. Gino hosed off the tarp and dragged it down the hillside where they shoveled dirt and garden debris onto it in preparation for its last trip to the dump. "What made you think of the septic tank?" Gino said.

"My brother and I were drinking beer one night thinking about all the ways you could dispose of a body that would never be discovered. Somehow the septic tank idea came up and it was a winner." He looked at Gino. "There was a lot of beer."

Back in the house, Francesca suggested that showers and clean clothes would be a good idea and not optional, so it was Morrie's turn to wear a bathrobe while the washer and dryer worked away. Fortunately for Morrie, his robe came from Gino's closet, and while the sight of a three hundred pound man wearing a robe sized for someone barely a hundred and forty stretched the limits of both the fabric and credibility, there was something about his presence that didn't invite snide remarks.

The house was back to rights except for the door which Carla had patched with a few pieces of cardboard box and duct tape. And when they finally sat down to their meal, dinner was as quiet as the day had been wild. Finally, somewhere between the second and third bottles of wine, Francesca said, "I never realized how dull my life was until I met you, Gino."

"Believe me," Gino said. "Only a little over a week ago, my life was going in a totally different direction. Not necessarily a good one, but definitely different. Now I keep thinking we're almost out of this, but then something else happens. I still owe money and I'm running out of time." He took a sip of wine. "Still, we've done all right so far. Just one more thing to do."

Francesca looked up from her plate. "Three. But at least we got rid of the bad mojo of four."

Carla twirled a piece of linguine around her spoon. "Yeah. Gino has to break into the DeMontana garage, and we've got to get the cops to look for the hit and run car there and find the art and arrest them for everything, and we got to get rid of Sal's car. But three's a good number," she said. "Like these pumpkin seeds I saved." She lifted the glass with the seeds inside. "Three. It's a good number."

"The car," Gino groaned. "I forgot about the damn car."

"I didn't," Morrie said. "It's doable. I figure we ditch it on our way to the city. We'll leave his wallet and keys in the car and toss the cell into the drink, just in case there's anything in the call history that has to do with us. And that ought to take care of Puglisi." He looked at Carla. "There are no prints on anything, except Sal's, of course. We're clean."

"If you say so," Gino said. "Dump the car. Why not? Just one more little detail."

Francesca patted his hand. "It's almost done," she said. "Don't worry. We'll take care of the rest. You just concentrate on how to break into the garage. You've been wonderful so far. Courageous and determined. I know that brilliant idea will come to you really soon."

"It better," Gino said. "It had better."

CHAPTER THIRTY-TWO

En Route

"This is as commonplace a vehicle as Ernesto could come up with on short notice," Morrie said, looking over the 2009 Ford Focus. They were gathered at the curb of his friend's home in Campbell checking out the merchandise. The car wasn't too clean. It wasn't too dirty. It looked like every other car on the road. It was practically invisible, and it had the added bonus of untraceable plates.

Ernesto Gagliardi stood at a respectful distance, hands in the pockets of his Madras Bermuda shorts jingling coins. His Hawaiian shirt stretched across a belly the size of Oahu, the palm trees in the pattern bent under the strain. His shaved head was working on a five o'clock shadow, and his jaw worked overtime on some bubble gum. Knock-kneed and pigeon-toed, Ernesto had cornered a niche market. "Ya want her?" he asked Morrie, who nodded and held out a hand for the keys.

"Not that I'm questioning anything," Gino said to Morrie, "but you sure seem to have access to a lot of cars with untraceable plates."

"Yeah, I do," Morrie said. He looked up and down the street. "If you guys are ready, let's get out of here. The sooner this is done, the better."

"I'm riding with you," Carla said over Morrie's protests. "I ain't never ridden in no Lincoln before, and I figure Sal owes me that after all he done to me. May he rot in hell." She crossed herself and reached for the door handle.

"Hold on a minute," Ernesto said. "Don't touch nothing." He turned and walked back into the garage, returning with a pair of yellow rubber gloves stained with varnish and several colors of auto paint. He handed them to Carla. "You can keep 'em. I got more."

"Gee, thanks Ernesto. You're sweet." She took the gloves and pulled them on. Morrie whistled. What Carla wanted, Carla got. He pulled on a pair of leather driving gloves, and they were off.

They left the Bug with Ernesto. Gino and Francesca climbed into the Focus and picked up 880 in San Jose. Morrie was one lane over and about a quarter of a mile ahead. As soon as he could, Gino slipped across lanes and took up a position a couple of cars behind the Lincoln. When Morrie took the Embarcadero exit in Oakland, Gino followed. Turning right onto Embarcadero East, Morrie pulled over to the curb right after the ramp ended and stopped the car within view of the marina down the street. He left the keys in the ignition and deposited the wallet in the door compartment. He stepped out of the Lincoln, walked the twenty feet or so to the shore, and hurled the cell phone as far as he could into the water. It made a small splash and disappeared into the depths. Then he joined Carla who was waiting by the driver side door. Gino idled while they wedged themselves into the back seat of the Focus and then made a U-turn back to the freeway. They merged into the flow of traffic crossing over to San Francisco on the Bay Bridge. It was several minutes before Francesca broke the silence.

"I think that went well," she said. "I mean there weren't any other cars or pedestrians on the street and no buildings where someone could have looked out a window and seen us." She folded her arms across her chest and hugged herself. "Yes, I think it went well. And even more importantly, we've crossed another item off the list, so we're back to two."

****

Carla, resting her head against Morrie's shoulder as they drove on, felt freer than she'd ever felt before. Sal was gone, and she had the money. Free and clear. She'd told Morrie the whole story, and he hadn't flinched or pulled away when she told him why she'd taken it. He'd told her she had guts and that you couldn't steal from a thief. They owed her. And he'd never let anybody touch her again. And that's when she knew she loved Morrie. She opened her eyes and realized she was still wearing the rubber gloves. She lifted her hands and twisted her wrists. The gloves slipped off her hands and onto the floor. She kicked them aside and took a deep breath. Then a dark thought intruded. If Frankie were still looking for her, she wasn't free. But if Frankie couldn't find Sal, after a while maybe he'd let it go. Let her go. She pressed her face against Morrie's chest. She was kidding herself. She'd never be free. She was an idiot to think somebody like her could make it. She'd always be looking over her shoulder.

Another thought occurred and she brightened. She could change her name. Nobody would look for her if she got to be high class and had a new name. What would it be? She closed her eyes and considered the possibilities. And then Marie Taglioni danced through her thoughts. Marie, the most famous ballerina in Italian history. Marie, who'd taught the Queen of England how to curtsy and who taught at her own studio. Marie, whose picture she kept wherever she went. Carla opened her eyes and smiled. When this was over, she'd become Miss Marie. The last name was a problem, though. She wasn't a Taglioni, and it would be a sin to pretend she was. She'd have to work on that. But something would come to her. She just had to have faith.

****

Traffic slowed to a crawl as they approached the toll booth, and Francesca watched out the window as an egret picked its way through the tide flats. Gulls circled overhead and a marsh hawk skimmed the waterfront. Each one was looking for food. Everywhere you looked, every creature had the same basic drives. It didn't matter who you were. Rich, famous, homeless. Satisfy one need and another quickly took its place.

"I just had an idea," Francesca said and Gino glanced at her, waiting.

"It's got to do with one of the two," she held up two fingers, "things we have to do. Not the breaking and entering part, though. It's kind of taking things out of order. It's about maybe finding a way to get the police to check out the DeMontana garage." Carla leaned forward and placed a hand on each of the front seat headrests to listen. "I think we need to stop by the shelter and talk to Mary, if she's still there. She could have remembered something about the car that killed Bobby. If she's gotten sober, she might be some help." She looked at Gino and then back at Carla and Morrie. "It's just a thought," she said.

"Can't hurt," Carla said.

"Might prove helpful," Morrie said.

Gino rested his head on the steering wheel. "Oh hell. Why not."

****

"Now what?" Gino said. They were parked on Fifth Street close to St. Vincent de Paul's homeless shelter, watching and waiting for something to happen. What happened was that dinner was being served and the line of clients stretched down the street and around the corner. From the length of the line, people must have begun queuing up at noon.

"That's an awful lot of people," Francesca said. "How are we going to find her? I had this dumb idea we'd just wait at the front door and would see her when she went inside, but there's no way anybody is going to let us cut the line, and that's exactly what they'll think we're doing."

"We only saw her once for half an hour or so," Gino said. "And if she's cleaned up and put on some decent clothes, I'm not sure I'll know her. For that matter, she might not remember us and will start yelling crazy stuff again, thinking we're going to hurt her. And that could bring the cops. And that..." He shook his head. "I don't want to go there."

"Well, she's got frizzy hair and that nasty scar down her cheek," Carla said, opening the door. "I'm gonna look until I find her. She's got to be here." She climbed out of the Focus and directed her words at Gino. "She'll remember us. And we can tell her we'll take her out to dinner. Denny's has some great meal deals. You can get stuffed for cheap." She paused with her hand on the door handle. "You know, this is an awful lot like when we were looking for that car at the Italian Embassy. And we found it, even though most of them cars was black. This ain't any different except we're looking for people and they're different colors. Well, just a few basic colors in different shades. Like my grandmother. She's white but she's dark. I'm gonna start at the end of the line and move up."

"She has an interesting mind," Francesca said, following Carla's lead. "Well, nothing ventured, nothing gained. I'll take the front and work towards the middle. You and Morrie can start somewhere in what looks like the middle and one of you can work forward and one back. With all of us looking, we might get lucky."

Gino stood transfixed by the length of the line and the humanity that filled it. He'd gambled away more money than most of them would ever see in a lifetime and the realization hit home hard. Francesca touched his arm.

"Life throws us some curves. We all make choices. Some are good and some lead us into a dark place. If we're fortunate, we find our way out." She looked at the entrance to the shelter. "This is a way out."

"Not all of them look like they're here because of bad choices. Some of them seem really out of it. Why aren't they somewhere being taken care of?"

"Some of it could be drugs or alcohol, but then there's the other part. They closed the mental hospitals. Some people thought it was the right thing to do. Get the mentally ill out in the community where they could live among the rest of society. Intentions were good but not realistic. Not everybody fit into the master plan. Not everybody got helped. Funding stopped and people forgot. And this," she looked at the line, "is the result. Come on. We can only do what we can do. Let's go find Mary."

CHAPTER THIRTY-THREE

San Francisco

Francesca found Mary. The woman was smaller than Francesca remembered. She was barely five feet tall and slight of build. It must have been her anguish that night of the hit and run that had filled the area around her, amplifying her presence. She was cleaner than the first time they'd met, and while her hair was still wild and frizzy, she'd exchanged the worn wool cap for a purple and red model with earflaps. Gone also was the men's oversized winter jacket replaced by a better-fitting woman's tartan plaid car coat. Pink tennis shoes and green socks completed her outfit, and it was obvious Mary had left drab behind.

Her feet shuffled ahead when the line advanced, but her head was bowed and her lips moved. Francesca pursed her lips and wondered what that meant. This might be difficult if Mary had retreated into her mind and was living there. But then there was a small hand movement as Mary moved the Rosary beads to a new position. She was aware and alert. She wasn't talking to herself She was praying. Francesca stepped back and looked for Carla and the men. She waved and Carla responded with a wave of her own.

"She's over there," Francesca said, pointing in the direction where Mary stood in line. "She looks good. Really colorful, actually, but she's praying. I don't know if it's right to interrupt her."

Carla turned to face the line. "I don't see her. What do you mean 'praying'?" "She's saying her Rosary. I couldn't see how far she's gotten, but the beads moved in her hands. How long does it take to finish? Regardless,

I don't think we can wait until she finishes. She's getting close to the door." Francesca let out a breath. "I'm not Catholic, and I don't know how these things work. You got any suggestions?"

"The Rosary? You can always pick up where you left off. It ain't difficult. You got your basic Hail Mary's and then when you get to the end of that part you got the Glory Be. That's a good place to stop if you got to—before you get to the Our Father. If you can't see where she is and we interrupt her, she can always start at the beginning of the part she left off at." Carla searched the line for Gino and Morrie. "Let's get the guys together and figure out what to do."

"Agreed." Francesca made for the top half of the line, and Carla took the bottom. When they'd rounded up the men, they reconvened close to Mary. They spent a few precious minutes wondering what to do. Once Mary had gone inside, she'd likely be there for the night. Finally, it was Gino who made the decision.

"Let me talk to her. I know you're thinking that as women you'll have a better chance, but I think I can connect on a different level. Give me a few minutes. If things are going well, I'll signal and you come over." His jaw was set and Francesca saw a look in his eye she hadn't seen before. It was one of purpose and she liked it. What he did next surprised all of them, including Gino. Some things you don't let go of even when you've given up everything else, including hope.

Walking toward Mary, he took his mother's Rosary beads out of his pocket and let them dangle from his hand. A tinge of guilt for tossing the other beads out the window on his way to see his grandfather niggled at him, but they'd been an annoyance. These beads—he looked down at them—had belonged to his mother. Through all the anger he'd felt and the hatred of God that anger had inspired, he couldn't let the beads go. He didn't know why, and if anyone had told him he was still a Catholic in spite of his denial, he would have laughed. But some things persisted for reasons beyond simple comprehension. Maybe that's why he'd taken them with him when he'd left his grandfather's house and why he carried them in his pocket now. Maybe they had a purpose. As he approached Mary, he showed her his own Rosary. She paused in her prayers and looked at his hands.

"You a priest?" Her tone was dubious.

"No," Gino said. "I'm about the farthest from a priest you could find."

"I know you," she said.

"Yes," Gino said. "You do. I drove you here the other night with my friends." He pocketed the beads. "After the accident. We didn't want to leave you all alone and didn't know what else to do." He paused and looked at her face which she'd raised to meet his gaze. "I hope it was the right thing. Are they good to you here?"

She shrugged. "I've been here before. It's okay. They try." She put her Rosary in her coat pocket. "It doesn't matter."

"But it does matter," Gino said. "You can't give up. I know. This is my last chance. And I'm not giving up. I've got to make it work this time."

"I don't have Bobby." Her face grew dark, as if losing Bobby had taken all the light. "That devil car killed my Bobby." She turned away. "Devil car," she repeated, almost in a whisper. Her eyes widened. "You watch out for that demon car. It'll get you if you don't." She moved ahead in the line.

Something clicked in Gino's head and he played back in his mind what Mary had just said. Devil car they'd heard before. Demon car, that was new. What had she seen? "Mary," he said, "tell me about the demon."

She looked at him in a way he hoped never to see again in his life. Her eyes grew wild and burned with some inner fire. She trembled. "Demon," she said. "The devil is a demon. I know." She took a quick breath. "He writes it on his car. On the back where you can see his evil work when he goes away. Demon. Black-haired devil man." She took out her Rosary again and fumbled with the beads.

Gino thanked her but she'd forgotten him and was talking with God. The line moved towards the door and shortly she was inside the building. Demon, she'd said. Odd word. He chewed on his lip, thinking about what it could mean. And then he knew. Of course. Mary had given them the answer they needed.

CHAPTER THIRTY-FOUR

San Francisco

"Are you absolutely out of your ever-loving freaking mind?" Carla was using the best weapon she had. Her mouth.

"I don't think this is the best tack to take," Morrie said. "I mean, really."

"I still have part of my good name left," Francesca said, standing in front of Gino with her hands on her hips, incredulous. "*If* we discount my theft of a major piece of art and all the aiding and abetting that has gone into this little production, that is." There were two small spots of red by her cheek bones, and from every indication, the entire Francesca body was just as hot at him as her tone of voice and not hot at him in a good way.

Gino raised his hands in surrender. "It was just an idea," he said, "and apparently a rather lame one at that."

"Lame?" screamed Carla. "I'm thinking murder here." She pointed at him. "You!"

"Okay. Okay. I get the idea. Point taken," Gino said. "Maybe it wasn't the best idea, but it seemed like it might work. But okay, okay." He clapped his hands to his ears. "No go. It was just a thought. Sheesh."

The thought that had brought on all this vitriol was Gino's suggestion that they call the police, tip them off to Mary's whereabouts, and hint that she had more information to tell them about the hit and run. Mary hadn't understood that DEMON was a personalized license plate for Michael DeMontana's car, but even if she believed the devil had written his name on the back of the car, all she had to do was tell her story to the cops, and they would take it from there. Putting two and two together to make four was what they did. That was Gino's line of reasoning, anyway. But tipping off the cops had to come after planting the art in the car. Timing the plant and the tip so they'd converge at the right time was something none of them had figured out yet. And the clock was ticking.

They were back at Dark Mountain, having left the Focus with Ernesto who promptly drove it into the garage where Jeffrey was waiting for it at the paint station. They'd reclaimed the Volkswagen, and now Francesca and Carla were seated on the leather sofa, Francesca with the shirt box and Carla with her pocketbook. Gino was practicing his breathing exercises in an attempt to lower his blood pressure.

"Desperation," Morrie said, "is counterproductive. We're so close to the end that we're not planning the way we did in the beginning. Not," he looked at Gino and Francesca, "that I was involved at the beginning, but I am now." He paused. "That gives me an idea, actually," he said, his face visibly relaxing. "I need to call Joe." His eyes locked on Gino. "Joe Alderman, my buddy's rabbi. I think he can help us."

Gino wasn't saying much, having had his brilliant idea shot down in flames. But he was listening. "So this makes like what? Two hundred and eleven people involved now?"

"You gotta do what you gotta do," Carla said. "Sometimes you need to call in the reinforcements. We're lucky that we got a bunch of reinforcements. Think of how many people are in our place and don't got nobody to call. That's sad." She drew her knees up close to her chest and wrapped her arms around them. "We're lucky. And things are going okay now that we offed Sal. Well, he offed himself. And Mary's doing good, and we're almost done."

"Finished," Gino said. "We're almost finished. I can't see this turning out the way we want. It's gotten much too complicated. Too many people are involved, and I'm fresh out of ideas." Francesca stood and set down the shirt box which Carla wrapped an arm around for safekeeping. "What Morrie said made sense. Everything is working towards the final outcome. And even though we've had some setbacks, we're okay now and moving forward. Think of everything we've done so far and you'll see that we're on track. Now we need Mary to talk to the police, but we also need one of those degrees of separation to safely distance us from her testimony. Rabbi Alderman can do that, provided Morrie can convince him we're on the side of the angels, so to speak." She sat down and Carla handed back the shirt box.

"Kinda like passing around a baby with colic," Carla said, and Francesca nodded in agreement.

Gino gave up on the breathing exercises and decided to raid the wine cellar instead. He emerged fifteen minutes later with a half dozen bottles of differing vintage which he set on the wooden table in the kitchen. "This is what I know," he said. "I don't know shit about anything else."

Francesca shook her head and walked to Gino, draping her arm around his neck. "You want to bet?" she whispered in his ear. He grinned.

"All right. Maybe I know something about two things. But I admit, I'm way over my head in this whole fiasco. We need to wrap it up and soon. Or I'm dead." He grimaced and then let out a heavy breath. "Well, better to be honest, I guess. But you're right. This can still all work. But it damn sure better work fast."

****

An hour later they were back in the Bug and driving back to San Francisco. "I feel like a yo-yo," Francesca said. "Let's just stay at my place until we're done. It's not going to be much longer now, and we'll save time if we're close in. Besides, we brought the wine along. That'll be good for celebrating after we tie everything up. Six bottles." She smiled. "Yum."

Gino's expression was grim and his jaw tight. Today, tonight, or tomorrow was it. It was all the time they had. Once this final detail was set in motion, it couldn't be taken back. Whether the outcome would be in their favor or against them, it was too soon to tell. Everything hinged on Mary's willingness to share what she had told them, first with a stranger and then with the police. It was too much to ask of someone so unstable. He shifted in his seat so he could see Morrie.

"What do you know about this rabbi?"

"Not much," Morrie admitted. "He and Ernesto go back a long ways. But if you're wondering if we can trust this rabbi, you can relax. If Ernesto has arranged it, it will work. Trust me."

"I trust you. All I know about Ernesto is that he comes up with whatever we need when we need it and he paints cars in his garage."

"And that's all you need to know. It's better that way."

Gino turned back and looked out the window. They were so far into this now that one more shady connection didn't really matter. If it was all going to blow up in their faces, it would. Thinking about everything that could go wrong wouldn't change that. His thoughts were interrupted as Francesca pulled into the parking lot of Bagels and Lox and rolled into a parking space near the door. Inside, they wove through the line of customers waiting to place orders and found the table where Rabbi Joseph Alderman was doctoring a soy chai with enough raw sugar to create syrup. He looked up at the approaching entourage and stood to greet them.

"Nice touch," Morrie said, looking around at the display cases filled with about a hundred different types of bagels, a wide assortment of spreads, and a drink menu that covered everything from juice to java.

"You have to be true to your roots." Joe gave a broad smile. "And this seemed appropriate, given the circumstances." Joe Alderman was about thirty-five. He had a firm handshake and a swimmer's physique and was dressed casually in polo shirt, jeans, and sandals. The maroon kippah he wore atop his head was nearly the same shade as his dark red hair. Now he pushed the sugar container away and began stirring his slurry. He looked up and his expression grew serious. "Come. Sit and we'll talk. I understand you have a problem. At least that's what Ernesto said. How can I help?"

"I'll let Gino explain," Morrie said. "It's a complex issue."

There was an uncomfortable silence when everyone's eyes turned to Gino. He spread his hands on the small table and braced himself to tell part of the story one more time. "I'm not sure I know where to begin."

"If you don't know where to start, just say what's on your mind."

"Rabbi, it begins a very long time ago. It's a complicated story, and we're actually writing the ending, but how it ends depends to a very large degree on your role. Believe me, the less you know about most of this, the better."

Gino hesitated. "But what we'd like you to do isn't wrong. In fact, it's right. It's probably one of the few right things I've ever done. And yes, it will help us, but that's just a side effect. What will happen, if you can help us, is that a murderer—two murderers— will be apprehended and justice will be done." He looked at Joe with a steady gaze. "That's all I am going to say but it's the truth. I swear."

"I don't think you should swear in front of a rabbi," Carla said. "It don't seem proper. And I ain't swearing anymore. I've been improving myself," she confided in a voice loud enough to be heard at the cash register. "I got the swear thing down now."

Joe smiled. "Always a good course of action."

With nothing else coming from Carla, the rabbi turned his attention to Gino. "So, what is it you want me to do?"

Gino didn't hesitate. "There's a woman who witnessed a hit and run in San Francisco," he said. "She's currently at St. Vincent de Paul's homeless shelter and she's not very well connected to reality, but you stand for something she respects. She can tell the police the license plate of the car that killed her companion. Whether she will or not, is the question." Gino paused for breath. "Everything hinges on that. If you can help her make that decision and be with her when the police question her, we may have a chance."

Joe considered this. "Why do you think she'll talk to me?"

"Because she's a good Catholic," Carla said. "We saw her with her Rosary and she was moving right through the Hail Mary's real quick. So it just makes sense that she'll take to a rabbi. That's you," she added. "Besides, we're kinda desperate, and you're our only hope."

Joe's stir stick traced another swirl in the chai as he considered this twisted logic. He looked up. "Desperation and hope in the same sentence. That covers quite a lot of territory. But if hope is stronger than desperation, we may have a chance."

"Does that mean you'll help us?" Gino said.

"I'll do my best," Joe said. "Today's my day to visit the homeless shelter. Call it serendipity or Providence that my work coincides with your need. I don't judge these things." He stirred his chai yet again.. "Sometimes people just need to talk. I don't ask their religious affiliation." He smiled at Carla. "Give me the best description you can. I'll talk to her if she's there, and I'll wait while she talks to the police, if she wants me to." He took a sip of his chai and winced.

"Too much sugar?" Carla asked.

"No. Not enough."

CHAPTER THIRTY-FIVE

San Francisco

Gino stood by the window, hands locked behind his back, watching the activity outside. A bicycle darted in and out of traffic and a car horn blared the driver's disapproval. Probably jealous the bike messenger was making good time. A pedestrian threw caution to the wind and jaywalked across the street, a cab nipping at her heels most of the way. Two joggers ran in place at the corner, waiting for the light to change and revving up the step count on the pedometers strapped to their ankles.

A city truck pulled up to the fire hydrant outside Francesca's apartment and the driver got out and strolled to the back where the orange traffic cones were stacked. He took the top cone off the pile and tossed it onto the ground. The cone wobbled and tipped and he gave it a kick that set it upright. He repeated the process four more times, completing an arc from the back of the truck to a point at the curb just past the storm drain. He returned to the truck bed and hoisted a sandbag onto his shoulder for the short trip down the street to the last cone where he let the sandbag drop. He then ambled back to the truck and opened one of the toolboxes mounted along the side, from which he produced a wrench. Leaning against the truck, he lit a cigarette and took a couple of leisurely puffs before wrenching the hydrant open to flush the system. Water gushed from the hydrant and flowed down the gutter, pushing leaves and dirt and other debris along with it like a small tidal wave. The sandbag redirected the water down the drain through the sieve that blocked everything else and left a pile of trash in a heap atop the grate.

At once everything fell into place for Gino. He turned to Carla who was lounging on the couch painting her toenails Tangerine Tango and stuffing cotton balls between her toes as she went along. "Remember that brilliant idea I've been working on? I got it. We've been approaching this from the wrong angle. We've been trying to find a way to get into the garage to plant the Rembrandt just before the police arrive. That's not going to work on so many levels. First of all, we don't know when they'll get there. And we've been thinking of the police as one big unit. They've got departments that probably don't even read the memos sent over by other precincts; maybe don't even do more than scan those from another department in their own station. The cop investigating the hit and run won't be the same one who's tracking the art thefts. That's the first problem, and it's a big one."

"Yeah, Gino, but you gotta look at this the way the cops will. They find the car that did the hit and run and then find our painting in the car, they're gonna check it out. And that's all we need."

Gino nodded. "I know. But then, even if we plant the art, we don't know how to avoid being seen. If we stake out the house to wait for the best moment to dump the Rembrandt into the back seat or the front or wherever, somebody either walking down the street or looking out a window is going to notice us after a while and call us in. And what if Bianca or Michael come out and catch us in the act? That would be the end of us." He turned back to look at the driver slouched against the truck door smoking his cigarette while the water did its work.

"Whatcha looking at?" Carla wedged in the last cotton ball and padded over to the window, walking like a duck stuck in popcorn with Pierre trotting at her heels.

"I think I've got the answer to one of our problems. What do you see?" He moved back to give her the full view of the street below. "I'll give you a hint. It's moving fast."

"Like my life. I gotta get moving with my life. I been in a holding pattern, you know? Just like a sock stuck in the dryer going round and round and never getting anywhere. I don't want to be a sock." Gino put his arm around her shoulder. "You're not a sock. You never were and you never will be a sock. Now look out the window and concentrate. What do you see?"

"I don't know what you're seeing, but I see a shitload of water running down the street, and it's going down into the garage. Francesca'd better move the Bug or it's gonna be underwater." She looked towards the kitchen where Francesca was poised over the counter, a cookbook in one hand and a mixing bowl in the other. "You wanna give me the keys so I can move the car out of the garage? It's getting swamped in there." She bent down to test her polish and grunted. "I ain't dry yet, Gino. I'll smudge. You're gonna have to move the car."

"My point exactly. You've got to love San Francisco. So many garages are built on a downward slope. They fill up like a bathtub when the gutters are obstructed." He paused by the door, car keys in hand. "Even in Pacific Heights."

CHAPTER THIRTY-SIX

San Francisco

"Late night?" Inspector Liz Paone looked up from her paperwork at the bags under her partner's eyes and accepted the mega two-pump skinny vanilla latte he'd schlepped in from the local designer coffee shop.

"My head hurts," Steve said, collapsing into his desk chair and inhaling the steam from his own triple shot drip. He pried open the lid and sucked in a mouthful of caffeine.

Liz winced. "Careful, there. You'll scorch your gullet."

"My gullet is beyond scorching. It would take a blowtorch to rouse feeling." "Details?" She took a sip and shoved the latest BOLO aside to make room for her cup.

Steve took another healthy slurp. "I met up with my buddy Rick Sanchez from Northern Station last night. There was a Niners game on. I think they won. There was drink. I remember buying at least one round. Possibly more. Yes, definitely more." He took another slurp and rested the cup against his forehead. "I should know better. I'm a weak person."

"Stop wallowing. Drink your coffee. You'll feel better tomorrow."

Steve's reply was lost in the depths of his cup.

"Not to change the subject, but we've got the latest printout from Interpol." She took the paper from the stack by the phone. "They've arrested a suspect in connection with one of the European art thefts, but there's no evidence linking him with the rest of the European ones or our domestic problems. He's one of your opportunistic types." She lifted her glasses and twirled them around her finger. "This guy was an art student and decided drawing nudes in the museum was too distracting—too many critics walking by—so he figured he'd practice from the security of his own home. After class, he packed 'Women Bathers,' a Renoir, along with his supplies and went home. It was a convenient size, about sixteen by twenty inches. He got discovered when he tried to return it and check out another painting. Sort of like a lending library system without the library card. He's currently not painting anything. So, my suggestion is we forget about Europe and the east coast thefts for the moment. That leaves us with the nine Espositos and the Rembrandt close to home. Since those are the most recent, our thieves may still be somewhere close by. I sure would like to close this case."

"I'd like to blink without feeling my eyelids crash against my eyeballs."

"Stop complaining. You know what I find interesting is that our Ms. Fabriani, the uber-event planner, has dropped out of the social scene entirely. And for that matter, so has Mr. Puglisi. He was conspicuous in his absence at last night's soiree at the DeYoung."

"Maybe they ran off together to some South Pacific island. That would piss off Bianca to no end. On the other hand, maybe somebody else in the organization decided it was time to make a career move and Sal and Fabriani are swimming with the fishes. No small loss on either end. Not our problem." Steve finished off the first coffee and reached for the second. "Be right back," he said. "I think I'm rehydrated."

****

"You're vibrating," Liz said, pointing to the cell on Steve's desk. "It's been doing the hoochy-koochy since you left for the can."

"Nobody calls me," Steve said. "I'm not taking calls today." He pressed his fists against his temples. "I may never take calls again." He glowered at the phone and picked it up. His buddy Rick's number flashed across the screen, and Steve grumbled. "What?" he said, putting it on speaker and sinking into his desk chair. "That's no way to say hello to the guy who's going to make your day," Rick said, his voice distorted in the acoustical nightmare of the squad room. "And here I

was, all prepared to take you along."

"I repeat. What?" Steve said.

"What? That the best you can do? You're getting old, pal. Any day now, it's gonna be the walker and drooling into your gruel. Take the phone off speaker. The echo is driving me nuts. I bring glad tidings."

Steve pushed a button on the side of his cell. "That better?"

"Yeah. Anyhow, we got the paint analysis back from PDQ on that hit and run. And we had a major stroke of luck. The witness turned up at a homeless shelter and spilled the story to a rabbi who called it in. Sometimes, the stars are aligned in your favor. The witness was coherent and gave us a plate to run and a few sketchy details on the driver. *DEMON*. God, how I love vanity plates. Car belongs to a Michael DeMontana. Ring a bell?"

"Rings more than one bell. Yeah, I'll come along. Could get interesting. I'll be right there." He disconnected. "Gonna be our lucky day, after all, compadre," he said. "Sometimes I amaze myself. Who woulda thunk it? We were just swapping war stories last night and look at the result."

"Don't mean to sound obtuse here, but what are you talking about?"

"They made the car on that hit and run we were thinking DeMontana might have done. And, as usual, our customary brilliance was affirmed. Rick's waiting on a warrant to go over the car, and I," he made a small bow and then pressed his fingers to his forehead and grimaced, "am riding along on the bust."

Liz moved so fast her chair slid across the linoleum and bumped the water fountain. "Not alone, you aren't. I'm coming with you." She grabbed her keys and propelled Steve toward the door. "I'm driving. Move it."

CHAPTER THIRTY-SEVEN

San Francisco

The city truck with Jimmy Falcone at the wheel and Gino riding shotgun turned onto Van Ness. The transaction had taken less than a minute since Falcone was not opposed to augmenting his city salary with a tidy five bills just for making a short jaunt on his lunch hour. Besides, as Gino had pointed out, he was only improving the safety of the residents along the street in question.

"Gimme that address again," Falcone had said as he pocketed his windfall, crushed out the cigarette butt on the curb, and climbed into the driver's seat.

"We're on," Gino said to Francesca, who'd answered the cell midway through the first ring. "Get Carla and Morrie and bring the dog. Don't forget his leash. Grab the first parking space you can find near the DeMontana house." He disconnected, leaving Francesca staring at the cell and blinking hard.

She yelled to Carla who responded by dropping a tray of cookies onto the floor. Francesca picked up Pierre, snapped the leash onto his collar, and tossed Morrie his shoes. She handed the dog to Carla, grabbed the shirt box, and took the stairs two at a time down to the street.

"You want to fill me in?" Morrie said, as they rocketed down the street, "And slow down. This is no time for a traffic stop."

"Right." She hit the brakes which caused them to hit a red light at every intersection.

Morrie frowned. "Okay. Maybe a little faster. We've got to find the sweet spot to get through these at green or at least high orange." Pierre was on his lap, eyes fixed straight ahead, his little body on full alert. Morrie's eyes were also fixed straight ahead and he could feel his stomach muscles tightening. Carla was clutching the shirt box as if it would jump out of the car and fly away if she didn't have it in a death grip.

"What exactly did Gino say?" Morrie checked the rear view mirror.

"He just told me to get you and Carla and the dog and his leash and head for DeMontana's mansion. Oh Lord. This could be it. By tonight it could be all over and we could be free and clear. Or not," she added as traffic came to a halt. A Muni bus had hit a fire hydrant and a good imitation of Old Faithful was erupting at the corner. A growing crowd of interested spectators was watching the waterworks, among them the not so happy owners of the cars getting a free car wash at the curb. A flashing orange light caught Francesca's eye and she pulled over as far as she could towards the curb to let the city maintenance truck pass. Gino nodded from the passenger seat as they passed.

Pierre yipped a greeting and wagged his stub of a tail.

"I either had way too much coffee this morning or not enough," Carla said. "Whatever was supposed to happen doesn't appear to be going to happen anytime soon," Francesca said and Morrie agreed as the insistent wail of a fire siren grew closer.

Within a minute the engine had pushed past them and joined the city maintenance truck by the gusher. There seemed to be some kind of jurisdictional dispute between the city and the responding engine company, the hammering out of the details of which took precedence over the maimed hydrant.

Added to the mix was a waterlogged convertible which had been the primary recipient of the hydrant's outflow. The car's owner was irate, ignoring the fact that he'd parked illegally in front of the hydrant. His face had gone from red to purple and he was letting anyone within earshot know he was an attorney and he planned to sue the city for negligence, malfeasance, conspiracy, and a few other procedural motions nobody else understood or cared about. All in all, it was a splendid show. San Francisco at its best. Any other time, it would have been an interesting diversion. Now, it was a roadblock of mammoth proportions and there was no way around it. The Bug was hemmed in with no place to go until the problem was taken care of.

"So here we sit," Francesca said, pounding her fists on the steering wheel. "This could be bad if they don't get traffic moving again soon. Mary's told the cops her story, and I'll bet they're already on their way to arrest Michael. We've missed the only chance we had to plant the shirt box." Tears of frustration were almost ready to break free and run down her cheeks. "So close, so close."

Carla leaned forward from the back seat and patted her on the shoulder. "You gotta have some faith. I already said a prayer to St. Jude, so we're gonna be fine. He's working on it right now." Carla gave a look upwards at the patch of sky from which St. Jude would be getting the matter under control.

"Right." Morrie said. "Peachy." He looked at the mess around them. "And just what is this St. Jude of yours going to do about our situation?"

"Dunno. That's where the faith thing comes in. But I do know one thing. You gotta recognize the opportunity when it shows up and make your move pronto. These saint guys are busy people. They don't hang around waiting for you to get the idea."

"Ah," Francesca said. "Subtle. Sounds almost Buddhist."

"I don't know from Buddhist," Carla said. "But like I said, you gotta recognize the opening."

****

Three cars back, Inspectors Liz Paone and Steve Cranston were also playing the waiting game. "That's a classic," Liz said, her eyes on the Bug. "It's even orange. I always wanted one of those. I used to dream about taking it down the coast to Mexico. Just me. Lost in the '60s." She sighed. "There was so much positive energy then. That was a generation that asked a whole lot of questions and got answers. Today we've just got more and more questions and no answers."

"So why didn't you?"

"Why didn't I what?

"Buy the car and take the trip."

She shrugged. "Life intruded. I grew up. I got married, had a kid. It was a dumb dream anyway. Come on. Let's see what's happening up ahead since the boys in blue aren't here yet." She took a last slurp of coffee and opened the car door. "Watch out for your designer loafers. We've got a river here," she called over her shoulder. "Nice wheels," she said to Francesca as she passed by.

At the accident scene, the attorney had lost whatever control he'd had and was banging on the door of the Muni bus with a jack handle he'd taken from the trunk of his drowned car while the driver sat inside doing paperwork. Francesca watched the woman who'd admired the Bug flip open a wallet and show something on the inside of it to the attorney who hesitated only briefly before dropping the jack handle and stuffing his hands into his pockets. Francesca slipped down in the car seat as far as she could and groaned. They'd been made. The nice lady was a cop.

****

Gino wasn't slinking down in the passenger seat of the city truck. He'd remembered the second lesson of his online course in body posture and was portraying himself as confident and in control. The instructor assured that if you modeled the behavior you wanted, you'd internalize that behavior. So far it seemed to be working. Nobody was eyeing him suspiciously or paying him any attention at all. He'd taken a clipboard Falcone had set on the dash and was busy not reading the page he'd flipped over to. A pencil gripped in his teeth, he looked like he belonged in the truck. And that was just fine. Especially since the cops had arrived.

"We have to abort," Francesca said. "There's no way we can let the Bug be seen in Pacific Heights. She'll remember it and she'll start to wonder. No. As soon as we can turn around, I'll head back home. Maybe something else will come up. Maybe not. Nothing's working right." She fished her cell out of her purse and called Gino.

"We'll be moving soon," he said, by way of greeting. "They've got the water shut off and the yellow tape's around the hydrant area. We're waiting on the tow for the bus, and that'll open up the road. Just hang tight."

"We can't," she said. "The cops have noticed my car and even talked to me about it. That lady cop up there. The one dealing with the angry guy. There's no way we can take the VW for the drop. We have to go back." She didn't even think to ask him why he was sitting in the water truck. Carla grabbed the phone out of her hand.

"What are you doing in that truck? And talk some sense into your girlfriend here. We can't go back. We gotta get this done now before I get a case of the heebie jeebies. We ain't making no forward motion here, and that's not good. And I mean more than the traffic jam. So spill it. What's the plan? We know what it is, we can figure out another way to get it done. Talk to me, Gino." She put the phone on speaker and handed it to Morrie. "Don't let her have it back until we find out what's going on." Francesca glowered but didn't try to take the phone back. They stared at the phone, waiting for Gino to come up with something.

"Can't talk now," Gino said. "The driver's coming back. Just get to the DeMontana house as soon as you can. Gotta go."

"See?" Carla said.

"See what?" Francesca said. "I don't see anything except years in the state penitentiary." She banged her forehead against the steering wheel.

"No. Don't be like that. Look. You gotta trust Gino. You do, don't you?" Francesca's head bobbled on the steering wheel. Carla took that for an affirmative. "You sure are taking out a lot of negative energy on that steering wheel, but you don't want it to collect there. You gotta get rid of it." She opened the window and made shooing motions with her hands. And just then, the opening she'd predicted came. Just like that. She slapped Morrie on the shoulder and let out a hoot. "Come on. There's no time to waste. You got change in your purse?"

Francesca lifted her head and looked at Carla as if she were speaking some extinct foreign language.

"Change?"

"Yeah, honey. Change. You got change?" "Sure. I guess so."

"Good. We're getting on that bus that's coming to take those passengers." She jerked her head towards the bus waiting across the street for the stranded passengers who were weaving their way through the traffic towards their new ride. "Once we're on, we'll get the route schedule and transfers if we need them. If that bus isn't going to Pacific Heights, another one will. So you've got your purse and the shirt box. You can do that. You gotta. You're an event planner. So goddammit, plan! I'll take Pierre. They let dogs on the bus. We'll meet Morrie there as soon as he can arrange some different wheels. Right, Morrie?"

Morrie held up a hand for silence. He was already on the phone. Francesca looked at Carla and groaned. She reached for her purse and the shirt box, squared her shoulders, and the women left the Bug to join the queue waiting to board the bus.

CHAPTER THIRTY-EIGHT

San Francisco

SFPD arrived at the scene of the waterworks to mop up and take custody of the attorney who'd been stuffed in the back seat of Liz and Steve's sedan. He'd finally shut up and acted like a spoiled child that for once hadn't gotten his own way by screaming and throwing a tantrum. Disturbing the peace and vandalism with an illegal parking citation thrown in for good measure would keep him from ambulance-chasing for the next twenty-four hours.

"First kill all the lawyers," Steve muttered.

Liz raised an eyebrow. "We're feeling better, I see. You're back with Shakespeare. But they're not all like our friend here. Sort of a necessary evil. Like Internal Affairs."

Steve grunted. "Yeah, well, I wouldn't want my sister to marry one."

"Your sister *did* marry one. Remember Bob? Your brother-in-law? The guy you shoot pool with every Friday night?"

"He's different. He's corporate."

"Changing the subject," Liz said. "Do you believe in synchronicity?"

"Do I believe in what?"

"Synchronicity. It's like when you see one thing that's different, pretty soon you see another of the same thing. Especially if you've never seen or noticed anything like it before. For example, like if you have a headache," she looked pointedly at her partner, "you start seeing ads for pain relievers everywhere. And like that car I was drooling over. I can't remember the last time I saw an orange Volkswagen, but there's another one. The last one had a woman driving." She watched as the unsnarled traffic began moving along and the Bug passed by. This one's got a man at the wheel. Synchronicity."

"It's time to go, Liz. You've been thinking way too much. Let's go catch some bad guys."

CHAPTER THIRTY-NINE

San Francisco

Jimmy Falcone worked at the carefully measured pace of a city employee. He parked the truck ahead of the fire hydrant and leaned against the passenger side door, doing a couple of stretching exercises as mandated by the Working Safe video he'd spent yesterday afternoon viewing without the benefit of popcorn or a cold drink. He handed Gino a sandbag while he set out the orange safety cones. "We put them down just after the storm sewer so the water flows into it." Gino nodded and Falcone turned away to attend to the hydrant. Gino set the sandbag down at the curb by the edge of the DeMontana driveway, a good twenty-five feet away from the drain.

"You gotta admire the power of water," Falcone said, as the torrent rushed down the gutter until it reached its diversion point, after which it made a forty-five degree change of direction and surged down the driveway, pooling at the garage door before finding a weak spot that gave it entrance to the interior.

Ten minutes later, Falcone checked his watch and reached for the wrench. "That'll do 'er," he said, closing the connection and tossing the cones back into the truck. "Sometimes people play with them sandbags," he said, retrieving the bag. "Kids usually. Can't watch everything." They climbed back into the truck, and Falcone dropped Gino off two blocks away.

Their exit was complemented by the appearance of the Larry's Lawn Maintenance truck that pulled into the driveway. Morrie got out, picked up a brochure from the front seat, kicked the door shut, put on a pair of gardening gloves, and strolled to the front door. Along the way, he pulled up a clump of grass and examined it with care. Greenery in hand, he leaned on the doorbell until Michael DeMontana answered it.

Michael DeMontana was not interested in any promotional discounts for lawn maintenance, had no plans to change providers, did not want to hear anything about the lawn mites that were consuming his grass, nor did he want the sales flyer. Morrie, aka Larry, was disappointed his sample wasn't enough to convince the homeowner of the necessity of proper drainage, so he stepped back and offered the wet driveway as further evidence.

Michael pushed past Morrie to check out the situation. He punched the code into the keypad and the door opened, revealing inches of water swirling about the garage floor. Morrie tried his sales pitch once more, but Michael was not hearing any of it.

"Get out!" Michael yelled. "Get the hell out of here!" He looked frantically at the water soaking into everything.

Morrie returned to the truck and removed his gloves. He backed out of the driveway and found a parking space half a block away. He called Gino. "I love freestyling," he said.

****

Michael's outburst had brought Bianca to the garage from the second floor where she'd been pacing, waiting to hear from Sal. "What on earth is all the yelling about? Oh my God. What is this?"

"It's water, Bianca. What the hell does it look like? The question is where is it coming from?" He looked down at his feet which felt wet. He cursed again. "This is insane. Look at my shoes." He slammed his fist against the wall, making a sizeable dent in the sheetrock. He recoiled from the impact and cradled his hand.

"We've got to get the cars out of here," she said. "Then maybe we can see better where the water's coming from. We'll have to get the place mopped out. I'll get the keys." She turned back to the stairs. "Wait. I can't take the

Mercedes out of the garage. It's hot. I need at least a month before I can move it and get it fixed. You want to bring the cops down on us?"

Bianca stood by the door, hand on the knob. "Take it out and cover it. There's a tarpaulin on the top shelf over there." She gestured toward the far wall. "Nobody will notice anything. Everybody covers their cars to keep the dirt off when they're not in use. Just do it, Michael. I'm calling the plumber."

"What good is a plumber going to do? Go wading? Call the city. It's probably a storm drain or a sewer backed up."

She gave him a hateful look and slammed the door. Michael hurled a string of curses at the place where she'd stood.

****

The route Francesca and Carla took was a straight shot on the number 24 to Fillmore Street at Pacific Heights. From there they walked, Pierre on his leash, trotting along and checking out every spot of interest along the way.

"Relax," Carla said. "We're just walking the dog. I think I know what Gino's up to. We're gonna walk right on past the DeMontana house, and nobody ain't gonna look at us twice. Everybody walks their dogs."

"I know," Francesca said. The shirt box was beginning to crumple at the edges from the constant pressure of her hands. She pushed back a strand of hair from her forehead and looked at her burden with a mix of fear and loathing. "When this is over, I'm never going to look at cardboard again." She laughed. "Okay. That sounded stupid."

"No. At least you're talking more positive now. Couple of hours ago, you didn't think you had no future at all. I told you." Carla pointed at the heavens. "You gotta have faith."

"I feel like I'm out in the open with a big sign on me that says *Art Thief* and everybody knows what's in the box and the police are just waiting for the right moment to pull up alongside us and arrest us."

"Could happen, I suppose," Carla said. "Anything's possible. But it ain't likely. We're just two dog-walking buddies. And for all anybody knows, that box is full of dog biscuits." At that moment, her phone rang. "It's Morrie," she said, "and he's got us a sweet ride. Or so he says."

"Where is he?"

"Waiting for us in the next block. Gino's with him and he wants a war council. So, let's get our asses in gear and find out what's next."

****

"Larry's Lawn Maintenance?" Francesca's jaw dropped. "Is this for real?" Morrie handed her a flyer. "Real as it gets. I'm doing cold calls for my buddy.

Would you be interested in our special of the month?"

"No thanks. I'm good. But if it's not too much to ask, now what?"

"Good question," Gino said. "Morrie's about to do a drive-by and see if our plan to smoke, or rather, soak Michael's car out of the garage worked. If it did, all that's left to do is tuck the Rembrandt into the front seat just before the police show up with their warrant."

"That's all, huh?" Francesca said.

"Yep," Morrie said. "Easy. Timing is everything, but we'll figure it out. Diversion is my middle name. I'll be back in a minute. Hold the fort." True to his word, Morrie was back within a couple of minutes. "Beautiful," he said. "Primo. The car's out of the garage, and DeMontana is struggling with a tarp he's trying to put over it. I'd give him a couple more minutes to be sure. He doesn't look like he's had a whole lot of practice with the process."

"All right," Gino said. "Francesca and I will walk Pierre down the street. While he's doing his business at the curb by the house, I'll plant the art and then rejoin Francesca as she's poop-scooping."

"Thanks so much," Francesca said, "but I stole the art, and I'm going to do the planting. You can poop-scoop."

"Listen, if something goes wrong. And I'm not saying anything will, but just in case it does, I will not let you take the brunt of it. You're not going to jail. Period. End of discussion. Subject is closed. I am planting the art."

"You're not telling me what to do with the art I stole. Stealing it was my idea. I've been carrying it around like a newborn baby, and I am going to stuff it in the car." She shook her head. "That didn't come out right. Regardless, I have no intention of getting arrested and going to jail."

"Both of you stop. Now. This is no time for a power play. We've all got jobs to do, and if any one of us screws up, we're all going up the river. So bag it." Morrie took what looked like an oversized cell phone and brought up an app. "I'm going to park across from the house. When you get to the driveway, I'll unlock the car with this." He held up the device. "You," he pointed to Gino, "reach under the tarp, open the car door, and drop the painting on the front seat. Close the door and let the tarp fall back down. Then, I'll relock the car. While this is going on, Carla will be into her political survey spiel with whoever answers the door. When they're at the door, they can't see what's happening in the drive. The garage is to the right of the drive and will be out of their view. Carla will keep them distracted. While they're trying to figure out what the hell Carla's talking about, or even better, trying to get rid of her, Gino gets safely back to Francesca who's been waiting for Pierre to finish up his business." He looked at Pierre. "That's your job, and we're counting on you to do a big one." Pierre wagged his tail and yawned. Morrie frowned. "Whatever. I'll relock the car door and drive around the corner where we'll meet. Once we're all in the truck, we're out of here. The rest is up to the police. God help us. We've only got one shot at this." Francesca huffed but nodded and turned over the shirt box to Gino. Carla produced a poop bag from her purse and handed it to Francesca. Morrie handed Gino a pair of latex gloves. "Don't forget to use these. And here's a shopping bag for the art. It'll be easier to get at it if it's not in the box." Gino nodded and slipped the painting from the box into the bag. Morrie took the empty shirt box and tossed it into the truck bed.

Carla was studying a clipboard with a list of the current propositions under consideration before the next election. "Where'd you get this?"

"Larry does this in his spare time for extra money. He's always on the hustle. Just read what it says word for word. Be persistent. It's one of your stellar qualities. There's probably a city ordinance against going door to door to solicit people's opinions," Morrie said, "but if anybody calls you on it, just smile." He kissed her on top of the head. "Okay folks. It's showtime."

CHAPTER FORTY

San Francisco

"Michael, would you come away from the window. The car isn't going anywhere. It's covered up, and it's going to sit there until the garage gets cleaned out and the water problem fixed." Bianca was checking her cell messages for the twelfth time that hour, waiting for a call from Sal. It wasn't like him not to check in, even after the row they'd had. He'd never kept her waiting like this. She tried his number again. Nothing. She walked to the kitchen, set her cell down, and lit a cigarette.

She walked back to the living room window and checked the street. They had to move the art out of the house and get it safely to Palermo. No worries about the police there. Everything would be fine. And for that, she needed Sal. Three packing crates in the library were waiting to be loaded and shipped. She ran her fingers through her hair and let the blonde strands fall back against her cheeks. She felt cold and she wrapped her arms around herself. It wasn't the temperature. It was worry. She'd thought it all out. She'd made no mistakes. But now everything seemed unsettled. It wasn't a good feeling. She left the window and returned to the library.

"Come on, Michael. Help me with this and stop wasting time. Sal will be back sometime this afternoon, and these need to be ready to go when he gets here."

Michael picked up the remote from the coffee table and turned on a local station. "Shut up and get off my back. If there's nothing to worry about, there's nothing to worry about. Or so you say. Maybe. I still don't like having the car out in the open. Covered or not, it's still there."

"If you're waiting for breaking news on your accident, it's old news, Michael. Nobody cares. Nobody cared then, and nobody cares now. Nobody gives a shit about what happened. Relax. It's been days. The police have more to do than devote their energies to hunting you down. Nobody is looking for you. Now help me." She flicked a bit of cigarette ash from her sleeve and dropped the butt into a flower vase on the sideboard.

"Just a minute." He turned up the volume and tossed the remote onto the recliner. "All right. Anything to get you to shut the hell up. What do you need?"

"Set up the work table and cut the foam core. The box cutter's over there with the plastic wrap." She waved a hand in the direction of a pile of Styrofoam sheets stacked by the wall. "Take two sheets for each painting. Set them on the table and lay a painting on top. Cut the foam two inches bigger than the frame all the way around. Then put one piece on top of the painting and the other on the bottom. You hold the foam in place while I wrap the plastic around it. Then we'll slide each painting into its slot in the crate. Three slots, three paintings in each one. Then you nail the crates shut. You need me to write it down for you or can you manage to remember all by yourself?" She reached for the first painting and waited while Michael got the foam. "After that, we wait for Sal."

Michael smothered a curse and grabbed the first sheet of foam core off the pile. He knocked it against the table as he turned around and the foam split in half. He shoved both pieces aside and kicked them into the corner. He reached for another piece. "This is a bunch of crap. It falls apart if you look at it." He picked up a roll of packing tape and ripped off a healthy piece that immediately flipped back on itself and stuck together in a wad which didn't want to release its grip on his hand. He shook his hand back and forth until the tape flew off and joined the broken foam core on the floor. "I don't see..."

"Shut up. Where's the remote? Dammit, where is it? Where did you put it? Hurry up!" Bianca was staring at an image on the television screen and waving her hand at Michael.

"It's on the table. Open your damn eyes. What the hell's the matter with you? First you didn't want the television on. Now you're all bitchy about the sound. Make up your goddamn mind."

Bianca strode from the library and grabbed the remote from the chair seat where Michael'd thrown it. She stood facing the television, her mouth slack-jawed, the remote dangling from her hand. The television showed an area cordoned off by police tape and some police moving about the scene.

"...the body found in the trunk allegedly identified as that of Jennifer Fabriani, society caterer. Police say the vehicle is registered to reported mob boss Salvatore Puglisi, currently under indictment for federal income tax evasion. Stay tuned for further developments as they become available."

The news anchor looked appropriately concerned, and Bianca powered off the television and sank into the recliner, her face ashen.

"That bitch finally got hers," Michael said. "Did you tell Sally to off her, or was it his own idea? Told you it wasn't a good idea to piss him off. He plays rough. No wonder he hasn't come back. He's probably half way to Sicily by now. You're not going to see him again anytime soon."

"*Minchia. Merda.*"

"Eloquent as usual, Auntie. Now what?"

Bianca ran her hands through her hair and then rubbed her forehead. "Cut. We've still got to box these up and get them ready to ship. I want them out of the house. There's too much at stake to stop now. I don't need Sal. I'll call Frankie, and he'll send someone else to help with the cleanup." She left Michael surrounded by foam and fled to the kitchen where she retrieved her cell. Five minutes later she returned to find Michael still wrestling with the second sheet of foam. "Frankie's been arrested. He's being held incommunicado. I couldn't get any information on him at all. Nobody wanted to talk."

"Phone's probably bugged. And that means they know who called. You can probably expect a knock on the door any moment. Guilt by association and all that. You can kiss your ass goodbye. Way to go, Bianca."

She cradled the cell in one hand and covered it with the other, as if to keep it from listening to her. "What if I destroy it now?"

Michael shook his head. "Too late. You called. They got your number. But so what? They have to know by now you and Sally are related. Me too. So what? It's no big secret. It just means you've got to be careful. That's what you've been telling me all along, at least. Now you need to take your own advice. What else did they say? And who did you talk to? How do you even know you were talking to the Club? You could have had a direct line to the Feds for all you know."

Bianca released her grip on the phone and pressed her palms to her temples. "Vito Alfredo. He's the new manager. No. It was the Club. I could hear background noises. Music. Loud voices. When they told me Frankie'd been arrested, I asked for Rico. You know what they told me?" Her eyes were wide in disbelief. "He's dead. And so's Tony. Both of them. Shot in the head and dumped in the canal. Dear God, this isn't good. What's happening? Maybe Sal didn't leave. Maybe he's dead too." Her voice rose to a frantic pitch. "We've got to get out of here. We can't wait for tomorrow. They could be coming for us, for all we know. We've got to get the art out of here. That's the only thing they can tie us to. When it's gone, we don't have anything to worry about."

"The car?" Michael reminded her. "Remember the car that wasn't anything to be concerned about?"

She chewed on her lip. "Maybe a fire in the garage to get rid of your car." She shook her head and dismissed the thought as quickly as it had come. A flooded garage doesn't burst into flames, and a fire wouldn't hide the front end damage anyway. They had to get rid of the car, too. Should have done that at the beginning. It was too late to get rid of the car. Today was all they had and maybe not all of that.

Michael turned the television back on. "We might have other problems. If Sal's gone, who's next in line? Who's he loyal to? Or is another family moving in?"

"I don't know. Maybe DellaPietra? He and Sal go way back, and there's no love lost there. If there's a takeover, we're not going to be safe. But we've still got the art. He doesn't know how much I kept back and shipped back to Sicily. It's worth millions. Plus, we've got all the DeMontanas my husband left me." She frowned. "But we've got to get the Espositos and us packed up and out of here today. We need to get back home. I'll call the transport van and have them come right away." She looked at Michael, still wrapping the paintings. He could handle this part on his own. She didn't have to hang around and wait for the transport van. Let Michael do that. It was the least he could do, and not even Michael could screw this up. No. She watched him slip a painting into the slot in the packing box. Time to get out while the getting was good. She took the cigarette packet out of her pocket and palmed the last two inside. She crumpled the cellophane and tossed it on the table. "I'm out of cigarettes. I'll be right back. You finish up."

Michael resumed cutting the foam core. "When is Cargo Transport picking this up?

"Four-thirty, they said."

"I'll have this ready within the hour. We clean up so there's no trace of what we did, and we're out of here and at SFO before cocktail hour. Which," he added, making a slice in the foam core, "is not going to come any too soon."

CHAPTER FORTY-ONE

San Francisco

There wasn't much traffic outside Northern District station house and when a patrol car passed by en route to a call, Steve Cranston looked up from his coffee. "I have lived too long. My way of life has fallen into the sere," he muttered, testing the temperature of the dregs with an index finger.

"Good," Liz said. "When you start quoting Shakespeare, I figure you've decided to live. But if you're referring to the donuts, your way of life is secure. By my count, you've eaten five, including the one I was saving for later."

Steve opened the window and dumped the cold coffee onto the pavement. "No, not the donuts, although that's part of it. I miss the old days. The cop on the beat, twirling his baton, passing the time of day with pedestrians, and stopping to check the doorknobs on the block to be sure everything was safe and secure. You don't see cops doing that anymore."

"You don't hardly see *pedestrians* any more unless they're running or jogging, and even then, they're tuned out to the world around them. Everybody's gone mobile. They've all got ear buds blasting music into their heads while the scenery passes by, oblivious to everything else around them." She tapped her fingers on her coffee cup. "I hate to wait. How long does it take to get a search warrant? And you were never a beat cop anyway. You worked homicide."

"It takes as long as it takes," Steve said. "And there's nothing wrong with a little nostalgia. Humor me. But as for DeMontana, we don't cross all the *t's* and dot all the *i's* and his *consigliere* will be at the station house with a fully legal demand for a motion to suppress and for us to release his client before we've even parked the car. And this is one time I want the charges to stick like glue. So, when you've got that plus chasing down a judge who'd rather be finishing up his golf game, it can take a long, long time." He opened the car door and stepped outside. "Patience."

Steve and Liz were cooling their heels and their coffee in the parking lot behind Northern Station on the corner of Turk and Fillmore, waiting for Sanchez to track down a magistrate judge to sign the search warrant.

"This building has no charm," Liz said. "It looks like they remodeled a bus station or a car dealership and bricked in the windows with blue tiles. Then they tried to artsy-fartsy it up with those enormous concrete sculpture faces of cops. They scare me. It's an architectural nightmare. The old station was better. It had an understated charm. It had presence. And those really cool light fixtures with the spiky feathers at the top. That, Cranston, was a police station. It was a solid building that conveyed exactly what it stood for. Now, we've got this thing." She curled her lip at the current architecture.

"Times change," Steve said. "That was my point, if you remember how this conversation started. You didn't have to pass through security to get inside a police station once upon a time, either. Now it's all locked down tight. We didn't wear Kevlar back in the day. Now it's a different game. But we're not the ones who changed the rules. Adapt or die, partner." He flexed his knuckles and stretched. "I'm getting out. You coming?"

"Might as well." She tipped the empty donut box and coaxed out the last few crumbs. "Seeing as we've run out of food here. Let's see if their coffee's any worse than ours."

****

Inside the briefing room at Northern District, Sergeant Rick Sanchez, Incident Commander for the warrant service, was at the computer console at the left front corner of the room. Above his head, a monitor displayed an aerial map of the DeMontana neighborhood, and the image was duplicated on a larger screen on the center wall. On the interactive white board mounted next to the screen, Sanchez had drawn an operational diagram indicating where each officer would be positioned. "Almost ready," he said.

"I have to admit," Steve said to Liz as they took their seats, "this beats the hell out of the old days of chalk dust and bad photocopies." He nodded a greeting to Sergeant Doug Brown, the fourth member of the team who joined them as Sanchez got up from his position at the console and walked to the center screen.

"Good afternoon," Sanchez began. "The judge has signed the search warrant, so we'll begin the briefing. Inspectors Paone and Cranston will be assisting Sergeant Brown and myself." He pointed to the front display monitor.

"We'll start with known elements. The house has two approaches to cover— front and back doors—in addition to low casement windows that could provide a means of egress along the east side of the structure. Inspector Paone will cover those windows, and Inspector Cranston will secure the rear entrance." He turned back to the officers. "Sergeant Brown has done the drive-by. There is an automobile in the driveway. It's covered by a tarp, and it may or may not be the vehicle in question. Subject vehicle is a black 2012 Mercedes SL, LC: DEMON. The vehicle may have sustained significant front end damage."

Sanchez picked up a piece of paper from his desk and moved to the inside of the front row. He shifted his weight so that most of his two hundred pounds was balanced on the edge of the desk.

"Just so you know." Sanchez looked down at the printout. "Forensics identified our homeless hit and run as Marine Lance Corporal Robert Richard Scofield, combat-wounded in Afghanistan. Purple Heart recipient." He looked up at his team. "Just so you know," he repeated. He set the paper down. "There are two known occupants at the address— Michael DeMontana, registered owner of the vehicle, and Bianca DeMontana. We are not aware of any dogs or children on the premises." Sanchez pointed the remote at the center screen and a photo of Bianca and a mug shot of Michael appeared. Liz leaned forward, and Sanchez responded to the unasked question.

"DeMontana has a rap sheet that goes from here to Marin. No convictions. All right," he said. "On to unknown elements. This operation has high-risk potential. We'll need to take all precautions. You can expect the residence to contain weapons. The DeMontanas are related to the Puglisi Crime Family.

"I'll do the knock and announce. Inspector Brown will assist. Once the target has been detained, Inspectors Paone and Cranston will conduct a safety sweep of the residence. Be aware there is a basement and also a second floor. Access to the second floor is via a staircase to the right of the main entrance. Questions?" Sanchez waited and then nodded. "If not, all right then. Let's roll."

CHAPTER FORTY-TWO

San Francisco

Gino squeezed Francesca's hand for luck as they crossed Steiner to Washington and started down the sidewalk, Pierre trotting ahead on his new blue leash. A jogger surged past them on the left causing Pierre to yip. Gino shifted the grocery bag so it was protected by his chest.

Up ahead the lawn truck was waiting and Carla, pen in hand and the clipboard cradled in the crook of her arm, was three doors away from the DeMontana house when she stopped short. Bianca DeMontana emerged from the house, got into an Escalade, backed out of the short driveway, and sped away down the street. Carla tightened her grip on the clipboard and turned slightly to check on Gino and Francesca's progress. They were right on schedule. Time to ring the doorbell and get Michael DeMontana away from the windows so he wouldn't be able to see what was happening in the driveway. She squared her shoulders and continued up the path to the front door. She rang the doorbell.

Michael answered the bell on the second ring, but when he saw that Carla wasn't the driver for the pickup, he told her he wasn't interested in whatever she was selling and attempted to close the door in her face. She stepped closer. He backed slightly and she pressed forward, blocking his side view and insinuating herself between him and the door.

"This coming election could be the most important in the history of San Francisco," she read and then looked up from her clipboard and smiled. She ran her tongue across her lower lip and leaned forward. Her voice was husky. "Do you vote?" She lowered her eyes and continued reading. "This election needs your vote." She smiled again. "Will you support a ban on plastic?" she asked. "Plastic?" Flustered, Michael found himself in the awkward position of needing to push past the young woman to get back inside his own house.

"Do you mind?" she asked, thrusting the clipboard at him and shrugging out of her sweater. "It gets so hot when you're working. I get hot," she said and smiled for the third time. She reached for the clipboard and heard the sound of the lawn truck starting up. "Okay. You change your mind," she said, turning to give him the full benefit of her profile, "you can always sign up later." She turned and walked back down the path to the sidewalk, her heart pounding and her pulse racing. A man and woman with a small black poodle at the intersection waited to cross the street. She came up beside them and they crossed together.

"My teeth are chattering," Francesca said. "They've done this ever since I was a kid. When I get nervous they sound like castanets."

"How'd you do?" Carla asked and Gino folded the empty shopping bag in half in reply. "Empty is good," she said. "Now Francesca won't have to go to the pen."

"There is that to be thankful for," Francesca said.

"We're done, but it's not done until the cops arrest Michael and follow the art trail from the car to the house" Gino said. "And we're not going to know about it when it happens. That part is killing me."

"The police can come anytime now," Francesca said. "I'm all planned out."

****

Ten minutes later, at four-thirty on the dot, the overseas transport van arrived at the DeMontana mansion. The driver opened the back doors, released the ramp, and wheeled the dolly to the front door. He kicked the door twice with the steel toe of his work boot, his hands being otherwise occupied with entering the address and his arrival time on the electronic data device. He waited another thirty seconds and gave another kick. This time he met with success.

"What the Sam Hill do you think you're doing?" Michael stood in the doorway, his eyes traveling to the scratches and dents that now bruised the bottom panel of the mahogany entrance. That was the last he had to say on the matter, as he looked up into the unconcerned face of a three hundred pound behemoth with no neck, biceps the size of bowling balls, and *Bill* embroidered on the left pocket of his gray uniform.

"You got a pick up." The voice didn't invite any argument.

Michael shot one final disapproving glance at the man's footwear and motioned him inside. "The crates are in the library. Down the hall, first room on the left."

Bill maneuvered the dolly down the hall, managing to sideswipe two tables and the baseboard before he negotiated the entry to the library.

"These three," Michael said. "And be careful with them. They're well packed, but they're still fragile."

"I don't take no responsibility for fragile," Bill said. "That's between you and the company. You got them packed right, we got no problems. You don't..." he shrugged and tipped the edge of one crate as he slid the dolly underneath. "You wanna get that front door for me?" He swiveled the dolly around and carved a gouge in the claw foot base of a Tiffany lamp.

Michael gritted his teeth. "Watch that thing, will you? I'll get the door. Hold on a minute." He waited by the opened door until all three crates had left the house and were secured inside the van. He signed his name with the electronic pen and the driver printed out a copy of the bill of lading which Michael folded and stuffed in his pants pocket. What was keeping Bianca? He looked up and down the street but there was no sign of her car. He'd give her five more minutes and then he'd call her. How long did it take to buy a lousy pack of cigarettes? He slammed the door and went back to the library to finish cleaning up. Fifteen minutes later, he'd tried Bianca twice on her cell but got no answer. Where the hell was she? When the doorbell rang, he went to answer it, ready to rip her up one side and down the other. Her filthy habit was costing them time.

****

"Police Officer, Search Warrant." IC Sanchez's strong voice would have carried through a metal door, let alone a wooden one that looked as if it had gone ten rounds with a chainsaw. He stood to the side, rang the doorbell, announced, and knocked twice more. Brown, positioned at the other side of the door, kept a time count.

"Where the hell have you been?" Michael opened the door and his mouth snapped shut. He froze, trapped, his eyes darting from the police at the door to the car in the driveway. He made one move but it was doomed from the get go. Before he could slam the door against the officers, he found himself on the ground, with a split lip, spitting out grass, and cuffed.

Lifted to his feet, Michael smirked, but the effect was lost when a glob of mud fell from his lip. "Police brutality! Look at my lip! Somebody take a picture of my lip! You don't know shit! You can't prove anything! I know my rights." He barely took a breath before he resumed yelling. "I want my lawyer. I wasn't driving. He was just a piece of worthless scum, anyway. He was nobody. He was nothing."

Inspector Doug Brown hauled DeMontana to the squad car and deposited him in the back seat without ceremony. "I'm going to set you straight at least on one thing," Brown said. "Not that you'd care. But I do. He wasn't a nobody. He was a Marine." He slammed the door, leaving DeMontana to his own demons. He wiped his hands on his trousers as he returned to the driveway, where he watched the photographer capturing every moment of the operation, including the one when the tarpaulin was lifted from the car, revealing the body damage to the left front fender and grille.

"And what's this? The fun never stops." Sanchez walked around the front of the car and pointed to the Rembrandt in the front passenger seat. He whistled. "Is that what I think it is? How the hell did that get there? Get Cranston and Paone," he said to Brown.

"Very nice," Steve said, taking in the unexpected but very welcome bonus package. "Very nice indeed, and it's about bloody time."

"Kind of feels somebody's given us an early Christmas present," Liz said. "I wouldn't have thought he'd have been that stupid." She turned to Sanchez. "In the hopeful event that where there's smoke there's fire, how long to get a warrant to search the house?"

"Maybe four hours. Again. Maybe sooner. Depends. I'm hoping sooner. Anyhow, the safety sweep of the house revealed no other occupants, so we'll secure the premises until the warrant arrives."

Steve rubbed his hands together. He felt like a kid who'd spotted Santa coming down the chimney. About time they'd gotten a break. He caught

Brown's eye as he prepared to transport DeMontana for booking. "*Semper Fi*," he said.

Brown nodded. "*Semper Fi.*"

****

Mirandized and cuffed, Michael DeMontana was taken from the premises, his departure witnessed by the crew in Larry's Lawn Maintenance truck who'd risked a one-time pass by to check on the outcome of their labors.

"We got him," Carla said. "They got the car." She planted a kiss on Morrie's cheek. "We got him."

"What about the art?" Francesca said. "Why aren't they going into the house to get the art?"

"I don't know," Gino said. "Maybe they didn't find the Rembrandt. Oh, crap." "No. They had to find the Rembrandt. It was right in plain view." Francesca looked at Gino. "It was in plain view, wasn't it? You didn't drop it under the seat or anything?"

"It's in plain view. It's on the seat. I saw it. It didn't go anywhere. It didn't fall down or off or anything like that. They had to have found it. Maybe they need to do some more legal stuff or something before they go inside the house."

"The rest of them aren't leaving. That's a good sign," Francesca said. "They're probably just waiting for impound to come and get the car. We're going to be leaving, though," Morrie said. "We stick around any longer and we'll become people of interest. That's never a good thing."

"We failed." Francesca said what they'd all been thinking. "It's over. They've got Michael on the hit and run, maybe. If they can prove he drove the car, but for the rest of it—we failed."

"I just don't see why the painting didn't work," Carla said. "Francesca had a good idea, and it shoulda worked. Why didn't it work?"

Morrie increased his speed and they drove away, unanswered questions swirling about them like vapors in the exhaust.

CHAPTER FORTY-THREE

San Francisco

"Well, that's that," Gino said, motioning for everyone to join him at the table in Francesca's apartment for a farewell toast. "We tried. Damn, we tried. And we did get the diary. Maybe some day down the road, I'll figure out how to use it to prove *papa's* claim to authenticity. It's more complicated than I thought. It's full of notes and figures. I don't know where to start with it. But in the meantime, they're still holding the trump card." He poured the wine, a not too shabby Pinot chosen from the batch they'd saved for the victory celebration.

"And, we got the cops to run down the DEMON car," Carla said. "That's good too. Maybe they'll pin the hit and run on Michael. Maybe not, but we got Mary to remember what happened, and that's good. Maybe she'll remember something about the driver and that'll prove it was Michael."

"We got rid of the Rembrandt," Francesca said, taking a healthy swallow. "That was way up there on my To Do list." She swirled the rest of the contents of her glass and watched the garnet liquid catch the light of the chandelier.

"Oh yeah," Carla said. "And we got rid of Sal, that piece of scum. That was super important."

"But it still leaves the work unfinished," Morrie said. "The capstone to all this was getting to the art. That was the ultimate goal, and that's where we came up dry."

The late afternoon sun had broken through the clouds and cast a beam of light across the table, not so much a ray of hope but a sunset on their aspirations.

"So you're saying we're not done? I know that," Gino said. "But I have to step back for a minute. This was a gamble. My last gamble," he said. "And depending on one last big roll of the dice wasn't going to work. It's how I got into this mess in the first place. I still need the money, but it's going to cost me the vineyard and the estate. The casino will sue, and they'll get their pound of flesh. I'll still be short, but I'll just have to work out something with the court. Maybe payments over time. I don't know. First thing is to get a job." He winced. "I've never worked for anybody before. I'm not sure I'll be all that good at it, but I guess I'll have to learn." He drained the rest of the wine from his glass. "That's it. Time to break up the party and go legit." He stood and took his glass to the sink. "I need a ride back to Dark Mountain, Morrie, if you don't mind one last favor."

"No problem. Carla and I are headed to the coast for a couple of days to talk things out."

"Wait a minute," Carla said. "Wait. Wait just one minute." She pushed back her chair and got her pocketbook off the sofa. She shoved the bag into Gino's chest. "This could help," she said. "I don't need it no more. I got Morrie." She kissed Gino on the cheek and took Morrie's hand.

"Ain't she something?" Morrie said.

"Your pocketbook? I need this?"

"Open it, Gino. You'll see."

Gino opened the bag and then sat down hard on the first chair he could find.

"Holy Mary, Mother of God," he said and crossed himself three times.

Carla jabbed Morrie in the ribs and nodded. "See?" she said.

Gino was hyperventilating. The online course on Mastering Your Body stressed the necessity of deep, even breathing, but Gino held one hand to his chest and gulped air like a diver come up from the deep. Screw the online courses. He needed air and he needed it now.

****

"What?" Francesca appeared at his elbow and peered into the bag. "What's the matter? Oh. Oh my. Oh. Wow. Oh." She reached into the bag and pulled out a fistful of bills, fanning them to be sure she was seeing what her eyes were telling her brain was actually there. "It's money!" She jumped up and down, waving the bills. "It's money!" She hugged Gino so hard he lost the first decent breath he'd managed.

"Yeah," Carla said. "It's not all there. I used a few hundred bucks to get some new clothes at the big box store. And I had to buy some stuff for Morrie and Jeffrey, too, on our way out here. But the rest of it's there, except they screwed me at the Club. There was supposed to be a hundred thousand, but I counted it and there was only nine hundred and seventy-two. Bastards." She frowned. "You can't trust nobody. Anyhow, it's yours. I was gonna open my dance studio with it, but I'll work something out." She turned to Francesca. "I figure they owed me that much for what I had to do when I worked there. You know, time and a half and all that." She looked at Gino. "If you gotta get a job, make sure you check the benefits. I didn't have no benefits, so I took my own."

"Carla," Gino began, but she held up a hand.

"Famiglia è tutto. Ti amo, Gino."

"E ti amo troppo, Signorina Marie."

"That's my new professional name," she confided to Francesca. "It's more high class than Vixen. That was my last professional name. But change is good. I got class now so I need a classy name." She beamed.

"I like it. Why Marie?"

"Marie Taglioni. I got her picture here somewhere." She grabbed the pocketbook from Gino and rummaged through it, finally dumping it upside down on the kitchen table and sifting through the contents until she located the tiny picture wrapped in tissue paper inside a zippered compartment of her wallet. "Ain't she beautiful." Carla held the photo at arm's length. "She was one classy broad." "Just like you," Gino said, and there wasn't a trace of sarcasm in his tone. "But you keep the money, Miss Marie. I appreciate the gesture, seriously, but I haven't given up on the art chase," he said to Morrie. "I just need a little time to get things back on an even keel. When I'm ready, are you in?"

Morrie put his arm around Carla. "I'm in."

"Me too," Francesca said.

"Don't forget me," Carla said. "Just because I got class don't mean I ain't up for another round. And I got all this money now. All the money in the world!"

CHAPTER FORTY-FOUR

San Francisco

"I can see why people smoke," Steve said to his partner. "Chewing gum doesn't cut it, and you can't very well eat a hamburger and drink a soda while you're waiting for the wheels of justice to turn."

Liz nodded. "Image is everything. Ketchup dribbling down your chin doesn't send the right message. But there's a lot you can do while you're waiting."

"For instance?"

"Well, you can conjugate Spanish verbs, if you're trying to learn the language. Or you can memorize the Periodic Table of the Elements, or try to think up a dozen new uses for duct tape." She looked at her partner over the rims of her glasses. "The possibilities are endless and limited only by the bounds of your imagination."

"So you're bored, too."

"Terminally. And if that warrant doesn't get here soon, I'm going to have to follow one of my own suggestions. And they sound even more boring than standing here watching the windows not open."

"I think you're saved," Steve said, tilting his head in the direction of a tan Crown Victoria pulling up to the curb. Sanchez took the warrant and waved it at Steve and Liz who wasted no time vacating the car and joining him on the front porch.

"We're looking for anything that leads us to the art," Sanchez said, leading the way into the house. They spread out, and it didn't take long to hit pay dirt.

"I think we may have found what we're looking for," Liz called from the library where she'd found the odd bits and pieces of foam core, plastic wrap, bubble wrap, and sealing tape. "My guess is the art's gone and we're back to chasing it down."

"Hold on," Sanchez said. "I've got an idea." He placed a call to the station house and spoke to the officer who'd processed DeMontana. "Anything turn up when you bagged his personal effects?" he asked. "I'll wait." He turned to Liz. "Just a hunch, but we could get lucky." He spoke to the voice on the line. "That's all? Nothing else? A receipt for what? That's it! Get all available units to meet me at cargo dispatch, SFO, and don't spare the horses." He disconnected and called to Brown who was on the second floor. "DeMontana had a receipt in his pocket from an air cargo transport company for a flight to Rome in," he looked at his watch, "thirty-five minutes. It's going to be tight." The officers took off running to their cars. Liz took the wheel of their car, and Steve hit the lights and siren. Both cars moved out with Sanchez and Brown in the lead.

CHAPTER FORTY-FIVE

The not so friendly skies

Bianca DeMontana swerved to change lanes to take exit 423B from 101 and merge onto I-380 South. A minute later she exited onto the El Camino and pulled into the parking lot at the first strip mall she found. She took a notepad from her purse and the cell from her pocket. Her first call was to the Air Transport Service who confirmed the pickup had gone as scheduled and the van was en route to SFO.

She unzipped the side pouch in her purse and checked that her passport was there. Then she looked up flights on United's mobile app and booked a round-trip to Rome, departing at nine p.m. with a layover in Zurich. She disconnected and went into the discount clothing store. Ten minutes later, she was back in the car with a cheap carryon crammed with an armful of clothes she'd grabbed from the women's sale rack.

She parked in the garage at SFO and rolled her suitcase to the kiosk where she scanned the barcode to get her boarding pass. No worries. With a round trip ticket and luggage, she was just another business traveler among the hordes filing through security. Three hours later, she was comfortably seated in first class with a window seat, sipping a martini with a twist and waiting for takeoff.

It was so easy, but Michael would have bought a one way ticket and tried to fly without luggage. He'd have been detained for hours by TSA, and then he would have started yelling, which would have been the beginning of the end for him. He was just that stupid. She took another sip. He was on his own. If he tried to screw her, he screwed himself. By tomorrow night, she'd be beyond anyone's reach, safe and secure in Palermo where you could buy anything, if you had enough money. She smiled. Money was never going to be a problem again. She pulled down the shade, and the flight attendant took her empty glass and brought a pillow. As the Boeing 777 lifted off, Bianca settled herself comfortably and dozed.

CHAPTER FORTY-SIX

Dark Mountain

The curtain of coastal fog had parted, and Gino sat on the upstairs deck off his bedroom, working on balance sheets as the stars shone down with a cool silver light. The vineyard slept under the full moon, and off in the distance, a screech owl complained its way through the woods, in search of deaf mice, Gino supposed.

He tossed the ledger onto the floor and stood. He'd been working the numbers for hours, ever since Morrie had dropped him off. Maybe he could work a deal where the casino would buy into the vineyard and take a percentage of the profits over a certain number of years. It was worth pursuing, at least. He felt a sting and slapped at a mosquito on his arm. He gathered up the financial reports and the ledger and went inside, flipping on the wall mounted television and half-listening to the news as he got ready for bed. A minute later he was on the phone trying to rouse a sleepy-voiced Francesca. "Turn on the news. Hurry! Hurry!" He set the phone down on the bed and stood in front of the screen, not daring to believe his eyes.

The eleven o'clock nightly news had come back from a commercial with a breaking news story that Gino was watching unfold right in front of him. The anchor continued.

"Police tonight are crediting a homeless woman with supplying the last, vital clue in solving a hit and run fatality that occurred last week in Pacific Heights and that ultimately led to what you're seeing on the screen behind me. These police cars are blocking a Pistoli Airline cargo plane from taking off at SFO. According to a reliable source, the plane's cargo contained nine art masterpieces stolen from museums and art galleries around the world. "Police are not revealing the name of the woman, but are giving her high praise for helping them break the case wide open. And Raul," the news reporter turned to her co-anchor, "she's going to be a very wealthy woman once the reward money has been delivered. I wonder what her plans are for the reward money. I guess we'll have to keep an eye on these developments."

"It's quite a story, that's for sure, Joy. We'll keep you all up to date on the story of this unfortunate woman who is now the heroine of San Francisco. It promises to be a miraculous life-changing event. But back to our lead story. According to that reliable witness, who prefers to remain anonymous, police have arrested Michael DeMontana and Bianca DiCicco DeMontana, both members of the Puglisi crime family, in connection with the thefts. Bianca DeMontana was taken off a United Airlines flight that was diverted to Chicago and met by federal authorities. Back to you, Joy."

"That's right, Raul. Stay tuned to your *Eyes and Ears on the Bay, KPDQ* for the latest developments in this fast-breaking story." Joy flashed a smile that strained the limits of her makeup and held the camera with her eyes until they went to commercial again.

Gino sank back on the bed and closed his eyes. They'd done it after all. He brought the phone back to his ear. Francesca was screaming. "Did you hear that? Did you hear that? We did it! We did it after all. But how? I don't understand."

"The cops weren't waiting on the tow truck. They were waiting on the search warrant. They followed the Rembrandt into the house and somehow the whole thing ended up at the airport. Beats the shit out of me how they did it, but I'll take it." He sat up and looked at the financial mess on the floor that belonged to another life. It wasn't one he was going back to. Hell, maybe the old man would float him a loan. After all, he'd come through on a promise. There was a first time for everything. "Gino, you there? Talk to me."

God, he loved her voice. "I'm here, honey. I'll always be here."

CHAPTER FORTY-SEVEN

Castel del Mare

It was the time between storms. The first rains of autumn had settled the dust and washed the landscape clean, and Francesca insisted they stop the Audi every time she saw something in the golden countryside to photograph. A small flock of goats coaxed down the hillside by a young boy with a dog by his side was her current subject. The boy's name was Alfonso, and he lived in the village by the sea with his mother and five brothers. His father was a fisherman. All this she discovered in the brief few minutes she had chatted with him as Gino waited in the car.

"My Italian is getting better," she said, waving goodbye to the boy. "I think he understood me."

"You could have been speaking in tongues and that boy would have understood you," Gino said. Francesca just didn't understand the effect she had on men of any age. "But your Italian is coming along nicely, *signorina*."

"It was just an online course and only a week long, but it covered the basics." She kissed his cheek. "*Ti amo, Gino.*"

"*E ti amo troppo*, Francesca."

They were on their way to *Castel del Mare,* and this time Gino hadn't had any trouble getting the car he wanted. He wasn't sure whether it was due to his negotiating skills or to Francesca's presence, but *Peppino da Palermo* hadn't batted an eye when Gino told him what he wanted, and he delivered the vehicle without argument. He seemed almost afraid when Gino told him the car would be returned when he was done with it and not a moment before. Peppino had found this acceptable, desirable even, and had personally escorted them to their vehicle, holding the passenger door open for Francesca and wishing them a pleasant stay on the island. It was all very strange but it felt good and it felt right.

"It feels like we're going home. It's so much like Dark Mountain. The trees, the hills..."

"The mud."

She patted his arm. "The mud is mostly dry, except for a few puddles, and there's no way you could have known that last one was as deep as a crater with those sharp rocks at the bottom. I mean, it looked like a puddle. And you were very competent with the jack. The spare tire works just fine."

"It looks like a tricycle tire. It looks ridiculous."

"Never mind. We're almost there and besides, it made for a great picture." She looked out the window at the passing scenery. "I hope he likes me."

"He'll like you. Just smile that smile and he'll fall in love. Guaranteed."

****

Celestina was the first test, and she welcomed Francesca like a daughter, cradling her face in her hands and kissing her on the forehead. "So you love my Gino," she said. She patted Francesca's cheeks and smiled. "Come, your grandfather is waiting." She preceded them down the hall to the bedroom where the door was open and the old man was propped up in bed, three pillows behind his back for support.

"It's me, *Papa*," Gino said, "I'm back, and I've brought someone for you to meet. *Papa*, this is Francesca."

Emiliano opened one eye. "Is she Italian?"

"No, *Papa*, she's American."

"American what?"

"Korean. And French."

"French?" Emiliano sighed. "It would have to be the French. But she's Catholic."

"No, *Papa*."

The old man opened both eyes. "Then what?"

Francesca coughed. "Buddhist, sir."

"*Madre mia*. All hope is lost. All right. Let me see her. Help me turn. Hurry up." Gino laughed and winked at Francesca. "It's all right. He's in a good mood." Francesca's eyes widened but she put on a pleasant smile and waited for

inspection.

"She's a pretty one," Emiliano said. "Do you love him?" he asked her.

"Yes, I do," she said. "Very much."

"Well, that's too bad. That's that then. If it's my blessing you want, you have it. God help you."

Gino put his arm around Francesca. "Good. That's settled. If you're feeling strong enough, *Papa,* it's my turn to tell *you* a story." He took the diary from his jacket pocket and handed it to his grandfather. "It's done, *Papa*, it's all done."

The old man listened while Gino, with occasional input from Francesca, gave the whole account. He asked few questions and it was apparent his strength was ebbing, but he perked up when Francesca gave him a small notebook. "Another book? What is this?"

"An accounting of our expenses during the...recovery operation," Francesca said. "I kept a running total, and the receipts for everything we needed to buy are clipped to the last page. There were almost two thousand Euros left over. One thousand eight hundred and fifty, to be exact, and I've clipped them to the back cover. For your records," she added.

Emiliano nodded and placed the notebook on the bedside table. He folded his hands and bowed his head. He was silent for a while. "She keeps good records." He lowered his hands and gave Gino a penetrating look. "That will be important. Now, I must rest. Come back later. But send Celestina to me now."

****

There was to be no later. Emiliano Esposito died that night, the diary clutched in his hand and satisfied that his legacy would survive and that his fame would grow. Before he slept, he had Celestina summon his lawyer, and she witnessed the final addition to his last will and testament. She kissed the old man and sent for the Jesuit. It was never too late for redemption. Especially in Italy.

CHAPTER FORTY-EIGHT

Dark Mountain Vineyards

"So what do you think?" Carla asked. She and Morrie were seated at the dining room table at Dark Mountain across from Francesca and Gino. Pierre was curled up asleep on the sofa. Francesca was organizing the scrapbook that had seen hard duty during the recovery of the diary and the rest of their exploits. She'd trimmed the torn newspaper articles Emiliano Esposito had stuffed between the covers and now was positioning them on the pages where they belonged.

She had three new clippings to add to the book. The first one showed Inspector Liz Paone holding a news conference to announce the apprehension of the art thieves and the recovery of the stolen paintings. "SFPD Breaks Art Theft Ring" the *Reporter* proclaimed.

"Interpol's reopened their investigation into the death of Donna Napolitano," Gino said. "That makes two murders for Michael. He's trying to cop a plea bargain by implicating Bianca, and Bianca's trying the same thing on Michael. There's no love lost in that family."

"It's a mess," Morrie said. "But it's not our mess. However it plays out, they're both going away for a long, long time." He stretched out his arms and cracked his knuckles. "The thing that blows me away is the cops finding that body in the trunk. I can't believe I drove that car all the way to the city with Fabriani's corpse in the back."

"What do you suppose Sal was gonna do with her?" Carla said. "No. Forget it. I don't want to know. Forget I said anything. He's gone and she's gone. It's done."

The second clipping showed Mary O'Rourke accepting a check from the Combined Insurance Group in the amount of one million dollars in gratitude for her part in solving the crimes and recovering the stolen art. Rabbi Joe Alderman stood by her side. "Homeless Woman Starts on the Long Road Back" was this story's headline.

"Joe's looking into setting up a trust for her," Morrie said, "so she won't get taken advantage of. She's savvy enough to know she needs the help, and she trusts Joe."

"But this one's my personal favorite," Francesca said. "Executive Charged with Embezzlement, Grand Theft, and Income Tax Evasion." She drew a mustache on the photo of Bryan Bishop III, her ex-boss, as he was led from the offices of Current Events in handcuffs. "I don't know how you did it, Morrie, but thank you."

"No problem. I know a guy who's a geek to the max. Only took him a few minutes and only cost me a six-pack. Plus, you can trust him. He'd done work for me before. Your slate is clean and your ex-boss is going down for the count."

"So, like I said before, what do you think? The red one or the blue one?" Carla had two photos in front of her. "I'm kind of thinking the red one but maybe it don't send the right statement, if you know what I mean."

"It's your wedding," Francesca said. "You should wear whatever makes you happy. What does Morrie think?"

"He don't say much, but I think he likes the red one, too."

"Then go with the red. You'll be a beautiful bride whatever color dress you wear."

"And I solved the name thing too. Now nobody's gonna find me if I don't want to get found. '*Miss Marie's School of the Dance, Marie Landow, Proprietress.*' Morrie thought of that last part. He's real good with words. And when we get back from Vegas, we'll have a grand opening."

"Another entry in my professional portfolio," Francesca said. "Planning your open house at the dance studio. Too bad I can't include the major event we just completed. It would be a doozie. But something tells me the less I say about that, the better." She looked down at the photo of Inspector Paone. "She's a really nice lady, but I don't think she'd let it pass."

"Good thinking," Gino said.

"Then the story is complete," she said, closing the scrapbook.

"Not quite," Gino said. "There's still the matter of papa's Will. He was very specific. He paid off my debt, but I inherit only if I marry you and you keep the books." He took a small box from his pocket and offered it to Francesca. "It's a ring," he said. "It belonged to my mother. I think she'd approve. But that's not why."

"Not why what?"

"Why I'm asking you to marry me."

"I know that."

"You do?"

"I do. You love me. You can't help yourself." "You're right. I do. Are you ready?' he asked.

"I think I've heard that question before," she said.

"Remember your answer?"

She nodded decisively and kissed him. "You bet your ass I'm ready."

ABOUT THE AUTHOR

Karen K. Brees is the award-winning author of *The Esposito Caper*, along with *Crosswind* and *Headwind* (*The World War II Adventures of MI6 Agent Katrin Nissen* series). She holds a master's degree in history and a doctorate in adult education. She is also the author and co-author of seven nonfiction titles in the health and general interest field, including *Preserving Food and Getting Real about Getting Older*. She has been a bookmobile librarian, classroom teacher, university professor, cattle rancher, and goat herder. She currently resides in the Pacific Northwest where she is at work on Whirlwind—the third *Katrin Nissen* novel.

NOTE FROM KAREN K. BREES

Word-of-mouth is crucial for any author to succeed. If you enjoyed *The Esposito Caper*, please leave a review online—anywhere you are able. Even if it's just a sentence or two. It would make all the difference and would be very much appreciated.

Thanks!
Karen K. Brees

We hope you enjoyed reading this title from:

www.blackrosewriting.com

Subscribe to our mailing list – *The Rosevine* – and receive **FREE** books, daily deals, and stay current with news about upcoming releases and our hottest authors.
Scan the QR code below to sign up.

Already a subscriber? Please accept a sincere thank you for being a fan of Black Rose Writing authors.

View other Black Rose Writing titles at www.blackrosewriting.com/books and use promo code **PRINT** to receive a **20% discount** when purchasing.